HIGH STAKES

KIDNAP AND RANSOM

LEE BISHOP

This is a work of fiction. Names, characters, places, and incidents are products of the author's imagination or are used fictitiously and are not to be construed as real. Any resemblance to actual events, locations, organizations, or persons, living or dead, is entirely coincidental.

World Castle Publishing, LLC
Pensacola, Florida
Copyright © Lee Bishop 2021
Hardback ISBN: 9798499567029
Paperback ISBN: 9781956788075
eBook ISBN: 9781956788082
First Edition World Castle Publishing, LLC, November 8, 2021
http://www.worldcastlepublishing.com

Cover: Karen Fuller
Editor: Maxine Bringenberg

CHAPTER 1

Tom Bradshaw walked down the narrow second floor hallway in the run-down Mexican barrio hotel. The smell was overpowering: a combination of cigarette smoke, urine, and spoiled food that almost made his eyes water. Sweat popped out on his forehead, and he began breathing faster as he stopped in front of Room 219. Bradshaw took a deep breath and knocked on the door. It opened a crack, and he could see a man in a black ski mask studying him. The door opened, and he was motioned inside. Three men carrying AK-47s, all wearing ski masks, confronted him. Bradshaw slowly walked into the room, carrying an iPad in one hand.

"Are you ready?" one of the men growled.

A second man moved forward and jabbed the barrel of his automatic rifle in Bradshaw's side.

"Make one wrong move, and I'll blow your guts out," he said in a menacing voice.

"All of you, knock it off," a man commanded from across the room. "Give him space to do his work."

The leader sat in a chair next to the bed, one leg crossed over the other, almost casual in his manner. His clothing was far different from the other three kidnappers, who were dressed in raggedy T-shirts and dirty pants. The leader wore blue slacks and a white dress shirt under a blue cashmere sweater. His highly polished black shoes reflected the light. He also wore a black ski mask.

"Shall I call you Ajax, or would you prefer to use your real name?" the leader asked.

"Ajax will be fine. And you are Carlos. I recognize your voice," Bradshaw said.

"We should know each other's voices by now. This is our sixth transaction together, and by far the largest at three million dollars," the leader pointed out. "Shall we begin?"

"Yes," Bradshaw responded.

"Use that small desk in the corner," the gang leader said. He got up from the chair and handed Bradshaw a piece of paper containing an offshore account number.

Bradshaw sat down at the desk, opened his iPad, and went to work. In less than five minutes, he completed the transfer of three million dollars to an offshore account in the British Virgin Islands. The leader of the kidnapping gang then used his iPad to confirm that the transfer of funds had gone through.

"Splendid," said the gang leader. "Ajax, your package is in the room directly above this one on the third floor. After we are gone, wait five minutes, then go collect your package. Physically he's not bad, but mentally and emotionally, only time will tell."

The leader walked over to Bradshaw and held out his hand. He was five feet, nine inches tall, trim, and sounded as if he was well educated. Bradshaw, at six feet, two inches in height, dwarfed his adversary. Tom was muscular but not bulky, his face was lean and handsome, and his thick, curly, brown hair was cut short. Bradshaw's hazel/green eyes took in every detail, storing every aspect of the meeting. Tom took Carlos's hand and shook it, feeling relieved.

"Until next time, Ajax," said the kidnapper.

Bradshaw thought his opponent's light brown eyes sparkled as he spoke. The four men filed out of the hotel room, and Bradshaw went over to the chair previously occupied by Carlos. He sat down and noted the woody, sweet spice scent of the kidnapper's cologne. His eyes moved about as he looked at the frayed carpet, the stained bed cover, the chair that was about to fall apart, and the cheap wooden bureau covered with cigarette burns. Five minutes passed, and Bradshaw quickly got to his feet, walked out of the room, and down the corridor to the rickety staircase leading to the third floor.

He took the stairs two at a time and felt a wooden step crack under his weight as he neared the top. He walked to Room 319 and slowly opened the door. A small man dressed in a maintenance man's bib-top overalls and dirty T-shirt was lying on the bed in a fetal position.

"Victor Chapa?" Bradshaw asked.

"Go away. Leave me alone," the small man responded in an angry voice.

"I'm Tom Bradshaw, the insurance company negotiator that your corporation uses. I paid a ransom and am here to take you home. You're a free man."

The senior vice president of Banco Royale lifted his head and stared at Bradshaw, eyes blinking in the half light, nose running, and salt and pepper hair standing on end. A six-week growth of beard covered his face in grey, scraggly knots.

"Are you telling me the truth? If you're playing with my emotions again, you can kiss my ass."

Bradshaw walked over to the banker and held out his hand. "Let's go. I'm taking you home."

Chapa's hand shook as he reached up and touched Bradshaw's fingers. Then his body became racked with convulsive shaking as he began crying. Bradshaw sat down on the edge of the bed and gently put his hand on Chapa's shoulder.

"If you would like, I'll take you to a salon and spa where you can bathe and have your hair cut and put on new clothes before I take you home."

"Thanks. I don't want anyone seeing me this way. I smell like shit and must look the same way." The fact that he was free but without protection suddenly registered in the banker's mind. "I'll want security while I'm there. Can you get me a couple of really good bodyguards to join us?"

"Certainly."

"What's your name again?"

"Tom Bradshaw. I'm a kidnap and ransom negotiator with California Fidelity Insurance Corporation. Your bank took out kidnap and ransom insurance on you, and I was in negotiations for six weeks to get you back."

Bradshaw helped Chapa down the stairs and out to his car that he hoped would still have its wheels in place. It did. He placed a call to a security company he frequently used, then called the spa to tell them they had an important guest arriving. He drove by the security company, and two bodyguards got in the back seat.

Fifteen minutes later, they arrived at the spa. Chapa soaked in a private spa for half an hour, then had his face shaved and hair trimmed. His eyes suddenly took on a worried look. "You're not leaving me, are you, Tom? These are rough looking security men. Please come with me. You're the only man I trust."

"I intend to drive with you to your home. Let's go."

Bradshaw was anxious to report to his office and to Chapa's bank that the transaction had been successfully completed and the victim was free. But, out of compassion, he decided to spend another half hour with Chapa, who did not show the usual sense of hopelessness, which many victims displayed. Tom vowed never to let himself be kidnapped, even if it meant risking his own life.

Chapa quietly looked out the window of the Toyota Camry for the next ten minutes as the neighborhoods gradually became more upscale. One bodyguard drove, and the other man sat next to the driver. Bradshaw and Chapa now were in the back seat. The banker turned and looked at Bradshaw. His appearance had changed entirely. Chapa's hair was neatly trimmed in an executive cut, his face was clean shaven, and he was wearing a silky gray sweat suit and new tennis shoes. But his face was gaunt and almost white from lack of sunlight. His eyes were red, surrounded by dark circles, and his forehead and cheeks were deeply lined.

"When does this sense of fear leave?"

"Gradually. It won't go away overnight."

"I've always been a very strong person, but I can't think about my family without wanting to cry."

"That's normal. You're just hours away from coming out of a locked, black box. No one spends weeks in a darkened room with no one to talk with and comes out of the experience with any kind of normalcy intact. The sooner you begin therapy, the sooner you get better," Bradshaw explained.

"How long does the therapy last?"

Bradshaw was quiet for a few moments while he determined how to answer. "You're much stronger than the average man from an emotional standpoint. You're asking questions that ninety-nine percent of the kidnap victims are unable to think about at this point. They have all they can do just to focus on their surroundings. Many are basket cases for weeks," Bradshaw replied. "To answer your question, it will be a far shorter therapy period for you."

Their eyes met and held.

"If ever you need anything in Mexico City, contact me. I feel that I owe you my life, and I'll help you in any way I can," Chapa said.

"Thanks, Victor." Inwardly, Tom's sense of accomplishment was at its peak.

The Camry pulled up to the master planned community. Victor Chapa talked to the guard, who immediately opened the gates. They drove to the twenty-thousand-square-foot mansion.

Tears rolled down Chapa's cheeks as he saw his eight-year-old daughter playing hopscotch on the front veranda.

CHAPTER 2

"Goddamn it! I told you not to get personally involved. We hire people to do these things, like wire funds," Mark Danforth nearly shouted. "You're too valuable to be putting yourself in the hands of these assholes."

Danforth was vice president of the kidnap and ransom division at California Fidelity, which was rapidly becoming the top K & R insurer in North, Central, and South America. This lucrative specialty insurance niche had exploded in size over the past twenty years as kidnappings in Central and South America spiraled out of sight. Bradshaw was seated in front of his boss's desk in California Fidelity's downtown Los Angeles high rise building.

"It was a spur of the moment thing. You'd given me the wiring instructions because we were very close to making a deal. Carlos called and told me to meet him in half an hour at this run-down hotel. I did it because I knew we had a deal. I could feel it. You just have to go with your gut instincts sometimes," Bradshaw explained.

"Your gut instincts are going to get you kidnapped or killed one of these days unless you use your head and stop making snap decisions," Danforth emphasized. "Tom, I don't want you going face to face with these bastards."

Danforth's blue eyes were mere slits in an oval red face. He was bald on top, with close cropped brown hair along the sides of his head. The fifty-year-old insurance executive was slightly less than six feet in height and beginning to develop a middle aged spread around his stomach.

"Mark, I'm convinced there's a connection, and possibly some type of organized kidnapping ring going after the bankers in Mexico City. Victor Chapa was the sixth banking victim connected to Carlos. I think specifically picked bankers are being targeted by an organized gang," Bradshaw said.

Danforth sat back in his chair and stared at his top negotiator. "Other than a hunch, do you have any real proof?"

"Carlos wore a ski mask, so I couldn't identify him. But, from the cashmere sweater he was wearing over a dress shirt and the expensive wool slacks and glove leather loafers he had on, this man is definitely a professional businessman. The other three kidnappers were dressed in dirty T-shirts and baggy pants. Each of these six kidnappings was professionally planned and executed by Carlos and his men. Where did they get their information?"

"You tell me," Danforth replied.

"My guess is that all of these bankers belonged to the same banking association or club catering to bankers. Or, someone in the Mexican State Department of Banking is supplying information to the kidnappers. Carlos is getting the information somewhere," Bradshaw said.

"Have you told anyone else about your belief?"

"No."

"Well, don't," Danforth said emphatically. "Unless you come up with some kind of proof, I don't want the banking community in Mexico City to become unduly alarmed."

Bradshaw's expression was one of disappointment. "Okay," he responded.

"Let's change the subject. You know who Felix Ramirez is, right?"

"Sure. He's the richest man in Mexico," Bradshaw responded.

Danforth smiled. "He's contacted us, and wants to place kidnap and ransom insurance on sixty-five of his extended family members."

Tom's mouth fell open, and his eyes widened. "You've got to be kidding!"

"It's no joke. We've completed negotiations with him, and he's ready to begin paying us premiums. There's only one condition that he has, and it's a deal breaker if we can't meet it."

"What is it?"

Danforth smirked. "He wants to approve the negotiator."

A pained expression spread across Bradshaw's face. "You know we can't do that. Once a client starts dictating terms, he thinks he's the decision maker, and that can lead to chaos."

Danforth brushed aside Bradshaw's objection. "Tom, I've selected you to meet with Ramirez. Your communication skills are the best in the business, and your customer relations abilities are outstanding. If anyone can convince him to come on board, it's you."

Bradshaw's eyes were wide. "You're blowing smoke up my ass, Mark. We have a lot of very capable negotiators. What do you want me to tell him?"

"Wing it. There's no script. Convince him that we are experienced, successful and that you're the man for the job. You have a lot of things going for you. You're young, handsome, fluent in Spanish, and have developed an excellent reputation. You'll win him over."

Tom stared out the office window, not really seeing anything. He took a deep breath and exhaled loudly. "What's he like?"

Danforth picked up Felix Ramirez's file, opened it, and scanned it again. "He's tough, a bottom line man who has amassed a fortune estimated at forty billion dollars. He has a civil engineering degree and a background in economics, mathematics, and linear programming. His method of operation has been to buy troubled companies, overhaul the management, then sell them for a huge profit, or sit tight and feed off the suddenly exploding income stream."

"How many corporations does he own?" Bradshaw asked.

Danforth studied the file. "Too many to count. His firms manufacture or sell tobacco, soft drinks, real estate, tires, cement, mining, chemicals, financial services, and insurance. He owns an airline, hotels, and telephone landline and cell phone companies. At one time, he owned ninety percent of all landlines in Mexico and controlled eighty percent of the Mexican cell phone business."

Bradshaw shook his head from side to side. "Is there anything he doesn't own?"

"Not much. He methodically diversified into numerous industry sectors across the Mexican economy, making his empire virtually recession proof."

"I take it he's got all kinds of relatives," Bradshaw said.

"Ramirez is one of eight children. He and his wife have five children. You can see how this multiplies with in-laws, cousins, and dozens of relatives," Danforth pointed out.

"There must be a hell of a lot of security around those folks who are closest to Ramirez. These guards must be tripping over each other at family gatherings," Tom stated.

"Very funny," said Danforth, but he wasn't smiling.

"When do you want me to meet with him?"

"Day after tomorrow."

"Thanks for the advance notice," Tom stated. "I'll do it, but he needs to know who's in charge, and I intend to tell him."

Danforth's red face turned a shade darker. "For Christ's sake, Tom, don't do anything to screw this up. We're talking seven figures in premiums."

Tom sat back in the comfortable leather chair. "I have a method I use when first dealing with domineering, assertive business types. Believe me, it works."

Mark Danforth's eyes were wide, and his mouth was slightly open. "What are you going to do?"

Bradshaw leaned forward as if to convey a secret. Danforth also leaned forward, expectantly.

"I tell them to shut up, or I'll beat the crap out of them," Tom said with a straight face.

Danforth jerked back in his chair and began breathing hard. Bradshaw started laughing loudly, his whole body shaking with merriment. Danforth cracked a smile and shook his head from side to side.

"You know how to pull my chain, you son-of-a-bitch."

"Lighten up, Mark. You have to have some fun in life," Tom said, still laughing. "I'll get the account for us."

***

Tom took an elevator down to the lobby of the downtown Hilton Hotel in the high rise commercial center of Mexico City. California Fidelity rented suites for its negotiators there on an annual basis, and Bradshaw tried to get the same one, Suite 614, so it had a homey feeling over time. He took a cab to the Ramirez Enterprises conglomerate headquarters.

Three-story glass and steel buildings filled two square blocks, and the entire complex was surrounded with decorative block walls. Gated entrance points were manned by security personnel, who continually called various departments to authenticate appointments. Visitors were then escorted to the appointed locations for meetings.

Bradshaw was third in line, and within two minutes, was on his way inside, escorted by an attractive young woman. She introduced herself as Carmen, and they chatted about the huge size of the complex as they walked. At the center of the complex was a beautifully landscaped small park with tables and chairs situated among the trees and flower beds.

"This is beautiful. Do you have lunch here?" he asked.

"You do if you're one of the workers like myself," Carmen replied and smiled. "If you're one of the executives, you eat out, or lunch is catered."

"It's an amazing complex. I've never seen anything quite like it," Tom admitted.

The headquarters was a beehive of activity with well-dressed men and women constantly emerging from buildings and disappearing into others. They reached the building housing Felix Ramirez's private offices, and Carmen stopped.

"This district also has wonderful nightlife. It's filled with discos, restaurants, and bars. I'm meeting some friends at *The Latino* after work. If you have the opportunity, stop by," she said and gave him a seductive smile.

Her light brown eyes and beautiful smile were enticing. Bradshaw said he would try and make it. He entered the outer office and told the receptionist his name and that he had a ten o'clock appointment with Ramirez. The older, thin woman picked up the phone and announced his arrival.

Within a minute, an inner office door opened, and a handsome, middle-aged executive in a dark blue suit emerged. His eyes were not friendly, and his manner was overbearing as he walked forward and shook Tom's hand.

"I'm Anselmo Garcia, Mr. Ramirez's administrative assistant, and I have some questions for you to be answered before you meet with Mr. Ramirez," he stated in an arrogant voice. "Follow me." Garcia turned and marched back to his office. To his surprise, Bradshaw did not follow him. The administrative assistant turned around, mouth opened slightly as he glared at Tom. "Didn't you hear me? Come into my office."

"No. I don't have an appointment with you. Tell Mr. Ramirez I'm here."

Garcia looked confused and unsure about what he should do. He closed his door without uttering another word. The receptionist had an astonished look on her face, eyes wide and lips puckered. Tom winked at her, then walked over and sat down in a comfortable waiting chair.

Five minutes later, another door opened, and Felix Ramirez walked over to Tom Bradshaw and shook his hand. They exchanged pleasantries, and one of the world's richest and most powerful men led Bradshaw through his outer office, where two secretaries were hard at work. Then they went into Ramirez's inner office, which contained a large desk and an oval conference table with six saddle leather colored chairs. Ramirez sat down at the head of the conference table, and Bradshaw sat near him.

The business mogul's big, dark eyes examined every aspect of the young American sitting to one side of him. "I believe in being straightforward, so I have some questions for you," he said in a deep gravelly voice.

"Ask anything you would like."

Ramirez's silver and black hair hung down to his shoulders. A thick, salt and pepper moustache and closely cropped goatee of the same color framed ruddy cheeks and a large nose.

"Why should I contract with your insurance company?"

"We're the largest and most successful kidnap and ransom insurance company in Mexico and Central and South America. Our negotiators are very well trained before they ever take on their first assignment."

"Why did they send you?"

"I'm a very good negotiator with a successful track record."

"Why did you choose this type of work?" the business tycoon asked.

Bradshaw looked at the conference table for a moment while he formulated an answer. "I was in the army in Afghanistan and killed a number of men who were trying to kill me. Towards the end of my tour of duty, I volunteered to become a negotiator. I wanted to make a difference and do something constructive. I turned out to be pretty damn good at the job. When I returned to the States, I contacted California Fidelity and told them I wanted a job. They gave me the opportunity, and here we are today."

Ramirez's piercing brown eyes never left Bradshaw's face as he continued his penetrating, probing questioning. "How successful have you been?"

Bradshaw's hazel green eyes were unafraid as he gazed back at the businessman. "I've completed dozens of successful kidnapping negotiations and have brought back alive all but two of the victims."

"What happened in those two instances?"

"One died from a stroke while in captivity. The other died from anaphylactic shock after he was bitten by a scorpion and was not taken to a hospital for treatment. The bodies were returned to us at greatly reduced prices."

"You pride yourself upon being a top negotiator in hostage negotiations. What singular attribute makes you so successful?" Ramirez asked, as he continued to examine every aspect of the man sitting next to him.

"There isn't a singular attribute. My ability to analyze people, psychological skills, and gut instinct all play a part."

"But you never see the kidnappers."

"I read their voices, changes in their tone of voice, variations in pitch, and whether there is hesitation. You can learn a lot about a man just by listening closely."

Ramirez smiled for the first time, revealing large white teeth. But his in depth questioning continued non-stop. "If there are no hard and fast rules, what techniques are employed?"

"There are a group of very flexible, standard, safe operating procedures that I follow. My job is to control the situation, keep everyone calm, negotiate a price, and then the handover," Tom explained. "Involving one of your family members, the hostage scenario is financial and is definitely the easiest to handle."

"What do you mean?" Ramirez asked.

"The kidnap would be a straightforward cost-benefit equation, with everyone having a vested interest in the hostage being kept alive. There's no money to be made from a corpse."

Ramirez sat back in his chair and stroked his goatee with his right hand as he thought. "How long does the kidnap scenario usually play out?"

"Kidnappers don't want the situation to play out indefinitely. The longer it goes on, the more it's costing them, and there's a greater chance that something will go wrong," Tom explained.

Ramirez's large dark eyes bore into Bradshaw. "Involving the ransom, how much is enough? How do you know when you've reached that point?"

"It's a matter of judgement as to how far you can push a kidnapper at any given moment. They don't want the abduction to play out indefinitely. The longer it goes on, the greater the chance that something will upset the scenario. Conversely, you should never settle too soon," Bradshaw stated.

"Why?" Ramirez asked.

"You don't want the abductors to think you are an easy mark, and there's ample additional money to be had. I've known cases where the same victims were kidnapped again a few months later, and this time the asking prices were sky high."

Ramirez glared at Bradshaw and exhaled sharply, not liking the answers he was receiving. "My immediate family members have bodyguards. Where do most abductions take place?"

"Within ten miles of their homes. Most of the time, it's when you're on your way to work and your mind is on autopilot. You stop for a red light, and bam, they jump you. Your bodyguard will either surrender or be shot. Remember, these people are despicable, the lowest of the low, and kidnapping is a sure way to make big money," Tom explained.

"What happens then?" Ramirez asked.

"Now the victim enters his most dangerous time. During the next ten minutes to half an hour, the kidnappers are volatile, unstable, and explosive. Their anxiety levels reach their peaks as they transport the victim to a safe house. The victim is usually blindfolded so he can't identify the abductors, or a black bag or sack is pulled down over his head."

"Why?" Ramirez asked.

"The leader doesn't want his gang members to look at the victim as being a human being. He wants them to think of the victim as being a commodity rather than a person. He's something to be acquired and sold. He's no longer human," Tom said.

Bradshaw watched closely as Ramirez digested the facts presented to him. The entrepreneur stared at the table and finally looked over at Tom. "What shape are they in after the ordeal?"

"If a person is psychologically strong when he's kidnapped, he can come out of it in decent shape following therapy. If you're not psychologically strong, there can be lasting damage. In extreme cases, they end up as vegetables, never wanting to venture outside again," Tom pointed out.

Ramirez grunted as the thought of permanent damage to his close relatives became horribly distasteful. He suddenly changed the subject. "You speak Spanish fluently, with very little accent. Why is that?"

"My mother was Mexican, and she never wanted me to forget my heritage. I had private Spanish classes up until high school in Los Angeles. She died seven years ago from cancer."

The powerful businessman's search for answers was at an end, and his mind was made up. "If one of my children or extended members of my family are abducted, I want to be present during negotiations and make all decisions involving money."

"Of course you can be present during negotiations. We would set up a task force headquartered in one of your conference rooms here. But as far as making decisions during negotiations, that's my responsibility. That's why you have K & R insurance and a professional negotiator," Tom pointed out.

"I make decisions involving hundreds of millions of dollars every month. I'm good at it," Ramirez emphasized.

"Your decisions are based upon making money. Mine are about saving lives. There's a big difference," Tom stated.

The two determined, persistent men continued to stare at one another, neither one giving in.

Bradshaw sat back in his chair. "Let's play a little game. You play yourself, and I'll be the head of the kidnapping gang calling you for the first time since your son was abducted. Are you ready?"

"Absolutely," Ramirez responded.

Bradshaw acted as if he had picked up a telephone with his right hand and held it to his ear. "Is this Felix Ramirez I'm talking to?" he asked loudly.

"Yes," the business tycoon replied.

"I've got that miserable prick you call a son. I want one hundred million American dollars for his safe return," Bradshaw yelled into the imaginary telephone.

The powerful businessman's eyes opened wide, and he was momentarily speechless. Finally, he muttered, "I think we can do business."

"Screw business! I want that money, and I want it now, you miserable son-of-a-bitch," Tom yelled.

"I'd like to negotiate—"

Tom cut him off. "Listen, you rotten bastard, you have more money than all of the banks in Mexico combined. Don't give me any shit."

"If you would just calm down, we could talk about this," said Ramirez, sweat beginning to roll down his forehead.

"You goddamned filthy asshole. I'm going to cut off your son's right hand and mail it to you to show you I'm not kidding."

Bradshaw made a motion as if he was slamming the receiver down.

Ramirez had an astonished look on his face. "He's not

really going to do that, is he?" Ramirez asked, his voice cracking.

Tom returned to talking in a normal tone of voice. "No, he's not. There's a saying in this business. 'When you're in a china shop, don't break the porcelain.' Your son is worth a lot of money to the kidnappers. They're not going to start cutting off his body parts unless the leader is a psychopath."

Ramirez nodded his head in understanding, took out his handkerchief, and wiped his forehead. "Tom, I think the interview is over. You got your point across, and you can handle the negotiations. I'll finalize the paperwork with Mark Danforth immediately."

CHAPTER 3

Tom was feeling jubilant after leaving Felix Ramirez and took a cab back to the Hilton Hotel. He completed some paperwork, talked with his boss in Los Angeles and gave him the good news, then stretched out on his bed and took an afternoon nap. When he woke, the image of Carmen, the slender, good-looking brunette guide at Ramirez Enterprises, flashed through his mind. He showered, dressed in a sky-blue cashmere sports shirt and dark blue slacks, and took a cab to *The Latino* restaurant and upscale bar.

Budding businessmen and well-dressed young women filled the huge bar area that had a glass ceiling and plants throughout, giving it a greenhouse feel. Popular music flooded the bar, creating a sense of urgency as dozens of young business professionals turned into early evening partygoers. Tom chatted with several young women as he moved leisurely through the bar. Carmen Flores tapped him on the arm, and he turned and smiled at the vivacious brunette. She had changed clothes and was now dressed in a white top and blue mini skirt that accented her ample breasts and long legs.

"I'm glad you joined us. Come over to the table. I want you to meet my girlfriends." She took him by the arm and led him to a table where three lovely brunettes were chatting and drinking with several young men. Introductions were made all around.

Carmen ordered a house specialty drink for Tom. He downed the first drink, and his head suddenly felt as if a bomb had gone off. "What's in this?" he asked.

"Seven different types of tequila," she said, and grinned. "Do you like it?"

"It tastes great, but wow! I think I'll have to go back to drinking beer just to stay on my feet."

The group of young women and Tom began bar hopping. Young men came and went as they passed from nightclub to nightclub, and Tom's American Express card was in and out of his wallet at breakneck speed. He tried to focus but found it impossible. Tom remembered dancing at more than one location but couldn't remember eating. At the end of the evening, he paid to send the young ladies home in cabs, saluting them as they departed.

Carmen and Tom got into a cab. He remembered a blur of lights as they passed oncoming traffic, and then his memory began to dim.

***

At five the following morning, there was pounding on the front door of the apartment. A very drunken man was shouting and then began kicking the front door until it crashed inward. Tom sat up in bed, alarmed, but the room was spinning, and he had no idea where he was.

"My God! It's my husband!" Carmen yelled.

"Your husband! You didn't tell me you were married."

"We're getting a divorce." The naked brunette jumped out of bed and ran towards the bathroom.

The drunken husband kicked the pieces of the broken door out of his way as he staggered towards the bedroom, calling Carmen's name. He pulled a revolver from his jacket and fired twice at the bedroom door, hitting it only once.

Tom, totally naked, jumped out of bed and ran to the window. He raised it just as Carmen's husband began kicking at the bedroom door. Tom dived through the half open window onto the metal fire escape on the fourth floor. He scrambled to his feet as the drunken assailant entered the room and fired at the window. Glass shattered, and pieces cut into Tom's shoulder. Bradshaw raced down the fire escape to the third floor, pushed up a partially open window, and clambered inside.

An old couple in bed was awakened by the shouting and shots being fired. They watched in surprise as Tom grabbed the man's pair of pants and a T-shirt off an overstuffed chair and ran into the living room.

***

Upstairs, Carmen was screaming as her husband kicked the door open and entered the bathroom.

"I love you, baby. You can't divorce me. Say that you still love me!"

"I love you! I love you!" Carmen responded as if on cue. "Put the gun down, Luis. We can still make it work."

Luis dropped the cocked revolver, and it fired a bullet into the bathtub, making a booming sound. Carmen picked up the weapon and dodged her husband, who was advancing towards her with open arms. She ran into the living room, past the shattered door and out into the hallway.

"Come back. I love you. Come back, Carmen," Luis yelled as he tripped and fell on his face.

"Call the police!" she yelled to her neighbors, whose heads were protruding from their front doors. She continued running down the hallway, then took the stairs down to the third floor. Tom and Carmen nearly collided as he entered the stairwell with the same escape route in mind. The two naked escapees, one with a gun in her hand and the other clutching pants and a shirt, quickly reached the ground floor and ran towards the front of the building. They burst out onto the street as sunrise flooded the area with light.

"How did you get the revolver?" Tom asked.

Carmen looked at her hand holding the weapon as if it was a foreign object from outer space. Her eyes were wide and mouth open. "I must have picked it up." She handed it to him, and he dumped it in the bushes.

They heard sirens, and their faces mirrored anxiety and fear. Tom began hopping around on one leg as he tried to pull up the trousers belonging to the tiny old man. He managed to pull them up to his crotch, but they wouldn't zip up, and the legs were a full twelve inches too short. Tom began waving frantically at a passing cab. The driver took one look at the naked woman and half naked man and speeded out of sight.

"This isn't going to work," she said. "I'll go back in and get some clothes from the neighbors."

"Hurry! The sirens are getting closer," he said frantically.

Carmen re-entered the building, and Tom decided to do the same. He peered through the glass in the front door as an older women walked up to him. Her eyes moved up and down the young man. Then she brushed past him. "Pervert!" she yelled back.

His features took on a pained expression, and he groaned. Carmen reappeared with a pair of old, paint stained pants that were too short and far too large around the waist. She also carried a paint stained T-shirt. He pulled them on as quickly as he could. Carmen took one look at him and began laughing loudly just as a squad car pulled up in front and two policemen ran towards the front door. She was wearing a shift, several sizes too large, but still managed to look sexy.

Carmen explained to the police officers about what had occurred, and they ran up the stairs, guns drawn. She stopped one of her neighbors exiting the front door and chatted with him for a moment. He looked reluctant but finally nodded yes. She motioned for Tom to come out of the stairwell leading to the basement, and he complied.

"Wait a minute. This guy's a bum," her short, rotund neighbor said.

Tom wanted to wrap his fingers around the fat man's throat but controlled his impulses. "I'll pay you one hundred dollars American if you drive me to the Hilton Hotel."

His eyes shined as he realized Tom would be easy pickings. "Make that two hundred, and you've got a deal."

Bradshaw's facial expression was twisted, almost wrenched out of shape as a gurgling sound came from deep within his throat. "Okay," he managed to say.

"Follow me, but don't get too close. I don't want people thinking we know each other."

Tom trudged down the street behind Carmen's friend. His raggedy paint-stained T-shirt and oversized pants caught everyone's attention who drove by. They reached a twenty-year-old Honda Accord that had most of its paint missing, and Tom climbed in the back seat. The upholstery was torn and spotted and smelled of decay.

"Don't get any paint on the seats," the plump man warned as he belched loudly. They rode for five minutes before the fat driver turned his head. "Open the windows. It's beginning to stink in here."

Another five minutes of travel brought them to the front of the beautiful steel and glass Hilton Hotel.

"Drive up to the valet parking," Tom ordered.

"Are you kidding me? The security officers won't let you in the front door. I'll drive around to the service entrance at the rear of the hotel."

Tom was at his destination and no longer had to appease or pacify the driver. "Listen. You want to get paid, don't you? I don't have any money on me. I'll have to get the front desk manager to give me two hundred dollars and add it to my account."

"You don't have any money! They'll never give you

money. You look like a homeless person," the sweating fat man blurted out.

Tom got out of the Accord and slammed the door, causing the window to fall halfway down. He marched past the parking valet, who buzzed for security. Tom reached the front desk and was second in line behind two fat matronly women who were arguing with the day manager about the location of their rooms. Bradshaw was almost two heads taller than the ladies. The manager, Vicente Cantu, looked at the bedraggled tall man and couldn't believe his eyes. "Is that you, Tom?"

Bradshaw moved in front of the women. "Vicente, I was caught in a compromising position by an angry husband. He began firing at me, and I escaped with no clothes on. I don't have my clothes, my wallet, or my keys. See that guy peering through the planter over there? Give him two hundred dollars, and add it to my account. And for God's sake, give me a key to my suite!"

"Oh, he smells terrible," one of the women said.

"I hope this isn't the type of clientele we'll be subjected to," the other lady noted.

Cantu pulled a key from the back wall and handed it to Tom. "I'll see that the guy gets paid. Do me a favor, Tom, and take the service elevator."

Bradshaw thought he was joking, but when he looked in his eyes, he could see that Cantu was serious. Feeling humiliated, he marched through the nearly deserted lobby past the bank of elevators to the service elevator and waited for what seemed like an eternity before it arrived.

The ride to the sixth floor was quick. The elevator door opened, and he stood face to face with a young, thin maid, whose eyes were wide as she viewed the disheveled man wearing clothing covered in various paint colors. Tom held up his key. "Follow me," he told her.

When they reached Room 614, he unlocked the door and told her to wait. Seconds later, the door opened about four inches, and his hand holding the dirty clothing popped through the opening. "Burn these. I'll tip you later."

Bradshaw, naked again, walked into the bathroom and turned on the shower. He spent the next fifteen minutes lounging in hot water. Then Tom shaved, dressed in a light grey striped sports shirt and dark grey slacks, and put on black, glove leather loafers. Just as he was about to leave and go down to the lobby, there was a soft knock at the door. He yanked it open, not knowing what to expect but now ready to re-establish his everyday dominance.

Carmen Flores stood there holding his clothing and shoes. "I wanted to apologize. That whole mess was my fault." She was dressed in a white blouse and beige mini skirt. Her dark hair hung to her shoulders in ringlets. The aroma from her perfume flooded the doorway.

"Come in." He opened the door wide.

"My husband's in jail, so he's no longer a threat. I'll understand if you no longer want to see me. I just wanted to —"

Tom reached out, grabbed her by the arm, and pulled her into the room. "I may not remember last night, but I'm sure as hell going to remember this."

As the door shut, he began kissing her and running his hands over her body. She gasped and returned his passion. He picked her up, carried her into the bedroom, and they were between the sheets a few seconds later. His intense, emotional excitement was returned in kind, and they spent the morning in bed.

CHAPTER 4

A tall, handsome young Mexican man exited the nightclub shortly after midnight, one arm encircling a beautiful brunette. They staggered and laughed as they made their way down the block to where Alejandro Ramos had parked his convertible Mustang. Just as they reached the car, two men jumped from the shadows, grabbed Alejandro, and pulled him out into the street. An old Nissan Altima drove up, and the driver got out to help the two kidnappers.

Alejandro fought hard, knocked one of the men down, and began punching the second attacker. The third assailant came up behind him and smashed him over the head with a tire iron. The university student fell down, unconscious. The girl had been struck in the face and was lying in the street, crying out. One of the grabbers kicked her in the head, knocking her out. They drove off with their prize, leaving the girl lying in the gutter.

Alejandro's arms and legs were bound with duct tape, and a black blindfold was tied behind his head and pulled down over his eyes. Twenty minutes later, he awoke to a splitting headache and the realization that he'd been kidnapped.

"What do you want?" Alejandro asked.

"Shut up, kid," one of the kidnappers growled.

"My family has money. Do you want my father's cell

phone number?"

"We already have it. Now shut up."

Fifteen minutes later, the Altima entered Netzahualcoyotl, or Nez as it is commonly called. The slums to the east of the Mexico City airport had densely packed housing for as far as the eye could see from a helicopter. It was originally started by shady developers, who never owned the land, in the 1950s. They sold hundreds of thousands of lots for a few dollars down and a few dollars a month for ten to twenty years. People began building houses out of planks, cardboard, and reeds. Roofs were made from asbestos, scraps of tarpaulin, and sheets of corrugated metal.

In the early days, the shanty towns were without paved streets, water supplies, drainage, and electricity. Today most of the small homes were patched together with concrete and tin and had electricity and water. Many of the streets were so narrow that only small motorbikes could negotiate them.

The kidnappers drove up a steep, rutted road to a nondescript grey block building that had the windows boarded up. It clung to the hillside like a child clinging to its mother. The area smelled of sewage and burning diesel fuel mixed with sizzling carne asada. The duct tape around his feet was cut off, and Alejandro was half dragged into the small building and thrown on a bed. Tape around his hands was replaced by handcuffs. His right hand was cuffed to the steel headboard, and only his left hand was free.

"There's a pot to piss and crap in next to the bed. If you make any noise, you'll be tied up, and your mouth taped over. We'll tell you when we are coming into the bedroom. Make sure your blindfold is in place, or we'll permanently put duct tape around your eyes. Do you understand me, asshole?" the kidnapper growled.

***

Wealthy shopping center owner Sebastian Ramos received a call in his downtown Mexico City headquarters. The caller growled out the sentence that terrified businessmen throughout the capitol city. "We've kidnapped your son." The overweight, bald corporate owner froze in his chair as the phone went dead. The short, fat man cried out in anguish as he dialed his son's cell phone. There was no answer. He jumped up from behind his desk, sending the chair sliding into the rear wall of his office.

Next, he called his home, and his wife informed him that his twenty-one-year-old son, Alejandro, apparently never came home from partying the night before. Sebastian felt sick to his stomach, and his face suddenly became slick with sweat popping out, running down and dripping on the front of his white shirt. Like a crazed animal, he walked in circles, not knowing what to do, where to go for help, or who to contact.

He knew better than to call the police, having just read the newspaper article about the arrest of the entire police force in Madera, Chihuahua, in northern Mexico. Madera's police commander and all fourteen of his men were arrested for providing protection to drug traffickers and obstructing the work of state security agencies operating in the region.

Sebastian began pacing like a caged animal. He stopped a few seconds later and grabbed the telephone. Ramos dialed his banker, Leonardo Pena, and started breathing heavily into the telephone. Pena answered, and Ramos blurted out what had just occurred.

"What can I do?" he pleaded.

"Do you have kidnap and ransom insurance?" Pena asked.

"No. It's expensive. I never thought I'd have to use it."

The tall, thin, impeccably dressed banker thought for a moment. "A friend of mine in the banking business was kidnapped. His bank had K & R insurance with a California firm. The negotiator provided by the insurance company was very smooth, professional, and finalized his release in three weeks."

"What are you telling me? I don't have K & R insurance."

"You need someone to negotiate on your behalf. Don't try

to do it yourself, or you'll end up paying ten times more than what a negotiator will arrive at with the kidnappers."

"Well, what should I do now?" Ramos asked, his voice cracking as he talked. "They've got my only son," he blubbered and began crying.

"The negotiator was Tom Bradshaw. He lives at the downtown Hilton Hotel when he's in town. Try him first to see if he's in town. Meanwhile, I'll find out what company he works for and pass that information on to you," the banker stated.

***

Tom walked into one of three Hilton restaurants and moved past a table where a beautiful blonde was reviewing small interior design sketches while she was eating breakfast. She looked up and smiled at him, her bright blue eyes showing interest. Tom stopped in his tracks and said hello. She responded in English, and he knew she was an American.

"I'm Tom Bradshaw."

"And I'm Crystal Henderson."

He told her that he liked her sketches, hoping they were hers. She said she was beginning a huge interior design project for the wife of a Mexican oil company vice president, who wanted a complete remodel of their twenty-five thousand square foot home.

He stood near her, making small talk until it became obvious to her that he would like to join her. Seeing no wedding ring, she invited him to join her for breakfast. Tom sat down. A waitress came to the table, and Tom ordered.

"I'm guessing we both are expatriates from the States," he said, his emerald green eyes never leaving her face.

"I'm from the San Francisco area. The company I work for is there. I'm on loan, so to speak, in order to do this very large remodeling job. Isabella Pacheco stayed at a home that I had done interior design drawings for, and she ended up hiring me and the company I work for."

"How long will you be here?" Tom asked.

"Weeks, I suppose. Every client is different, and they all have different wants and needs. I'm staying in one of the presidential suites, which has a large working office. Living conditions are terrific," she said and smiled, revealing beautiful white teeth.

"Hey, that's no fair. I have to stay in a suite on the sixth floor." They laughed.

"What line of work are you in, Tom?"

"Insurance. It's a different type than you normally think of."

The longer they talked, the more interested Bradshaw became in the gorgeous young blonde. Her personality was charming, her smile was captivating, and her eyes were inviting. During the next five minutes, Tom's iPhone, set on vibrate, rang four times. The same phone number kept popping up.

"Aren't you going to answer it? It must be the same person calling," she observed.

"No. I'd rather talk with you. Would you like to have dinner with me tonight?" he asked, and smiled.

Crystal used her beauty to follow a path different from what most women would take. She'd learned to smile and speak in a soft voice when asking penetrating questions, which took away the sting of overstepping the bounds of propriety.

"Are you single?" she asked.

"Yes. I've never been married, but I've come close a couple of times," he replied, his eyes never leaving hers.

"I can't tonight. I have a business commitment. But tomorrow night I'm free."

Tom knew how to use his charm, good looks, manliness, and emerald green eyes to achieve his goals with the opposite sex. The force and strength of the man were manifested in the way he confidently carried himself and spoke in a direct manner. Women loved his assertiveness, aggressiveness, and boyish charm that created enormous sex appeal. Chrystal was no exception.

"I'll knock on your presidential suite door at seven tomorrow night," he said, and grinned.

***

Tom returned to his room, sat down behind his desk, and checked his iPhone. The same number had popped up three more times. He returned the call.

"Oh, thank God you've called! I don't know what to do. They've got my son, my beautiful boy. Help me, please!" Sebastian Ramos begged.

"Try to calm down. What's your name, and why are you calling me?" Tom asked in a soft voice.

"My banker says you're a very good negotiator. I'll pay you whatever you want. Please get my boy back. He's my only child," Ramos blubbered.

"What's your name?"

"I'm Sebastian Ramos. The kidnapper called and said he has my son, Alejandro, and then he hung up," Ramos said and began weeping loudly.

"Do you have kidnap and ransom insurance with any company?"

"No. I never thought I'd need it. Please help me. I don't know where to turn. I have money. I own shopping centers in Mexico City." Ramos began wheezing, unable to catch his breath.

"Look, Mr. Ramos, if you're not insured with our company, California Fidelity, there's nothing I can do for you. I can only do negotiation work for my employer. I can recommend a free-lance negotiator that you can use," Tom explained.

"I'm begging you. Please help me," Ramos pleaded, sobbing into the phone.

Bradshaw put his hand over the phone. "'Shit!" Then he exhaled sharply. "Give me your address. I'll come over and meet with you."

Ramos blurted out the address in an unintelligible voice.

Tom made him repeat it three times before he could understand the shopping center mogul. His next call was to his boss, Mark Danforth, who told him to forget about it.

"We're not a charity. This is a for profit insurance company, for Christ's sake," Danforth said sternly.

"I know you'll do it if the money's right. Give me the parameters. If he won't agree, I'll give him the name of a free-lancer."

Danforth thought for a moment. "He'd have to sign a contract back-dated to a year ago. The premium for the past year would be $250,000, wired to us before you can begin any kind of negotiations on his behalf. The cost of your services would be the standard $4,000 per day. If you're successful, there would be no payout from Cal Fidelity. In addition, he'll need to wire us another $50,000, from which the $4,000 per day will be subtracted."

"Okay. I'll tell him the good news."

Danforth snorted. "You don't seem too upset about the terms."

"I'm not. This guy cries continually. That's the worst kind of client."

"We don't know anything about this guy. We haven't done any background checks. We haven't seen his financials. Has he been a deadbeat?"

"He'll cry harder when he hears the terms," Tom said.

"You're supposed to be in the midst of your ten days off. What the hell are you still doing in Mexico? Aren't those beach bunnies in Santa Monica calling?" his boss asked.

"I'd tell you to go screw yourself, but you're my boss."

"It hasn't stopped you in the past." The men laughed.

***

The taxi took Bradshaw into the exclusive Polanco neighborhood west of the downtown high rise area. Guards at the front iron gates of the master planned community checked his identification. He was expected and was given a map showing how to navigate the interior streets to reach Sebastian Ramos's home.

The luxury home had a massive red-tiled roof and was surrounded by lawns and flower gardens. Ramos came running out of the gigantic glass-enclosed double front doors and nearly fell on the cobblestone walkway. He was short, fat, and bald except for hair on the sides of his head. His eyes were encased in circles of fat, and he had guppy-like lips and a pencil-thin moustache. Rosy red cheeks completed his facial features.

"Thank God you're here," he croaked.

They walked inside the house and straight to the back living room, where his wife awaited them. The room had fifteen-foot high ceilings and a full wall of windows looking out on the rear yard that was also beautifully landscaped. The room had two settings of white leather furniture, which complemented cream-colored walls and light honey-colored marble floors.

Sofia Ramos's eyes were wide, and her mouth would open and shut as she swallowed. Too frightened to say anything, she clutched her hands in her lap and began reciting silent prayers. The short, fat lady stared at Bradshaw, not really seeing him as an individual but as a potential savior. Fear had consumed her to a point that she was frozen in place, unable to function.

"Mr. Ramos, my company has rather strict requirements in cases where we don't have a policy in place. Normally, California Fidelity won't represent corporations or individuals unless we are contractually obligated with them."

"Just tell me what you want. Anything! I don't care what it costs," he cried out.

Tom quietly explained the terms, then sat back, waiting for a response. It came in a flash.

"Are you crazy? You want $250,000 on a post-dated contract? And you want $4,000 per day to represent us? That's robbery!" Ramos yelled.

"Plus another $100,000, from which the $4,000 would be

deducted daily," Tom said.

"I didn't get where I am today, owning ten shopping centers, by agreeing to such one-sided terms. I won't do it."

Tom got up from the white leather couch and held out a business card to Ramos. "This is Richard Edwards' cell phone number. He's a very competent negotiator with a great deal of experience in Mexico City. Give him a try."

Suddenly there was a high pitched, penetrating scream from Mrs. Ramos. She ran to Bradshaw, grabbed his hand, and got down on her knees. She looked up at him with eyes the size of eggs and continued to cry out with ear-splitting shrieks.

Ramos jumped to his feet. "All right. I agree to your terms."

CHAPTER 5

Tom had the recording equipment set up in an office next to Sebastian Ramos's private office at his corporate headquarters. He had a conference table brought in, additional phones added, and speakers strategically placed so that all telephone conversations could be recorded and played back instantly. Six leather chairs were placed around the table. A computer was installed with a large screen to be used for Facetime.

Bradshaw was chatting with Sebastian Ramos towards the end of the first day when Ramos's private secretary hurried into the newly completed center of operations.

"There's a man calling about your son," she said, a worried look on her face.

"Thank you. Put the call through," Tom replied.

"What do we do? What do we say?" the worried father asked.

"Just listen. Don't say anything, or there could be real problems," Tom warned. Bradshaw turned on the recorder and picked up the phone. "Hello. My name is Ajax, and I'm the negotiator who will be communicating with you as we negotiate a deal for the release of Alejandro Ramos. We do want to pay you for his safe release."

"Goddamn it! Put Sebastian Ramos on the phone," the

kidnapper yelled.

"I'll be doing the negotiating on his behalf. I'll be here in the office Monday through Friday during regular eight to five hours. Once again, my name is Ajax. If you call after working hours or on weekends, it may take longer to reach me, but the operator will find me," Tom explained in a business-like manner.

"Listen, asshole, I want to speak to Sebastian. Don't screw around with me," the kidnapper shouted.

"Remember, we do want to pay you for his safe release," Tom said calmly.

"You son-of-a-bitch. I'm going to cut off the kid's ear and mail it to you."

The line went dead. Sebastian began wailing, and tears rolled down his cheeks. "Is he really going to harm my son?"

"No. This first conversation went about how I expected it to go. The kidnapper wanted to show that he was boss, and he did. I was able to make several points. As he reviews the conversation in his mind, several things will stand out to him."

"What do you mean? He was angry and threatened to harm Alejandro." More tears ran down his cheeks, and he began sniffling.

"Here are the points I got across to him. Number one is that we do want to pay him for Alejandro's safe release. Secondly, he knows what hours to call here so he can reach me immediately. Third is that my code name is Ajax, and using that name will eliminate any confusion about who the call is directed to. He also has learned that threats won't work, and the negotiations will be carried out in a calm, business-like manner," Tom explained.

Ramos stopped crying, wiped his eyes and face with a handkerchief, and thought about Bradshaw's explanation.

"How much will they ask for?"

"A lot. They want to determine how likely you are to give in to ridiculous demands."

"Can't we just pay them what they want and have this

over with?" Ramos asked.

"No. You never meet the kidnappers' first ransom demand even if you're willing to pay the money."

Ramos had a pained expression on his face. "Why?"

"Every kidnapping is about control, and you have virtually none. What you do have is the fact that you're the only buyer in the market for your son. Think of the first demand as being an asking price for a precious object. There has to be some back-and-forth before a deal is struck."

Ramos shook his head back and forth and wiped his running nose. "I don't know what you mean. I can't focus."

"If you quickly pay an exorbitant price, the grabbers will think you're a golden goose. They'll take the money and release your son. Then, several months later, they'll kidnap him again. This time they'll ask for ten times more than what you've paid previously. You'll have placed yourself in a no win situation."

The shopping center owner groaned. "What happens next?"

"Chances are the kidnapper will make a huge demand over the telephone. I'll tell him that I'll have an answer for him within twenty-four hours. When he calls back, we'll start with a very low offer. Kidnappers will always scorn your first offer, no matter what it is. You want the kidnappers to know that you're not going to instantly meet their demands."

"How long is all this going to take?" Ramos asked.

"There's no set time. It could be days, weeks, or even longer. Don't expect it to be over quickly."

Ramos looked as if he was about to cry again. "My wife is not strong. I don't want her to have a nervous breakdown."

Tom opened his briefcase and wrote down two names and telephone numbers. "These are the names of two local psychologists. Get your wife into therapy as quickly as possible. Some people are stronger than others. You certainly don't want her to have a nervous breakdown."

"What's it going to cost?"

"Does it really matter? What's more important, your wife's mental well-being or money?"

***

That evening precisely at seven, Tom knocked on the door of the presidential suite at the Hilton Hotel. Seconds later, Crystal Henderson opened the door. She was stunning in a light blue silk dress and blueish-green earrings and neckless. Her blonde hair fell on her shoulders in ringlets.

"You look terrific," he said, and smiled.

"So do you. You look like an ad from a men's fashion magazine."

Tom was dressed in a light brown, summer weight wool suit, brown and gold striped tie, and white tab collar shirt.

Crystal learned early that she could travel through life shielded from trouble and displeasure, knowing that men were captivated by her allure and charm. She would take liberties when and where she felt like it. Men never seemed to care.

Tom laughed. "You've got a great sense of humor. I like that in a woman."

"Come on, I'll show you around. This suite has everything." She showed him the working office, a huge living room, a lavish bedroom, and an outside patio surrounded by glass partitions five feet high.

He stared off into the distance at high rise buildings in the foreground and sparkling city lights as far as the eye could see. Crystal studied him as his gaze traveled in a half circle. "Magnificent," he said in a calm voice.

Suddenly, she knew she was standing next to a different type of man, one she seldom encountered. Crystal looked away quickly as his gaze returned to her, not wanting him to recognize her momentary bewilderment.

They took a taxi to the Miralto restaurant located on the forty-fifth floor of the Torre Latino Americana skyscraper. It featured 360 degree views from its huge, glassed in dining room. Waiters in white button down shirts, black vests, and black ties moved slowly throughout the room as patrons relaxed to grand piano music and enjoyed fine dining.

"These views are amazing. I'm impressed, Mr. Bradshaw," Crystal said.

"I really love Mexico City. It has a European feel with its spectacular museums, impressive boulevards, and lovely squares full of flowers, surrounded by outdoor cafes. The city has an energized rhythm all its own," Tom said.

"Is that why you choose to work here?" she asked.

He hesitated, then decided to fully explain what his job entailed.

"I'm a kidnap and ransom negotiator for California Fidelity in Los Angeles. It's one of the largest insurance companies selling this type of insurance to corporations throughout Mexico, Central, and South America. We also sell coverage to American companies whose executives spend a great deal of time abroad. For the past two years, I've been doing most of my negotiating in Mexico City, although I can't talk about who our clients are."

Crystal stopped eating and stared at Tom. "I've heard of that type of insurance. But I never really gave it any thought."

"Cal Fidelity deals with corporate presidents, CEOs, and boards of directors. The people being covered by the insurance are never aware that the policies exist."

"Why? What's the logic in that?" she asked.

"Two reasons. If a man knows he's covered by K & R insurance, he may take risks that he would ordinarily avoid, thinking his company will bail him out. Also, he might brag about it, thus greatly enhancing his desirability if a kidnapping gang learns about his loose tongue."

Crystal thought for a moment and frowned. "Then there might be a policy covering me."

"Possibly. Hey, let's change the subject. You look beautiful tonight, and the surroundings are magnificent," Tom said. "It just feels right tonight. I don't know how to explain my feelings, but I'm happy you're here. Let's enjoy the moment."

They ate dinner, danced, talked, and enjoyed each other's company. The conversations were light, humorous, and they laughed often as they began to learn about one another.

"It's interesting how chance encounters can change your life entirely," Tom said. "I was going to have breakfast in my suite but changed my mind and met you."

She looked at him and smiled. Crystal used her beauty as a weapon and traveled through life protected because her friendly demeanor and charming smile captivated men, no matter what questions she asked. As if magnetized, she would gradually pull information from men. They didn't mind and felt privileged to be among her intimate confidants.

"You told me you'd come close to getting married a couple of times. Why are you still single? You're not getting any younger, you know," she said.

They were sitting side by side on an outside patio, looking at the twinkling city lights. The aroma from her French perfume was captivating, and Tom wanted to wrap his arms around the vivacious blonde.

"I live in my dad's Santa Monica condo on the beach when I'm in Los Angeles. This is usually ten days out of each month. Twice I've been serious about women, but my being out of the country so much eventually caused the relationships to fall apart. I don't blame the women for moving on," he explained.

She stared at him, her blue eyes trying to analyze Tom. "Are you going to do this forever?"

He laughed. "No. I've established a great many business contacts because of my work. I'm also completing a business degree from USC online. When I find the opportunity I'm looking for, I'll leave the kidnap and ransom negotiation business. International business acquisitions and management probably will be in my future."

"You're a complicated man, Tom," she said, and looked out at the never-ending array of lights illuminating the city.

"It's my turn to ask a personal question. How is it that a beautiful, charming woman like you is still single?" Tom asked.

Crystal smiled. "I've been divorced for three years. I got married just as I graduated from Cal. It was the thing to do, and most of my girlfriends did just that. But, I determined in a short amount of time that a marriage, a house, and kids were not what I was looking for, at least not now. My ex-husband had a different view on life, and so we divorced."

What she neglected to tell him was that she had a steady boyfriend in San Francisco, who was mounting a full-court-press to get married.

"Enough of this serious talk. Let's hit a couple of lively nightclubs, dance, and laugh," Tom urged.

During the next two hours, they visited El Cubano, decorated like a Cuban nightclub in Miami. They danced and swayed to the music that changed rapidly from electronic to salsa to funk. Next, they took a cab to Patrick Rios, a three-story, old converted colonial house. Bands played pop rock and dance music on all three floors, and the top floor featured an open terrace.

Tom put his arm around Crystal and pulled her close as they gazed out from the terrace at the city of flickering lights. He kissed her, and she responded with great intensity. They were consumed with emotion, each feeling the intimacy of the moment.

Neither one saw Carmen Flores as she rushed towards them. "You bastard!" she shouted. Tom and Crystal pulled away from each other just as she threw a drink in Tom's face that splattered down his suit. "You screw me in the morning, and then you're out with this whore tonight." Carmen grabbed a drink from a table next to them and splattered it down the front of Crystal's dress. "You rotten bitch," she yelled.

Both Tom and Crystal looked at their clothing in disbelief, their eyes wide and mouths open.

"I wish my husband had shot you like he tried to do!" Carmen shouted.

Crystal had had enough. "I'll get a cab. Tom, do something about her," she said, and rushed away.

Bradshaw was torn between going after Crystal and trying to calm the nearly hysterical brunette. "For God's sake, Carmen, stop it."

But he wasn't fast enough in making up his mind. She hurled a plate of guacamole at his chest, and her aim was perfect. The green dip covered his suit coat and moved down his pants like a slow moving lava flow.

Bouncers ran forward and were greeted with more flying food as Carmen dodged around the tables. Tom stood still, arms held out from his sides, looking like an immobile, slimy-green scarecrow.

CHAPTER 6

Tom was working on the computer when a secretary rushed in and told him a caller wanted to talk with Sebastian Ramos about his son. Ramos burst into the room seconds later.

"What are we to do? Do you think they've hurt my son? Can we pay them money?" he asked, sweat pouring down his face.

"Sebastian, we've discussed these points several times. I'll take the call, and you remain quiet," Bradshaw said calmly. "Put the call through," he told the secretary. He turned on the recording machine and picked up the telephone. "Hello. This is Ajax, and I'm handling the negotiations for Mr. Ramos."

"I told you, you son-of-a-bitch, that I want to talk with Sebastian Ramos. Put that fat turd on the phone," the kidnapper shouted.

"We do want to pay you money for the safe return of Alejandro. Is there a code name that you use? It would be helpful so that the calls are always immediately put through to me," Tom said.

There was silence on the line while the kidnapper thought about what to do. "You can call me Paco," he said.

"Good, Paco. How can I help you today?"

"You tell that money-grubbing bastard that I want three

million dollars American for the return of his son, or I'll start sending him body parts," the grabber yelled and hung up.

"What are we to do?" Ramos moaned. "Do we pay him? Is my son okay?

What am I to do? Why doesn't he stay on the line longer?"

Tom took a deep breath before he spoke, thinking about how much easier it was when dealing with corporate executives. Family members had a tendency to be too emotional, and at times were physically ill from worry.

"To answer your last question first, kidnappers' phone calls are always short and mean. They fear that the calls may be traced, so the conversations are short. He'll call back tomorrow expecting a reply, and we'll give him one he won't like."

"What do you mean?" Ramos's face mirrored dread, and his voice cracked.

"I suggest we offer two hundred thousand dollars," Tom said in a business-like tone of voice

"But he wants three million. Won't he be mad? Will he hurt Alejandro?"

Tom got up from his chair and walked over to Ramos. He pulled up a chair, sat down, and put his hand on the shopping center mogul's arm. "Once we begin negotiations, the deployment becomes business oriented."

"What's a deployment?"

"Sorry, I forgot to mention that the term we use for negotiation is deployment in the kidnap and ransom business. A ransom itself is called a settlement. We'll be working towards a settlement. I know what I'm doing. You have to trust me."

Ramos's bloodshot eyes, sour-full expression, runny nose, and quivering lips portrayed a picture of a man drowning in fear. Bradshaw tightened his grip on the businessman's arm.

"You have to stay strong and focused for the benefit of Alejandro. The pressure is going to increase because I'm going to ask for proof of life in the form of two questions before we begin negotiating. We don't want to negotiate only to find out that they don't have your son or he's dead."

Ramos cried out, mouth open and eyes shut. "God, help me, please."

"It's sad to say, but this is a business. The kidnappers know they will get only a small amount of money if the victim dies, so they will keep him alive," Tom said. "I'll continually ask proof of life questions to insure Alejandro's safety. They'll be simple questions, but only ones that Alejandro can answer."

The shopping center owner's eyes popped open. "What kind of questions?"

"Does he have a dog? What's its name? What's your mother's first name? They'll be questions like these," Tom explained.

"Yes, he has a dog named Pedro. My mother's first name is Andrea," Ramos said quickly.

***

The following afternoon Tom was busy on the computer, reviewing for a final exam in USC's online business degree program. Every few minutes, the connecting door to Sebastian Ramos's private office would open a couple of inches. Ramos would study Bradshaw and then silently close the door.

After the fifth time, Tom said, "I can see you, Sebastian. Come on in."

The door opened, and Sebastian scurried in. "Any word? Anything?" he asked.

"No. I'm taking an online course. It helps to relieve tension and stress if you can take your mind off the deployment."

"I can't think about anything else. My wife is talking with a psychologist you recommended, and it seems to be helping her. I tried talking with the doctor, but I can't focus," Ramos said.

A secretary opened the door and stuck her head in. "There's a call for Mr. Ajax," she said hurriedly.

Tom turned on the recorder. "Put the call through."

Moments later, he picked up the phone. "This is Ajax."

"I've got a surprise for you," Paco said loudly.

There was screaming in the background. "Leave me alone! Don't touch me again!" Then another scream came forth.

Paco came back on the line. "Tell that fat asshole that we'll continue to make his son's body twitch and jump until he pays us."

"There's no need to harm Alejandro. We are going to pay you ransom money. I have a couple of proof of life questions for you to ask, Alejandro. What is his dog's name? And what is his grandmother's first name, meaning Sebastian's mother?" Tom asked in a smooth, business-like voice.

"Is this some kind of a joke, you bastard?" Paco responded.

"It's no joke. I'm just trying to establish that you have the right boy. Please ask him the questions," Tom replied.

"Just a minute. What's your dog's name, and what's your grandmother's first name?"

Paco covered the phone while he retrieved the answers from Alejandro. Then, he came back on the line. "His dog's name is Pedro, and his grandmother's first name is Andrea. Now, what about the money?"

"Senor Ramos has instructed me to offer you two hundred thousand American dollars."

"Are you crazy?" the kidnapper shouted.

"That's about four million pesos, a nice chunk of money," Tom emphasized.

The kidnapper hesitated for a moment. "I want a hell of a lot more than two hundred thousand."

"We are always willing to negotiate," Tom pointed out.

The line went dead.

Ramos began his animated movements, jerking and twitching in his chair. His face mirrored pain, eyes mere slits and mouth fluttering open and shut. "They're killing him, Tom! We have to do something."

"Calm down, Sebastian. I found out several things today. Your son has not been seriously harmed. He's frightened, but he was able to give quick answers to the questions. He may be shackled and locked in a dark room, but he's surviving okay."

Sebastian shook his head back and forth. "I don't know. I can't think straight." He took a deep breath and exhaled sharply, causing his body to shake like jelly.

"Here's the important thing. We are beginning to negotiate. The kidnapper's spokesman, Paco, hesitated when I mentioned that four million pesos is a lot of money. It made him think. My guess is that he'll counter our offer tomorrow," Tom said.

"Do we accept the new offer?" Sebastian asked excitedly.

"No. It'll be too high. Remember what I told you. If you pay an exorbitant amount of ransom, they may try to kidnap Alejandro a second time and ask for…ten million."

Ramos winced. "Oh shit."

***

During the next week, Tom had three more short conversations with Paco. The grabber dropped his demands to two million and finally to one million. Bradshaw countered at two hundred and fifty thousand, and then two hundred and seventy-five thousand. Tom was anxious for the third conversation, knowing they were close. The call came in, and Bradshaw pushed the record button.

"Hello, Paco."

"Ajax, I want five-hundred-thousand."

"I've been instructed to offer you three-hundred-thousand American dollars. That's six million pesos. Think what you can buy with that much money," Tom pointed out.

He could hear Paco breathing hard, then the call was disconnected.

Ramos was pacing back and forth. His shoes squeaked as he walked. "He didn't make a counter offer. Is he angry? What do we do? I can't take much more of this."

"We are near the end. I think he'll call back today," Tom replied. "Go to your office and try to work. Do something, anything to get your mind off the kidnapping."

Sebastian walked to his office door, opened it, and glanced back at Bradshaw, much as an indignant child looked at a parent who had sent him to his room.

An hour later, the call came in for Ajax, and Ramos came rushing into the room. Tom hit the record button.

"Hi. This is Ajax."

"Three hundred and twenty-five thousand American. I won't take anything less. The kid is going to start losing body parts if I don't get it."

Tom put his hand over the telephone receiver, extended his arm, and pointed his finger at Sebastian. "Do you agree on the price?"

Ramos jumped out of his chair. "Yes! Yes!" he cried out.

Bradshaw put his finger to his lips, signifying silence. "Paco, we have a deal. How and where do you want the money delivered?"

Paco exhaled sharply and was quiet for a moment. "I have coordinates for you. The money is to be put in two satchels and dropped from a helicopter at this location. Don't land the helicopter. Just drop the money and leave."

"What are the coordinates?"

The kidnapper rattled off the numbers, and Bradshaw repeated them back to the gang leader as he wrote them down.

"What time do we make the drop?"

"How soon can you lay your hands on the money?"

Ramos was jumping up and down. "Right away. Right now. My bank is across the street."

"It's about 10 a.m. right now. How about 4 p.m.? And is the drop site an open lot or the top of a building? We don't want to make the drop at the wrong location by mistake," Tom explained.

"It's a field. Remember, if we see any cops or security people come into the area, you'll never see that boy alive again," Paco said, and hung up.

Sebastian began jumping up and down, yelling with delight. Then he suddenly stopped and looked horrified. "They didn't tell us where to find Alejandro. How do I get my boy back? Is he okay?"

"They seldom give a specific location for delivery. They're afraid that the police will be waiting. We'll know within a couple of hours after we deliver the money where he is," Tom said.

Ramos went to his bank and withdrew three hundred and twenty-five thousand dollars, which was divided and put in two canvass duffle bags. They drove to the airport, and Sebastian rented a helicopter and a pilot for the drop. Tom brought along his computer, and the coordinates were put in Google Maps.

As they neared the location, the pilot, Antonio Reyes, told his passengers that the target location was an old soccer field that now was partially covered with garbage and rubble.

"Kids still play there," he yelled above the noise of the helicopter motor. "Where do you want to make the drop?"

Tom pointed to an open area near the center of the field. He checked his watch.

"It's time. Let's do it," he shouted.

The helicopter hovered about twenty feet off the ground as Tom threw the duffle bags out the open door. One of them split apart as it landed with a thud, and money began blowing in the swirling wind.

"Take it up, Antonio," Bradshaw yelled.

The helicopter rose in the air and flew off at an angle. Two men came running up to the bags and stopped the upward flow of money. They commenced grabbing twenty, fifty, and one hundred dollar bills off the ground and did a good job of recovering most of the money. Only a few dozen bills were still blowing in the wind by the time children from the shanty town began running in circles catching the bills as the money returned to earth.

Sebastian's eyes were wide and his mouth open as he watched the running kidnappers disappear into the slums, swallowed up by the grey shacks with corrugated metal roofs. Tom shook his head from side to side and looked at Ramos. "They got almost all the money," he yelled at Sebastian.

***

Two men entered the dark room, put a black blindfold on Alejandro Ramos, removed the shackles, taped his hands together, and jerked him upright. Ramos had a three week growth of beard, had lost fifteen pounds off his slender frame, and now resembled a very thin cadaver. He was thrown on the back floor of an old Honda Civic. Two of the kidnappers put their feet on him to hold Alejandro down. The car sputtered and backfired as they drove away, heading for a main road on the periphery of the slums.

They reached the road, stopped the car, pulled Ramos out of the vehicle, and dumped him in the dirt. "Leave the blindfold on for ten minutes, or I'll come back and beat the piss out of you. Understand?" a gang member yelled.

Alejandro groaned. "Yeah," he replied.

Ramos waited five minutes before he was able to get the black mask off by rubbing his face on the ground. He lay on his back, staring at the sky, wondering whether or not he was really free. Then he worked his hands loose from the duct tape. The young man rolled over and made a crab-like attempt to get to his feet. It failed, and he fell back on the dirt.

Minutes later, he tried again, and this time was successful. He lurched forward, trying to get his legs working properly. Alejandro reached the two-lane road and began waving his hands, trying to get a vehicle to stop. The cars speeded up rather than slowed down when they saw him. Finally, after ten minutes, an old Toyota Camry slowed and stopped.

Two men jumped out, ran up to Ramos, knocked him down, and began pulling off his boots.

"Stop! Stay away from me. What are you doing?" he yelled.

"Those are good-looking leather boots, asshole. They belong on me," one of the robbers said, and laughed.

Alejandro began rolling around, kicking at the men and screaming. The taller of the two men kicked Ramos in the head, leaving him in a semi-conscious state. His beautiful alligator leather boots were pulled off, and the men got back in the car and departed.

Ramos regained consciousness and sat up. Coming towards him out of the shanty town was a small cart pulled by a burro. An old man with white hair and beard pulled on the reins, and the burro stopped. They stared at each other, neither one comprehending what the other was doing there.

"You look like you've been beat up, kid. It happens to me now and then. Lots of bad men around here."

Every bone in Alejandro's body ached, and his head felt like a pounding drum. He shook his head up and down, agreeing with the old man.

"Get in the back, boy. I'm going to the market," the old man said.

Alejandro's eyes opened wide. "A real market? One with electricity and water?"

"Why, sure."

"Oh, thank God! There must be a telephone there."

Fifteen minutes later, the cart slowly pulled up in front of an open air market. Multiple vendors were showcasing their fruits, vegetables, rolls, breads, clothing, and small toys. Women walked in, made their purchases, and quickly headed home.

Alejandro walked from vendor to vendor, asking to use their cell phones. All of them turned him down, thinking the starving vagrant would run off with their phone. Finally, the old man walked up to a fruit vendor he knew and asked him to let the boy use his phone.

"Let the boy use the phone, and I'll give you this watch," he said, showing him an old silver watch. Reluctantly, the vendor agreed.

Alejandro called his father's cell phone. "Dad, I'm free. The kidnappers let me go."

Sebastian screamed with delight and then broke down crying. It took two minutes before he was able to write down the location of the market, which really had no permanent address. Thirty minutes later, a line of cars carrying Sebastian Ramos, six bodyguards, a doctor, and Tom Bradshaw arrived at the market. The boy and his father wrapped their arms around one another, both crying and trying to talk at the same time. At Alejandro's urging, Sebastian gave the old man nearly a thousand American dollars that he was carrying in his wallet.

"Here, old man. The watch doesn't work. You can have it back," the vendor said, and handed him the watch as the cars pulled away.

"I never said it did," the old man replied, and grinned, showing a nearly toothless mouth.

CHAPTER 7

Chrystal Henderson stood in front of the door to Tom's suite. She was dressed in a pastel, blue and white flowered sun dress, her blonde hair falling in ringlets onto her shoulders. She hesitated for a moment, took a deep breath, and knocked. Tom got up from the computer, walked to the door, and opened it.

They stood there staring at one another. "Hello," she said in a soft voice.

"Hi. When you never responded to my voice mails, I didn't think you wanted to see me again."

"Can I come in?"

"Sure," he said. She entered, and he closed the door behind her.

Crystal inhaled sharply and gave him a perplexed look. Tom pointed to the couch, and they both sat down. He was dressed in a white polo shirt, blue shorts, and flip flops. His emerald green eyes never left her face, and his expression was one of firm determination.

"I was angry and hurt because I was just beginning to really like you. When that woman showed up, throwing drinks and food and screaming, everything just disintegrated. I wanted to get as far away from you as I could," Crystal explained.

"I understand. It was a hell of a shock to both of us."

"In the last voice mail you left, you said I never let you explain. I realized that was true, and it was part of the reason I came here today." Her bright blue eyes were questioning, but she received no response from Tom.

He rose from the couch and walked over to the picture window, looking out on the high rise buildings, colorful boulevards, and streams of cars and people. Tom turned and looked at the gorgeous blonde, who so attracted him.

"I don't think it can work between us. We both have the desire and are very much attracted to one another. But our lives pull us apart. I'm only in California about a third of the time. Absence does not make the heart grow fonder."

Crystal momentarily looked shocked. "I wasn't expecting you to say that."

"You need to find some nice guy in San Francisco, who's going to be available on a full-time basis," Tom said.

Unsteadily she got to her feet, her total confidence somewhat shaken. Crystal walked towards the door. Tom met her, and they stood there, a longing for one another appearing clearly on their faces.

"Damn it," he said. Tom grabbed her by the shoulders and kissed her passionately, holding her tightly. Crystal responded with intense emotional excitement. Their desire for one another became a craving as Tom carried her into the bedroom, all his good intentions having evaporated. They made love twice during the next hour and then contentedly held each other, letting the spontaneity of the moment carry them blissfully into a soft, quiet place.

"Are you falling asleep?" she asked in a very soft voice.

"No, I'm just thoroughly enjoying the moment. I don't want anything to disturb us and the way we feel at this moment."

Crystal smiled. "Yes. I feel the same way."

They were both silent, neither feeling the necessity to speak. Tom felt her smooth flesh, the warmth of her body, and the smell of her perfume. He wanted to savor the moment and let the feeling of bliss continue uninterrupted. An hour later, they awoke. She showered first and finally coaxed him out of bed. He showered, and they went to the restaurant where they first had met.

They ordered, and Crystal looked at Tom and smiled. "Are you going to tell me what happened that night after I left?"

Tom grinned. "I'll bet it was really hilarious to watch. By the time the bouncers captured her, she'd cleared the whole third floor of patrons. Men and women were running everywhere. There was food splattered from one end of the room to the other. They booked her into jail for disturbing the peace and a half dozen other charges. I called my attorney here, and he bailed her out. I also paid her fines when she went to court."

"How noble of you," she said in a facetious tone of voice.

Tom described how they met, the shooting episode involving her husband, and the fact he ended up on the street stark naked. He told her about the paint stained clothing he had to put on and the desk clerk asking him to use the service elevator.

Crystal began giggling, then chuckled, and finally was unsuccessful in holding back laughter. As the story ended, her beautiful, melodic laugh caused the other patrons to turn their heads and stare at the gorgeous blonde.

"I had a talk with her after she went before the judge. We both agreed that it was best to break off our relationship. I haven't seen her since." She was still trying to end her laughing jag when Tom added a postscript to the story. "When I finally got back here covered with guacamole, the desk clerk asked me again to take the service elevator."

Crystal covered her mouth with her napkin and tried desperately to keep from laughing aloud but was unsuccessful. When they finished eating, they agreed that Tom would pick her up at seven for dinner.

"Want to come up to my room now for a few minutes?"

Tom asked in a lascivious tone of voice.

"No. I have to work. Besides, it wouldn't be for a few minutes," she said. "Hey, tomorrow's Saturday. I would love to see the Dolores Olmedo Museum, which houses a huge collection of paintings by Diego Rivera and Frida Kahlo. Would you take me?"

"Sure. I've been through it once before. It's a fantastic display of art."

***

The following morning they were in a taxi headed for Dolores Olmedo's huge, rambling estate. The large stone home, dating back to the 16th Century, was the centerpiece of five buildings that housed some of Mexico's most important paintings, archaeological pieces, a collection of popular art, and art from the Far East.

"I'm surprised you don't own a car in Mexico," Crystal said.

"It's easier and safer just to call a taxi. I'd be continually searching for parking spots because I'm called to so many varied locations. Then, walking back to a parked car leaves me open to robbers and kidnappers," he pointed out.

"My client, Isabella Pacheco, sends a car for me every day we work on interior design drawings and ideas. She doesn't want me to set foot out of the hotel without bodyguards. It just seems like such a beautiful city to have such crime problems."

Tom thought for a moment. "It's a paradox. Mexico City is a bustling, enormously modern city with triple-decker highways and tunnels bored through the mountains. It has towering skyscrapers, enormous cathedrals, fantastic museums, and wonderful restaurants. But, it also has shanty towns and slums that hold millions of people."

"I guess I just never see that part of life here," she said.

"It's one of the most unequal countries in the world. The wealthiest one percent of the population earns about twenty-one percent of Mexico's total income."

Crystal glanced at Tom. "You sound rather cynical. Don't you usually deal, business-wise, with people in the top echelon of society?"

"I do. Don't get me wrong, I love Mexico and the people at all levels of society. But much of this living area around Mexico City is a gigantic worker's colony. Poverty is a residential way of life. Lower income citizens seem to be resigned to their plight. Perhaps they're too busy just scraping out an existence to express their true emotions."

She frowned and looked perplexed. "Do you mind if we change the subject?" she asked.

"Fine with me."

"You told me, briefly, about learning to negotiate in Afghanistan. Can you explain more about that to me?"

"After the Twin Towers came crashing down, a lot of men were inspired to fight the nation's terrorist enemies. I signed up and became part of the U. S. Army's Special Forces. A year later, I was in Afghanistan fighting for my life against a variety of men trying to kill me. Over there, you just never know who your friend is and who your enemy is."

"I don't understand," she said.

"Sometimes, we were led into ambush situations by members of the Afghan army. Many of my friends died. I killed numerous Afghan men, and I wasn't sure which side they were on. They all hate us and believe we don't belong in their country," he explained.

"That's not the impression I get from news stories," Crystal said.

"Often news is based upon information the government gives out. The number of Afghan districts under government control has dropped from seventy-two percent to fifty-four percent in four years. But those are not figures that the U. S. government releases."

"How do you know your figures are accurate?"

"They're accurate because I know the people who gave them to me. Anyway, let's get back to your original question about how I got into the negotiation business. I was on a security detail that provided backup for a negotiator trying to get one of our men released. He haggled back and forth with the Taliban for two days, ten hours per day, and finally got our soldier released in exchange for two Taliban fighters."

"Was that a fair exchange?"

"Yes. And I was so impressed with his skills, I asked him if I might be trained and join his unit. We hit it off well, and I ended up being a pretty good negotiator over there."

"So, it gives you a lot of satisfaction doing this type of work?"

Tom nodded his head yes. "I get a great deal of satisfaction negotiating to bring a man or woman back from the abyss. They're in a wretched condition where they've had their humanity ripped out. Taking a man or woman from a dark place from which there is no escape is one of the most satisfying feelings I'll ever have."

Crystal moved over closer to him, and he put his arm around her. She rested her head on his shoulder. "You're a complicated man."

"There's the entrance," he said, and pointed to iron gates at the entrance.

They walked about the lush, green lawns and beautiful gardens and watched peacocks fan their shimmering, iridescent plumage in hopes of getting lucky. The birds perched on tree branches, strutted about the lawns, and sat in rows like sentinels on the hacienda's rooftop.

They decided to purchase a private tour of the estate, and their guide was Alonzo Quintero, a short, thin, older man with white hair and a white moustache.

"Dolores Olmedo, known as Lola to her friends, was a famous philanthropist and businesswoman, who was known for her political and governmental contacts. More than one Mexican president stayed here," Alonzo said.

"I understand she was a good friend to Diego Rivera," Tom said.

"Yes. She met Rivera when she was seventeen, and he was in his forties. She posed nude for him, but of course never told her mother. They had a life-long friendship, and under his guidance, she amassed a vast collection of his paintings, which she donated to the people of Mexico," Alonzo explained. "It's the largest collection in the world of his paintings."

Tom and Crystal held hands much of the time as they followed Alonzo through the cavernous rooms in the main house. Tom enjoyed himself immensely, just being near her, touching her, and watching the beautiful blonde as she studied Rivera's paintings from an artistic standpoint.

Her elegance and delightful personality created almost an illumination surrounding her. Tom was charmed by her desirability and enjoyed being included in the circle of light. A sense of well-being enveloped him as the tour progressed, and he believed it was almost a perfect day.

They reached the building that housed Frida Kahlo's artwork. "Dolores Olmedo and Frida Kahlo had little regard for one another. But once Frida died, Diego insisted that she buy twenty-five of Frida's works of art, which she did," Alonzo explained.

"Why weren't they friends?" Chrystal asked.

Alonzo smiled. Tom knew the reason and said, "Frida and Diego were married, but nothing stood in Diego's way when he was interested in a woman. Dolores Olmedo was also known to captivate men."

"I guess that explains it," Crystal said.

They moved outside to a fenced-in green area that housed male Xolo, or Mexican hairless dogs, which are the descendants of a pre-Columbian breed. The bald, wrinkled, dark-skinned animals were a delicacy enjoyed by the Spanish conquistadors, who ate them to the brink of extinction, Alonzo explained.

The final portion of the tour involved artifacts collected by Dolores Olmedo from a large number of Mexican states. On display were works in glass, ceramic, wood, tin, and papier-mache. It was considered to be one of the most important Mexican collections of art in the world, the guide said.

***

They took a cab back to the Hilton Hotel and walked through the long lobby towards the elevators. "I need to check up on a couple of business matters and catch a shower. I'll be up to get you for dinner," Tom told her.

They stopped in front of the elevators and kissed. Crystal put her arms around his neck and kissed him passionately. Tom returned the ardor, holding her close.

"I had a wonderful time today," she said.

Neither one paid any attention to the man rapidly approaching them. "Goddamn you, Crystal!" he shouted. "I flew all the way here from San Francisco to ask you to marry me, and you're with another man. You rotten bitch."

Both Tom and Crystal were shocked, eyes wide, not believing what was transpiring.

The young man had perfectly groomed brown hair, blue eyes, was clean shaven, and dressed in expensive sports clothing. "How could you have done this to me? You cheap whore. I hate you!" he shouted.

Tom pulled away from Crystal as the short man charged at Bradshaw. Tom backed up as the man swung at him. He missed, and Tom grabbed his arm and pulled him forward, then threw him onto an overstuffed chair that flipped over backwards, depositing the angry suitor upside down on the floor.

"Mark, for God's sake, stop," Crystal said loudly.

"He's all yours. I'll talk with you later," Tom said, and walked towards the huge entrance doors to the hotel. Once outside, he walked down the street in a trance, thinking that his relationship with women placed him in constant turmoil. Several blocks later, he realized he was in a neighborhood he didn't recognize.

CHAPTER 8

An old beat up Nissan Altima had been slowly following Bradshaw as he wandered aimlessly, deep in thought. Suddenly it speeded up, stopped alongside Tom, and two men with revolvers jumped out.

"Get in the car, asshole," one of the young men growled. The second kidnapper jabbed his revolver in Tom's lower back. "Do it, you gringo bastard." They shoved Bradshaw into the rear seat alongside a third man holding a gun.

All three of the young criminals looked alike — late teens, early twenties, dirty T-shirts, old jeans, and baseball caps. Their attempts to look tough and mean included moustaches and short black scraggly beards. The leader, Salvador Torres, was behind the wheel of the car as it drove away. Twins Pedro and Felipe Castio kept their guns pointed at Bradshaw, who thus far had not said a word.

"Get out your wallet," said Pedro, the robber sitting next to him.

Tom pulled it from his rear pocket and handed it to the bandit, who then went through the credit cards until he found what he wanted.

"Here's a Bank of Mexico debit card."

"We'll try it at the bank branch a half mile from here,"

Salvador said.

The drive took a few minutes, and they stopped in front of the bank's ATM machine. Pedro got out and then remembered. "What's the pin number, and what's the maximum we can pull out?"

"7954, and the maximum is two hundred dollars," Tom replied.

The young kidnapper/robber was back in the car in three minutes time, counting two hundred dollars in twenties.

"On to the next," Salvador said as he drove away.

Ten minutes later, they were at another branch, and the scenario repeated itself.

"You're wearing some pretty fancy clothes. What do you do for a living?" Salvador asked.

"I sell insurance," Tom said.

Salvador glanced around at Tom. "I think you'll be worth some money. Maybe we'll keep you."

Those words sent a cold chill up Bradshaw's spine. Instead of letting him go after the express kidnapping concluded, Salvador was thinking about a full blown kidnap and ransom scenario. It was something Tom said he would never let happen.

At the next bank branch, Pedro encountered trouble and couldn't get the pin number to work. He came back to the car. "It won't work, Salvador," he said.

"All right, asshole, get out of the car and fix it," Salvador ordered. "Pedro, keep your pistol in your belt. Cover it with your shirt, but hold on to it."

"Right, Salvador."

Tom exited the car on the curb side, followed by Pedro, who slid across the seat and out the door. Standing in front of the ATM machine, Bradshaw pretended to put in the pin number.

"Look here, Pedro. I think it'll work now."

Pedro came forward and squinted at the screen. Simultaneously, Tom smashed his fist into Pedro's hand, holding the revolver under his shirt. The gun went off with a bang, and Pedro cried out as the bullet went through his right foot. Bradshaw grabbed the gun from his waistband as the young bandit began screaming from pain.

Tom turned to the car just as Salvador fired from the driver's seat. The bullet struck him in the fleshy part of his left shoulder and went through without striking a bone. Tom fired back. The slug hit Salvador in the lower jaw, taking out most of his teeth, and exited the other side. The third bandit, Felipe, scrunched down in the passenger's seat, trying to hide.

Salvador was holding his jaw with his left hand as blood gushed out, covering his chest and pants. He drove off using his right hand, but the pain was so intense he couldn't concentrate. He pushed the gas pedal to the floor, and the Altima lurched forward at high speed. Salvador cried out in pain and momentarily closed his eyes. The car crossed the center line and struck a semi-truck head-on. There was a boom like an explosion. The Altima was tossed into the air and landed on its top, further crushing the two dead men in the front seat.

Tom groaned and grimaced in pain. He watched the traffic accident unfold as if it were a scene from a dream. "My God!" he exclaimed.

Pedro stopped screaming when the crash occurred and stared dumbfounded at the mangled car. Suddenly the car exploded as escaping gasoline was ignited. The wreck of a vehicle blew apart, showering parked cars with fiery debris. The driver of the semi ran as fast as he could away from the scene.

"You bastard! You've killed him. You've killed my brother!" Pedro yelled. "My dad's a police captain. He'll kill you, you son-of-a-bitch."

Bradshaw shook his head from side to side. "Holy shit. Could anything else go wrong?" he said aloud.

He used the speed dial on his phone. A moment later, the connection went through. "You told me if I needed help, I should call. Believe me, I need help." Tom briefly explained what had occurred, and the man on the other end of the line asked about the location of the shooting and explosion. Tom named the streets at the intersection.

"Are you badly wounded?'

"I'm shot in the shoulder, but it's not serious. I received worse wounds in Afghanistan," Tom replied.

"Help is on its way."

Minutes later, the area was swamped with police cars and two ambulances. Pedro kept yelling that Tom had shot him and caused the accident that killed his brother.

"My father is Police Captain Rodrigo Castio. He'll kill this bastard," the sobbing kidnapper said.

The police weren't sure what to do after questioning Bradshaw. Both men were loaded into ambulances and taken to a nearby hospital. Two officers were assigned to guard the wounded men until their stories could be sorted out.

Tom's wound was treated, and he was moved to a hospital room. The sedative took effect, and he dozed off. There were loud voices in the hallway, and Captain Rodrigo Castio burst into the room, ran over to the bed, and began beating Bradshaw. The police officer assigned to watch Tom finally was able to pull the distraught father away from the bed.

"You killed my son, you asshole. I'm going to kill you," Castio shouted as he began to draw his pistol. The police officer struggled to keep Castio from drawing his weapon, and the two men ended up rolling around on the floor. Two more officers rushed into the room and assisted in subduing the angry father.

Also entering the room was Assistant Police Chief Franco Gomez. The assistant chief was tall and athletic looking, had dark penetrating eyes, a large head, and neatly trimmed moustache.

"Give me his weapon," Gomez ordered. "Take him into another room until I have a chance to speak with this man."

A policeman took Castio's pistol and handed it to the

assistant chief. Then he helped the other two officers drag the fighting and yelling captain from the room. Bradshaw's face was bloody from being struck several times, and he groaned from the pain.

"I received a call and came at once. You have friends in high places," said Gomez. "I'm going to repeat what I was told. You tell me if it's the truth."

The assistant police chief went over the facts pertaining to the kidnapping, firefight, and explosion. Bradshaw's eyes were closing as he said, "That's what happened."

Gomez motioned for a doctor to come forward. An officer had kept the doctor and nurses from entering the room until Gomez was satisfied that he understood the facts. The assistant police chief left the room and gave orders to two police officers to stand guard and make sure that no one harmed Bradshaw.

He walked to the room where Captain Castio was being held. "Have you calmed down enough to talk?" Gomez asked.

"He killed my son and shot my other son! I'm going to kill him, and no one can stop me," Castio shouted.

"Let me go over the facts as I know them to be," said Assistant Chief Gomez. He began talking to Castio in a calm voice, but the crazed captain kept interrupting him.

"He's a liar. My son told me what happened. I'm going to kill that gringo son-of-a-bitch," Castio yelled.

"Shut up. Listen to me, or I'll bust you to patrolman and send you to the slums," Gomez warned. He went through the fight and explosion scenario from start to finish, wondering if the mentally confused captain was even listening.

"I'm going to kill that no good bastard," Castio vowed.

Gomez exhaled sharply, giving up trying to communicate with Castio.

"Captain, you're under arrest for assault, and you're suspended from the police force. You're to be booked into the main headquarters' jail and held there until further notice,"

Gomez said.

Castio's eyes widened in disbelief, and his mouth dropped open. The reality of the situation brought him back down to earth. "No. Don't do that to me. My career would be over. For God's sake, Chief."

"I can't have you killing Bradshaw because your sons were involved in an aborted kidnap and robbery attempt. You leave me no choice."

The crazed look returned to Castio's eyes. "I'll remember what you've done to me and my family, you asshole."

"Strip off his uniform and dress him in hospital scrubs, then book him into jail. He's to be considered dangerous," Gomez said.

Four patrolmen were standing near the two officers, amazed expressions on their faces. Then they moved towards Castio, hating the thought of the scuffle they knew was coming. Gomez walked out of the room as Castio began fighting and screaming at the officers as they wrestled him to the ground.

***

The following day Bradshaw was transferred to a private hospital, and bodyguards took the place of police officers as his protectors. He put in a call to Crystal Henderson.

"Where are you? I've been trying to phone you for two days," she said in a frightened voice.

"I'm in a hospital. I've got a wound in the shoulder, and I've been beat up pretty good. None of the wounds are serious. I'll tell you about it when you get here," he said, speaking in a slightly slurred voice.

He gave her the name of the hospital, and she said she would be there as quickly as she could. An hour later, Crystal arrived and was escorted to his private room. When she took one look at his battered face, tears came to her eyes, and she bit her lip.

"What happened?" she asked in a worried voice.

"It's a weird story. I'll give you the highlights." He told her what happened when he left the hotel and didn't sugarcoat the kidnapping events, the shooting, and the explosion. He emphasized that the kidnappers' father was a police captain who began beating him in a hospital room. Tom wanted her to understand the dangers of walking on the streets without regard to the consequences.

Crystal's face turned white, and she looked as if she was going to faint. She sat down on the edge of the bed, eyes wide and trembling. "How could this have happened?" she asked.

"I wasn't paying attention when I left the hotel. I shouldn't have been walking on the streets. I've told you often to always be careful in Mexico City. I've got no one to blame but myself."

"Did this all happen after that episode with Mark Reynolds in the hotel lobby?"

"Yes," he said.

"Then I'm to blame."

"No. Not at all. I wasn't to blame concerning that episode with Carmen Flores. Bad things just sometimes happen, and there's nothing we can do about them."

Crystal moved closer to him, gently kissed him on the cheek, and lay her head on his chest. Tom smiled, feeling better than he had in two days.

"What are we going to do now?" she asked in a quiet voice.

"I have to appear in court in a week. There'll be a preliminary hearing involving the assault charge against the police captain. I'll have to testify. After that, I'm heading back to Los Angeles for a vacation. Want to come along?" he asked.

"I'm done with Mexico City," she said emphatically. "The interior design work is complete. My company can get someone else for the remodeling phase. Yes, I want to go back to Los Angeles with you," she said, and kissed him on the cheek again.

"You can do better than that," he said.

She kissed him on the lips and put her arms around him,

being careful not to touch his wounded shoulder. They were caught up in a moment of bliss, each one happy just to be near the other. Several moments passed, and she finally raised her head and looked into his eyes. "I love you, Tom. I want to be with you."

He smiled. "I love you, too. I don't know where this relationship is headed, but I'm willing to try."

They talked for a few minutes, and Tom started dozing off.

"You need rest. I'll be back tomorrow," she said in a quiet tone of voice.

***

A week later, Crystal was back in San Francisco, and Tom was walking into a district court building that looked like a four-story concrete prison, with tiny windows and streams of men and women moving in and out of the double front doors. He went through security and was escorted to the office of public prosecutor Alfonso Bettencourt. Tom shook the hand of a tall, clean shaven Mexican dressed in a dark suit and tie. Bettencourt looked at Bradshaw with an analytical eye, wondering who this man was who had friends in high places.

They chatted for a few minutes before Bettencourt got down to business. "How much do you know about the Mexican criminal justice system?"

"Not a lot."

"It's the opposite of what you are accustomed to in the United States. There are no jury trials, and the accused is deemed guilty until proven innocent. Release from jail prior to a trial is done on a cash bond basis only," the prosecutor said.

Tom's eyes narrowed. "Has Rodrigo Castio been released on bail?"

"No. That will be decided today. The judge in each case controls the process and has an active role in developing a case. He narrows the legal and factual issues, selects which witnesses he wants to question, and gathers evidence."

"That's certainly quite different from our legal process," Tom said.

"Yes. The public prosecutor's office is the door through which crime victims and criminals enter the criminal justice system. Unfortunately, a large percentage of the cases get stranded here, never go anywhere, and ultimately are dismissed."

"What percentage, if you don't mind my asking?"

"Three quarters. And the accused people are detained in Mexican jails until a final determination is made. There's about two-hundred-thousand alleged criminals in Mexico's jails, held for an indeterminate amount of time."

"That's ridiculous. Where does common sense enter into the process?"

"Our system is time honored, some aspects dating back hundreds of years. It's almost impossible for the legislature to make changes," Bettencourt noted.

The public prosecutor continued to study the man seated in front of him. Tom realized that Bettencourt was analyzing him, and there was no friendly interchange of conversation between them. Tom decided to be blunt.

"You can tell me what's on your mind," Bradshaw said.

"Several things. High-powered attorneys have contacted me regarding defense and prosecution in this case. And, District Judge Emilliano Robles has been brought in to preside over the pretrial investigation phase. He's very experienced and has quite a reputation."

"Good or bad?" Tom asked.

"Both. He's very political—or should I say, politically connected."

"Terrific. Castio wants to kill me, and politics is in play," Bradshaw noted.

"I've studied the pretrial investigation report. Assistant Chief Franco Gomez did an excellent job of assembling testimony from officers at the scene and piecing together everything I need to have Castio bound over for trial. It's a good case file."

"That makes me feel better. Anything else?" Tom asked.

Bettencourt looked uncomfortable. "There's movement in the shadows, things I can't put my finger on. I just sense that something else is transpiring."

CHAPTER 9

Judge Emilliano Robles entered the small courtroom, and the attorneys, court employees, and a few onlookers all rose to their feet. He looked around the room, much like a king reviewing his subjects, then sat down. Judge Robles was short and heavy-set, with a square, block-like face and neatly trimmed black moustache. His dark eyes matched his dark hair, and he had a direct, no-nonsense gaze that was riveting.

"Let us proceed," Judge Robles said in a deep, commanding voice.

The defendant was not in the courtroom as the public prosecutor touched upon the highlights of the assault case, emphasizing that Bradshaw was beaten while in a hospital bed. He noted that there were two police officers who witnessed the assault. Their reports were available, plus they were present to testify. Bettencourt's attempt to fill in background material about the express kidnapping, shooting, and car explosion were met with rejection by Judge Robles.

"That is not material to the assault case, and therefore will not be entered into this hearing," he said in his authoritarian, gruff manner.

Bettencourt objected, saying the previous events were the basis for the assault. But Judge Robles repeated his refusal to allow introduction of the events.

"Do you have anything more than what is in the pretrial investigation report?" Judge Robles asked.

"No, Your Honor," Bettencourt stated.

"Then, my ruling is that Captain Castio be remanded for trial at a time to be determined later. Is there any other business to come before the court in this matter?" Judge Robles asked in a booming voice.

A well-dressed attorney stood up, said he represented Police Captain Rodrigo Castio, and asked if he might address the court.

"Proceed," the district judge stated.

"I would ask that a reasonable bail be set for Captain Castio. His exemplary service record shows that he has been a tireless pursuer of justice. He deeply regrets the events that took place in the hospital room. They were due to the fact that he had just lost a son. He assures the court that if he is released on bail, he will not enter into future activities that might be construed as being dangerous," the lawyer stated in a smooth, almost rhythmic delivery.

In reality, Captain Castio had been reprimanded on three occasions for beating alleged suspects, twice for lying under oath, and six times for submitting false or misleading case summaries.

Attorney Daniel Moreno, who spoke so elegantly on behalf of Castio, had white hair combed back on the sides and a matching white moustache and Van Dyke beard that came to a point just below his chin. His urbane charm and ultra-smooth delivery allowed him to tell stories about his clients that were mesmerizing. They were delivered in such a manner that courtroom attendees almost believed him. Moreno charged more per hour for his services than Castio made legally in a month.

Every eye in the courtroom returned to Judge Robles, who looked around the small courtroom, thoroughly enjoying the moment. "I will allow bail to be set at five hundred thousand pesos." He banged his gavel, and court was adjourned.

People in the courtroom began talking excitedly.

"Wasn't I supposed to testify?" Tom asked.

"If the judge wanted to hear from you, he would have said so," Bettencourt replied. "The bond is twenty-five thousand in American money. Very few people can come up with that amount of cash. We'll see what happens."

"To you or to me? This whole damn thing is a sham, and you know it," Tom said loudly.

Bettencourt acted embarrassed and looked away from Bradshaw. "I'll be in touch with you at a later time," he said as he stood up and walked away.

Bradshaw called a cab and was about to enter it when Assistant Police Chief Franco Gomez walked up to him. The men shook hands.

"There's no way to sugarcoat this. Five hundred thousand pesos have been delivered as bail for Castio. He's being processed and released as we speak," Chief Gomez explained.

Tom exhaled sharply, feeling nervous and angry. "This was all a charade from beginning to end. He'll be out on the street and coming after me."

"My advice is for you to leave the country, at least in the short term. I'm surprised that such a low level police officer could have such strong backing and the ability to raise a large bail almost instantaneously," the chief said. "Apparently, he has connections that I know nothing about."

Bradshaw thought for a moment. "Does he have connections with the drug cartels and crime families?"

Gomez's eyes narrowed. "There were always rumors that he was on the periphery of criminal activities, but nothing of substance surfaced. I'll be looking into his background in greater detail now."

"Realistically, what are we looking for as a trial date?" Tom asked.

"It's difficult to say. It could be months or never. Judge Robles has complete authority over the trial date, and he said it would be determined later."

Tom shook his head from side to side, indicating disgust. "I'll be flying back to Los Angeles tomorrow to recuperate."

The assistant chief nodded his head. "That's a wise decision. I'll have a couple of my men give you security until you fly out."

"Thanks for your help. I appreciate it."

Two police officers traveled with Bradshaw to the Hilton Hotel. Vincent Cantu, the front desk manager, saw Tom and the officers walking toward the elevators. He quickly caught up with them and handed Bradshaw an envelope. Tom opened it, read the short message, and glared at Cantu. He was about to curse the manager but wisely decided not to do so. The letter said that Bradshaw was being asked to find other accommodations, effective the first of the month, because of strange events that had recently taken place.

***

Rodrigo Castio, previously a captain and now a patrolman, unsteadily got out of his car in darkness and swayed as he walked to the corner of a warehouse. Out of the shadows walked a Mexican dressed in a dark blue suit, white shirt, and color coordinated blue and gold striped tie. His distinctive woody, spicy cologne was pungent in the night air.

"What do you want?" Castio growled.

"You're drunk. Remember, you're not to do anything to Tom Bradshaw. I'll need him in the future."

Castio sneered. "That bastard killed my son and shot my other boy."

"I read the police report. Your sons grabbed him off the street, and the fight and explosion were their fault."

"I'm going to kill him, and there's nothing you can do about it. I lost my boy, and he has to pay," Castio said in a gravelly voice.

"You'll continue to be paid by me. In a few months, I'll see to it that your rank is reinstated. But nothing is to happen to Bradshaw," the well-dressed Mexican warned.

"I've worked for you for a long time and snatched a lot of bankers and other rich men for you. Don't forget that," the drunken police office growled.

"Your performance has been good, and you've been well paid. Right now, I want you to agree to leave Bradshaw alone," the Mexican emphasized.

Castio staggered and was barely able to stay on his feet. "My boy is dead, and I'm going to kill Bradshaw. Don't screw around with me. I know too much."

The street light made the man's light brown eyes sparkle. He drew a revolver from his belt. Without saying another word, he shot Castio twice in the heart. The police officer's eyes were wide in disbelief as he fell over backwards onto the pavement. The killer walked forward and placed a third shot through Castio's brain.

"Too bad. You were useful, but your time has come and gone," he said as he stood over the dead policemen.

CHAPTER 10

Tom boarded an American Airlines plane for the four hour flight to Los Angeles. He dialed his father's private cell phone. It rang twice before Douglas Bradshaw, an orthopedic surgeon, answered.

"Hi, Dad."

"Hi, son. It's great to hear your voice. I'm really surprised you called me."

"Can you talk for a few minutes?"

"Sure. I just got out of surgery." The elder Bradshaw suddenly was concerned. "Are you all right?"

"I had an altercation and was shot in the left shoulder. The bullet went through without striking bones, and I was given good medical treatment. I should recover one hundred percent."

"I'll meet you at LAX when you arrive. I'd like to have you checked out at the Bancroft Hospital just to make sure everything is okay," Douglas said in a worried voice.

Tom gave him the flight number and time of arrival. Then, he answered a variety of medical questions his father asked.

"Are you sure you're strong enough to be walking around on your own?"

"Dad, I'm only thirty-two, not eighty-two."

Douglas sighed. "Well, I'm fifty-eight, and I sure wouldn't

be up and around that fast. I suppose you don't want to go over the details about what happened right now."

"You're right. It's a long story, but I'll explain everything to you when I land."

***

Tom walked through the security check station and saw his father and his wife of two years, Marilyn, both staring at him with concerned expressions. Tom's mother had died seven years earlier from cancer, and his father married a physicians' assistant affiliated with the same hospital corporation two years ago.

Tom liked his choice. Marilyn was well liked by everyone she came in contact with. She had a wonderful sense of humor, a pleasant demeanor and was devoted to Douglas. At fifty, she was still very attractive, with light brown, shoulder length hair, pretty blue eyes, and a dazzling smile.

He immediately quickened his step so as to seem like nothing was the matter, although his shoulder wound hurt and his arm was in a sling. "Hi, Dad. Hi, Marilyn. You can see that I'm fine. No need for a wheelchair," he said, and grinned. Tom gently hugged his father and did the same with Marilyn.

Douglas Bradshaw studied his son. "You're right. You look healthy, except maybe a little tired."

"You've probably guessed that we have you lined up for an examination as soon as we can get to Bancroft Hospital. I guess we won't need an ambulance," Marilyn said. Father and son laughed.

Douglas and Marilyn pummeled Tom with questions about what had occurred. By the time they reached the elder Bradshaw's Lexus, he had briefly explained about his kidnapping, the short battle with the snatchers, and the auto accident that killed two of the kidnappers. He glossed over the part about being attacked in his hospital bed, although the bruises and facial cuts were quite evident.

"Do we have to go to the hospital now?" Tom asked.

"Yes," his father replied. "I want a complete examination just to make sure no problems arise."

"I was taken to one of Mexico City's finest private hospitals and given five star treatment, courtesy of a top echelon Mexican businessman. We've become friends, and he has a large number of his extended family members covered with K & R insurance from California Fidelity," Tom explained.

"Do you think they sterilized the needles?" Marilyn said factitiously, and grinned.

The men laughed.

"Marilyn, Dad made the right decision when he married you. Your humor and light-hearted demeanor are just what he needs to keep him from being so serious."

She smiled. "Thanks, Tom, for the kind words. I even got him to go to Disneyland with me."

Douglas Bradshaw looked slightly chagrined. "Hey, I enjoyed it."

They arrived at the hospital, and Tom quickly was subjected to a wide range of examinations. Two hours later, his father was pushing him towards the exit in a wheelchair, a process that was required by the medical facility.

They made the drive to Douglas Bradshaw's home in Brentwood, an upscale neighborhood on the west side of Los Angeles. They drove down tree-lined streets past a wide-range of homes with different architectural styles and wound their way up into the hills along Mandeville Canyon Road. The elder Bradshaw's house was a sprawling, historic Spanish style home with a red tile roof, originally built in 1936.

Marilyn Bradshaw was taking her time remodeling the main house that had three hundred and sixty degree mountain views. Finger-like ridges towered above the home on two sides and virtually enclosed Bradshaw's house in a gorge. The hills were covered in a variety of trees, shrubs, plants, and ferns, enhancing the spectacular green scenery.

Tom spent the next two days there in a detached guest quarters at the rear of the main home. They ate meals outside on the large patio that separated the two buildings. He knew the two medical practitioners were eying him closely and were satisfied that his recovery was much faster than expected.

"I've met a woman in Mexico City who I really like a lot," Tom said. "Her name is Crystal Henderson."

"Is she Mexican?" Douglas asked.

"No. She's from the San Francisco area and is an interior designer. Crystal was down there on assignment, and we were both staying at the Hilton Hotel."

"Does she know about the business you're in?" his father asked.

"Yes. But we haven't really talked about the logistical problems of me working in Mexico City most of the time and Crystal being in San Francisco. I guess you don't think about the practical aspects of a relationship at the beginning. Everything is so new and…great."

"Is she back in San Francisco?" Marilyn asked.

"Yes. And after my run in with the street corner kidnappers, she'll never go back to Mexico City again. I love Mexico City, but I couldn't get Crystal to come back. The whole debacle really scared her."

"I can sympathize with her. If you don't feel safe in a city, you don't want to be there," Marilyn commented.

"Which brings us back around to the question of how much longer you'll be a negotiator for California Fidelity. I'd sure like you to go into business here in Los Angeles. International business negotiations is a highly specialized line of work, and you'd be a perfect fit," Douglas emphasized.

"I know, Dad. I'm thinking more about it and realize it's on the horizon," Tom said.

"You tried to make it work with two other women, and it didn't. If you're serious about Crystal, you could be heading down that same road," Douglas said.

Marilyn and Douglas stared at Tom. He was quiet for a few moments, looking at the beautiful, green covered mountain ridges but not really seeing them. Finally, he shook his head from side to side. "At the moment, it's not an easy problem to solve." Tom's cell phone rang, and he answered it, thankful for a brief sojourn from the questioning. "It's nice of you to call, Felix."

"I hope you're better," Felix Ramirez said in a deep, gravelly voice.

"Much better. I'm on the mend and should be back in great shape before long."

"I don't know if you've heard, but that police captain, Rodrigo Castio, has been shot and killed."

Tom jumped to his feet. "My God! I can't believe it."

Douglas spoke Spanish, but Marilyn did not. She looked at her husband in a quizzical manner. He shook his head from side to side and remained silent.

"Assistant Chief Franco Gomez told me it was a professional killing. Two shots to the heart and one to the head," said Ramirez. "That takes care of a lot of your problems."

"Yes. I'm relieved."

"The Mexico City Police Department has a substantial number of men investigating, but so far, they've turned up nothing," Ramirez said.

"I'll be back in Mexico City, probably in two to three weeks. In the meantime, I have a suggestion for you involving the family members you have insured with us. This is just between the two of us."

"I'm listening," Ramirez said.

"I assume that most of them have worked for one or more of your corporations."

Ramirez was quiet as his computer-like mind went to work. "Yes, I believe that is the case."

"Each corporation would have its own human resources

department with complete data on those family members. Is that correct?" Tom asked.

"Yes. I think I know where you're going. All that information pertaining to my family members is sent and stored in my home office HR department, as well. I like to know what's going on regarding family members," Ramirez explained.

"Would it be possible for someone to tap into that information base regarding your relatives?"

"Anything's possible."

"Here's what I have in mind. I'm sure your computer systems are sophisticated to a degree that a program could be installed to monitor all entries into your families' HR data. You'd be alerted to these entries, where they originated and when."

It was silent on the other end of the line. "I understand. If you're going to kidnap someone, you want their current address, the company they work for, and the time-frame for working hours."

"A sophisticated kidnapping ring might try anything, especially when it comes to your family."

"I'll have a program set up immediately. And, I'll let you know if anything more is uncovered in the Castio killing."

The men talked for another minute before saying goodbye. Douglas and Marilyn sat at the patio table, staring at Tom. He was oblivious to his surroundings, looking off into space until his father cleared his throat. Tom's eyes opened wide as he felt the intense scrutiny.

Tom exhaled sharply. "The police officer who attacked me has been killed, apparently assassinated. No one knows why or anything else."

"Now you know why we're so concerned about you," his father said. "Are you really going to be safe when you return to Mexico City?"

Tom lied. "Yes. I don't know of anyone who has it in for me."

The three Bradshaw family members talked for a while longer, but repeated attempts by Douglas and Marilyn to change Tom's mind were unsuccessful. He packed his suitcase and drove one of his father's cars to Douglas Bradshaw's ocean-side condo in Santa Monica, about forty minutes away. He laughed to himself as he thought about leaving his father's house, driving away in his dad's car to a condo owned by his father.

"One of these days, I'll have to buy a few things of my own," he said to himself, and grinned.

CHAPTER 11

The Seaside Condominiums were oceanfront condos with floor to ceiling walls of glass that revealed unobstructed, expansive views of the crashing waves and sandy beaches. The smell of the Pacific Ocean came in through open windows.

Each of the four buildings contained four units, for a total of sixteen. The eight second floor units had roof-top patios, while the ground level condos had large front patios emptying onto the sandy beaches. An elevator was at the rear of the four glass, rectangular cubes and went down to underground parking, two spaces per condo.

Decades earlier, Douglas Bradshaw had just completed his medical internship when they were being constructed. He chose a center unit with the elevator behind his condo and stairs on the side leading down to the beach. The fifteen-hundred-square-foot units were now selling for three and a half million dollars or more, making them some of the most expensive condominiums for their size on the Pacific Coast.

Tom carried his suitcase from the elevator to his front door. He unlocked the unit and was about to enter when a grey-haired, elderly woman, very prim and proper in a dark blue dress, approached him.

"Young man, I wonder if I might have a moment of your

time?" she asked in a strong voice, which reminded Tom of one of his early school teachers.

"Sure. How can I help you?"

"There's a terrible smell in my condo next door to yours. Do you have any suggestions?" she said.

"I'm Tom Bradshaw. And you are?"

"Vivian Fairchild. My sister just died and willed me this condominium. It's the first time I've been here, and the smell is horrible," she said loudly. "I don't think anyone has lived here for more than a year."

"The sewer traps probably are dried out. I can give you the name and phone number for a good handyman, Jim Donaldson."

Vivian's eyes narrowed, her lips snapped together, and her expression became one of suspicion. "What is it going to cost?" she asked in an indignant voice.

"I think Jim's service call is about two hundred dollars. What it will cost to make the repairs, I don't know."

"You mean he charges two hundred dollars just to come out here? That's outrageous!" she said in an arrogant voice.

"Jim's in the business to make money. He doesn't drive all around Los Angeles for free," Tom pointed out.

"Young man, won't you at least take a look at the problem? After all, we're neighbors," Vivian announced.

Tom exhaled sharply, set his suitcase inside his condo, and walked to the nearby unit. She opened the door, and the rotten egg smell immediately made Tom wince and back away. "That's sewer gas, all right. The water traps have dried out under the floor drains and wash basins from lack of use. That would be my guess."

"And what would your handyman charge to fix it?" she asked in a firm voice. Vivian's eyes bore into Tom in a domineering manner.

"Maybe two hundred or more, depending on the scope of the job."

"That's outlandish! You mean it would cost me four hundred dollars or more to correct this problem?" she asked, haughtiness in her voice.

"It could be even more if he has to do snaking or rodding in the main sewer line to clean out clogs. Or, it might need hydro jetting, which is really expensive."

"You seem to know a lot about these things," she pointed out.

"Over the years, I've had a lot of apartments with similar problems. You sort of learn the steps that need to be taken," Tom explained.

"Can't we just dump something down the drains to fix it?"

Tom didn't like the word "we" and looked at her skeptically. "You could try a concoction of baking soda and distilled white vinegar. Then, wash it down with boiling water."

"I don't have those ingredients here."

"Neither do I," Tom replied.

"I don't have a car yet. I'm going to rent a small one soon."

"Look, Vivian, I really need to check in with my office. I'll give you Jim's phone number, and you can take it from there."

"I'd prefer it if you'd address me as Mrs. Fairchild. I don't have a cell phone, and the house phone is not hooked up."

Tom grunted in frustration. "Come in and make the call from my cell phone."

"Young man, can't you get those ingredients and try to fix the problem? After all, we are neighbors, and I've been placed in a very serious situation," she stated in an autocratic voice.

Tom's eyes widened, and his face took on a shocked look. "Who, me? I'm not a plumber."

"You said you've had experience with these problems."

"Well, limited. I'm sorry, but I really don't have time for this."

"So, you're going to leave me standing here on the porch with no phone and no transportation. How could you do such a thing? I thought you were a nice man," she said in a soulful voice.

Tom groaned, and his face took on a pained expression. "All right, come in. I'll drive to the nearby market and bring back the ingredients needed to try and clear the line and eliminate the sewer gas problem. But remember, it may not work, and you'll have to use a handyman or plumber. Is that clear?"

"Absolutely."

Bradshaw was back in half an hour. He poured a quarter cup of baking soda down the drains in the bathrooms and kitchen. This was followed five minutes later by a half cup of distilled white vinegar in each of the drains. Fifteen minutes later, he poured boiling water down the drains. All the windows were open, and breezes took away the chemical and rotten egg smell. "Thank God," he said to himself.

He walked back to his condo, where Vivian was seated on the outside patio, drinking hot tea and munching chocolate chip cookies. "This tea of yours is not the best. It's a good thing I brought my own cookies. Bring me another cup of tea, will you, young man?"

Minutes later, he returned with another cup of hot tea. "Did you decide what kind of car you're going to rent?"

"I hadn't thought about it."

"I'll be happy to drive you to a rental car agency."

"I don't drive," she said emphatically.

Tom growled like a wounded animal. "What do you mean, you don't drive? You just told me you were going to rent a car."

"Don't raise your voice to me, young man. My niece will be arriving in a week or so, and she'll be driving me."

"What are you going to do in the meantime? There are a couple of restaurants within walking distance. Perhaps that will solve the food problem."

"I can hardly walk from one room to another. Arthritis, you know," she said in a matter-of-fact voice.

Tom's eyes were wide and his mouth open. A terrified look

spread across his face as he imagined the worst case scenario, being stuck with her. He paced back and forth as he tried to rally his thoughts. "What exactly are your plans? Are you going to live here? Are you going to put the condo on the market?"

"Calm down, young man, or you'll have a stroke. I haven't decided yet."

"How do you expect to live with no food and no transportation?" he asked, sweat beginning to course down his forehead.

"I'm sure some kind soul will take me to the grocery store. I'll stock up on groceries and rough it until Cynthia arrives. Then, I'll rent a car so she can drive me around."

"Do you feel good enough to go to the grocery store now?" Tom asked.

"Perhaps we should go to a restaurant first. I'm hungry. Then, we can go to the grocery store."

Bradshaw emitted a sound somewhere between a growl and a whine. They took the elevator down to the basement garage and got into Douglas Bradshaw's Lexus. During the short trip to the restaurant, Vivian questioned him about the condo complex, and he supplied her with as much information as he could think of.

"I'm only here about ten days out of each month. My dad owns this condo and also the car you're riding in. Most of my time is spent in Mexico City."

"What line of work are you in?"

"Insurance."

"It must be difficult to sell insurance in a foreign country."

The tension and stress evaporated briefly as he laughed heartily. "It's not that kind of insurance."

"Aren't you a little old to be living in your father's house and driving one of his cars?"

Tom wanted to reach out and grab her by her wrinkled neck but refrained and tried to swallow the mouth full of food that was caught in his throat. He cleared his throat several times before speaking.

"I pay for the homeowners' insurance on the condo and the monthly HOA fee, plus the annual taxes on the property. I also pay for all repairs and maintenance. It's free and clear, so there is no monthly mortgage payment," Tom said. "My dad wants to keep the property because it keeps appreciating in value, and he would pay a huge amount in taxes if he sold it. Does that make sense to you?"

"I'm finished. Let's go," she replied.

They went to Ralph's supermarket and spent the next hour going up and down the aisles. He marveled at how much food she could get into her cart and into the one Tom was pushing. The grand total at the cash register was slightly more than three hundred dollars.

"Well, silly me. I seem to have left my wallet in the condo. Take care of it, will you, young man?" she said, and smiled.

Tom stared at her, dumbfounded. "You don't have any money?"

"Not with me. I'll reimburse you later," she said, a hint of arrogance in her voice.

The female clerk stared at Tom, wondering how these two were related. Bradshaw pulled out his money clip and handed her a Visa card.

"Can you get a bagger to push this cart?" she asked the clerk, as she turned and walked out of the store.

The clerk stared at Bradshaw, a look of wonderment on her face.

"Don't even ask," he said as he pushed the second cart towards the door.

***

Crystal Henderson arrived at LAX. Tom drove her to his condo as fast as he could, enveloped her in his arms, and they were quickly in bed. His frustrations melted away as his full attention was on lovemaking and the passion and contentment that came from being with the beautiful young woman. Two hours later, Crystal went to the refrigerator for a Coke, and food came tumbling out as she opened the door.

"What on earth? Tom, what's going on?" she asked.

Bradshaw started at the beginning, telling her about the sewer gasses and ending with the debacle at Ralph's. Crystal smiled at first, then giggled, and finally burst out laughing as the story progressed.

"Tom, you're an easy mark. You're a nice guy who can be manipulated by an elderly lady who plays on your sympathy," Crystal said.

"I don't know what to do. I had to put the perishables in my refrigerator because she has neglected to turn on the electricity. And, she hasn't called to reconnect the house phone," he explained. "And, she doesn't know how to drive."

Crystal burst out laughing and went back into the bedroom, and the two of them returned to the bed. They were kissing passionately when there was a knock on the door. Tom sat upright in bed, eyes wide, a look of fear on his face.

"Young man!" a muffled voice called out.

"It's her! What should I do?" he asked.

Crystal got out of bed and put on a shorty nightgown that ended several inches above her knees. "I'll take care of it. Women understand women."

She picked up her cell phone and opened the front door. Vivian Fairchild stared at Crystal, lips pinched together and eyes bulging from her head.

"Good heavens. What are you wearing?" the grey-haired woman said loudly.

"Something guaranteed to catch a man's attention," Crystal replied.

"I need to speak to the young man. I need food from his refrigerator."

"Tom told me all about your situation. Have you contacted the power company about reconnecting the electricity?"

"I don't know what business that is of yours," Vivian snapped.

"If you don't get your electricity turned on, all of your perishables will go bad."

"I'm through talking with you. I want to speak to the young man," Vivian said in an indignant voice.

"He won't be available today. Try back tomorrow," Crystal said in a matter-of-fact voice.

She began closing the door when Vivian cried out, "Wait! Wait! I don't have a phone to make those calls."

Crystal held up her cell phone. "I do. But you'll need a credit card to pay for the deposits. Go back to your condo and bring back a credit card." She shut the door before Vivian had a chance to speak.

Tom came out of the bedroom wearing a polo shirt and shorts. "Do you think that's really going to work?" he asked incredulously.

Crystal smiled. "She'll be back within five minutes." She walked over to Tom, put her arms around his neck, and kissed him passionately. "I'll need the telephone numbers for the power company, the phone company, and a cab company."

Tom quickly pulled up the telephone numbers on his cell phone, wrote them on a slip of paper and handed it to Crystal. Within five minutes, there was a knock on the door. Crystal had changed into shorts and a blouse and answered the door. Vivian tried to move through the doorway, but Crystal blocked her path.

"We can do this outside the condo," she said as she stepped outside and closed the door.

Vivian acted arrogantly, then settled down as Crystal phoned the power company. The transaction took fifteen minutes. Next, she called the telephone company, and this call lasted ten minutes. Both scheduled turn-ons late that afternoon.

"I hope you're satisfied. I'm not used to being treated this way. I'd like to get some of my groceries, if you don't mind," she said in an insolent tone of voice.

"Do you have three hundred dollars?" Crystal asked.

"Now, just a minute. You are being extremely rude."

"No money, no groceries," Crystal said firmly.

"I've never been treated like this. I'll be back in a minute," she said as she hurriedly walked to her condo. She returned quickly with three, one hundred dollar bills.

It took several trips before Tom, Crystal, and Vivian took all of the non-perishables to the elderly lady's condominium.

Vivian looked at Tom. "I'll need a ride to the nearest beauty parlor."

Crystal handed her the slip of paper with the cab company's phone number on it. "They'll know just where to take you. Make sure you have a credit card or cash to pay the cab driver and the salon."

CHAPTER 12

During the next week, Tom and Crystal thoroughly enjoyed what could be described as a honeymoon. They surfed, played beach volleyball, sunned themselves daily on the beach, spent part of each day in bed, and twice had dinner at Douglas and Marilyn's home. Crystal and Marilyn developed a good relationship, as Crystal recommended numerous interior design ideas for remodeling the Bradshaw home.

At the start of the new week, Tom called his boss, Mark Danforth.

"How's the recovery going?" Danforth asked.

"I'm back in good shape again."

"We've had a couple more bankers snatched since you went down. There may be something to your idea that there's a connection between all of these banking kidnappings," Danforth related. "Any new ideas?"

Tom was quiet for a few moments. "I do. But I'll have to talk to some people in person, not on the phone. The woman I've been seeing is going back to San Francisco day after tomorrow. Then I can fly to Mexico City and talk with several of my contacts."

"Do it. If this is some type of organized banking abduction gang, we need to look into it. Stop in and see me before you go."

"I will. Hey, Mark, is there another hotel besides the Hilton that we have an ongoing contract with?"

"Yeah. But the Hilton's rates are the best by far. Why do you ask?"

"They've asked me to move to a different hotel. The shooting and car crash and a couple of other embarrassments that I don't want to talk about prompted the request that I find other accommodations."

Danforth laughed. "You get yourself involved in the strangest situations. I'll take care of it. Don't worry, you won't have to change hotels. I'll bet your social blunders involved women."

"You can say that again."

***

Crystal Henderson was unusually quiet on the drive to the airport. She looked over at Tom, concern registering in her eyes and face. "I don't mean to belabor the point, but are you considering making a career change? Or are you telling your father and me that just to quell our anxieties?"

"I'm not being dubious. I'm just not ready to make the change now. I have unfinished business in Mexico City. That's why I'm flying there tomorrow," he replied.

Crystal exhaled sharply. "I'm worried that something's going to happen to you. I don't want to get so emotionally involved with you that all I can think about is your safety."

Tom glanced at her and their eyes locked. He'd had these conversations twice before. Both relationships ended badly, and he could see where this one might go. "Is our being apart much of the time part of the equation?"

"Yes, I suppose so. If you were working in Los Angeles, I could easily get a job here. We'd be together, and you'd be safe."

Tom thought for a few moments. "The timing now isn't right."

"That's all you have to say," she said in a hurt voice.

"Crystal, I care about you deeply. But I just can't leave

what I'm doing. I'm sorry," he said.

"Your business is more important to you than I am. That's obvious," she said.

"I don't think that's a fair comparison."

"I do. We won't be together for several weeks. I don't know when I'll see you next, and that really bothers me," Crystal complained.

Tom took a deep breath. "It bothers me, too. I want you with me all the time, but there's a very difficult problem I have to try and solve."

"Can you give me a time frame?" she asked.

"No."

"Are you trying to break up with me?" she asked.

"Of course not. I care for you very much. You know that," Tom responded.

"I don't know anything, except you're putting me on an airplane and saying goodbye."

"You're making it sound as if I'm insincere, and that's not true."

Both were quiet for several moments.

"Give me some idea where we're headed. Right now, I don't have a clue," she said in a quiet voice. Tears welled up in her eyes.

"Let me try to take care of this problem in Mexico City. Then we can address our relationship."

"Unless another problem arises. Then I'll be pushed farther down the line again."

Tom pulled into the parking garage, found a space, and turned off the ignition. "Do you realize we're arguing like a married couple? I hate arguing, especially with someone I care a great deal about."

"I don't like it either," she said as tears rolled down her cheeks.

Tom reached over, took her in his arms, and kissed her

tenderly. Crystal groaned and hugged him tightly. "Next time we're together, give me some answers," she said quietly.

"I will."

***

Tom had successfully negotiated the release of Victor Chapa, the vice president of Banco Royale, one of Mexico's most successful commercial investment banking institutions. His office was on the twentieth floor of Bando Royale's high rise building in downtown Mexico City. Security guards were everywhere, even accompanying Tom in the elevator to Chapa's suite of offices. He was shown in immediately, and the investment banking genius rushed over and grabbed Tom's hand.

"It's great to see you, Tom," said the short, dapper banker.

Tom noted that Victor's sunken cheeks had filled out, as had his gaunt body since the kidnapping and his release several months earlier. His salt and pepper colored hair now had more white than black, and the lines in his forehead were more pronounced. However, his energy level appeared to be back to its normal high.

"It's good to see you, too, Victor. I bet you were surprised when you got my call," Tom said.

"I was."

They were sitting in overstuffed leather chairs in front of Chapa's desk and chatted for a couple of minutes before Bradshaw began discussing the reason for his visit.

"There are too many bankers being kidnapped in Mexico City for it to be a coincidence. My boss, Mark Danforth, and I both think it's a conspiracy based upon acquiring personal and business information when choosing victims."

Chapa nodded his head, indicating he understood. "That's quite possible. How can I help?"

Tom pulled a list out of his suit coat pocket and handed it to Victor. "Here are the names of ten bankers who have been kidnapped. Your name is on the list. This is a private discussion between the two of us, and I would appreciate it if you would not divulge this information to anyone else."

"Of course. This is strictly between the two of us," said Chapa.

"There has to be a relationship between all of these men, other than knowing each other through business. Any ideas?" Tom asked.

"I'm sure they're all members of the Mexico City Banking Association. The association has all of the information about these men and where they work. If a kidnapping gang has an informant within the MCBA, there's a lot of information to be had," Chapa pointed out.

"Here's all I know about the leader. He's slender, about five feet, eight inches tall, has very light brown eyes, and dresses in expensive clothing," Bradshaw explained. "He also wears a very different woody, spice cologne. He was wearing a mask, so I didn't see his face."

"Was this the guy involved in my kidnapping?"

"Yes. I was in the hotel room below where you were held hostage and wired the money to an off-shore account in order to get you released," Tom said. "That's the only time I've seen him."

"They took me blindfolded to that hotel room at night. I was only there for a few hours before you found me," Victor said.

"Do you remember anything about the leader?"

"I never saw him," Chapa replied. "I only had contact with the low level gang members, no one with any education."

"Well, anything you can come up with would be helpful," Tom said.

"I know the chairman of the banking association and will make a discreet inquiry," Chapa promised.

"I'd appreciate it. Victor, you look in great shape. Have you come full circle back to normalcy?"

Chapa smiled. "Pretty much so. I still have dreams about being held in a windowless room, struggling to keep my sanity, but not as often as before. Now I'm being kidnapped by bodyguards. I ride with escorts every day of the week to and from the office. I'm never really free, but I'll deal with it."

The men talked for another fifteen minutes before Bradshaw excused himself and headed by cab to the Hilton Hotel. He entered the front lobby and walked to the check in counter. The front desk manager, Vincent Cantu, looked at Tom, a worried expression on his face.

"Welcome back, Mr. Bradshaw. We are happy to see you," he said in a less than enthusiastic voice, and cleared his throat. "I suppose you would like your usual room?"

"Yes, I would, Vincent. I promise to be a good guest. You don't have to worry about a thing," he said. "Any parties going on tonight at the hotel?"

A look of anxiety and uncertainty flooded Cantu's features. "I...I don't know."

Tom grabbed the hotel room key and headed for the elevator. He turned his head and said, "Just kidding, Vincent."

CHAPTER 13

Nine-year-old twins, Daniel and Mario Rios, jumped out of the limousine as the door was opened by their bodyguard, Antonio Pena. They gathered their backpacks and jackets as they prepared to sprint to the front door of one of Mexico City's premier private schools, the Chapultepec College Preparatory Academy.

Two men wearing ski masks suddenly jumped from nearby parked cars. A large man with huge arms fired his revolver. The slug hit Pena in the upper right leg, and he fell to the ground screaming. The thug ran to the downed bodyguard and relieved him of his pistol.

The boys were frozen in place, afraid to move, as the kidnappers grabbed them. Daniel suddenly began fighting until he was struck hard across the side of his head, rendering him semi-conscious. Mario was consumed with fear, unable to function, and did not put up a fight.

Chaos ensued as children and their parents entering the school began yelling, screaming, and running in different directions. Bodyguards for these children stayed with their wards, guns drawn, many shielding their children.

An old blue Chevrolet van pulled up to the limousine, the back doors were flung open, and the twins were tossed inside.

Both of the kidnappers followed them inside, leaving their stolen cars on the street. A third snatcher used duct tape to tie their hands and legs. Daniel began cursing the abductors. Mario began crying. The van raced down the street, ending the episode that had taken less than three minutes.

"Both of you, shut up, or I'll put tape over your mouths," the huge kidnapper yelled at the boys.

The driver and the three kidnappers in the rear of the van all wore ski masks. They quickly put hoods over the boys' heads, then removed their own ski masks for the drive through the city. The drive east took forty-five minutes and ended in the midst of Neza, a vast community of four million poor Mexicans and the largest mega-slum in Mexico.

Their destination was a small building on the side of a hill that was one of the few remaining structures that hadn't collapsed and slid down into a huge gully. The kidnappers removed the duct tape from the boys' feet and arms and pushed them into the shack. The windows were boarded up, and the only light came from cracks between the wall boards.

The big man, Bruno de la Garza, was a former member of Columbia's Special Forces. His daily weight lifting had generated a huge torso and long muscular arms. Bruno's head was shaved bald, his ears stuck out sideways, a bulbous nose hung down to his upper lip, and a black beard completed the amazing ugly facial ensemble. The grotesque combination of physical oddities struck fear in the hearts of his subordinates, who complied immediately with his orders.

"I want you to keep your goddamned mouths shut. Any yelling, and I'll come in and duct tape your arms, legs, and mouths. Understand me?" Bruno growled.

The boys quickly nodded, yes.

He walked out of the shack and addressed the other three snatchers. "Paco, you're to stay near the front of the building, making sure the boys are securely locked in. If they shout and yell, go inside and rough them up a little. Not much, just a little."

"Okay, boss," Paco said. The small gang member's dull eyes reflected limited intelligence.

"Pepe and Pedro, you are to get food and fresh water for the boys. They're to be fed morning and evening. Tomorrow, I'll change the job assignments around, so each of you does night duty only once every three days. Is that clear?" Bruno asked loudly.

The three young men babbled their consent while looking at the ground. De la Garza turned, trudged down the hillside, and disappeared in the maze of run-down hovels that constituted housing for thousands of families.

The tandem of Pepe and Pedro returned before dark on their motorbike that made a loud pinging noise. The twins' hoods were removed, they were fed and then were locked up for the night. Then, the two young snatchers walked down the hill and departed on the motorbike, the loud pinging indicating a short future for the machine. As dusk settled upon the Neza slums, Mario began wailing, yelling for his mother. Paco had pulled a bottle of tequila from his jacket and had nearly finished the liquor when the crying began.

"Shit," the drunken young man said as he moved unsteadily to the door. He had difficulty unlocking the door and nearly fell down as he entered. "Keep quiet, or I'll beat the crap out of you," he yelled. Mario stopped crying.

Paco stumbled outside, raised the bottle to his lips, and let the remainder of the fiery liquid burned its way down his throat. He walked to his sleeping bag, flopped down, and was asleep moments later.

Daniel Rios had his arm around his brother, trying to comfort him when he realized that he hadn't heard the door being locked. He got up and made his way to the door in the darkness that was illuminated only by the moon's rays through cracks in the building's sides. He turned the door knob and pushed. It opened with a squeaking noise, and he walked outside. To one side was Paco on his sleeping bag, snoring loudly.

He walked back inside. "Come on, Mario, we can escape."

"They'll be mad if we're gone," Mario whispered.

"I'm leaving now. Give me your hand," Daniel said in a firm voice.

The two boys walked silently past their guard, who began snoring even louder. The moonlight helped them pick their way down the side of the large gully. The twins began running as soon as they entered the maze of paths between buildings, primarily constructed of cardboard and wood slats with corrugated tin roofs.

The twins ran through the twisting, narrow streets and paths, looking for anyone who could help them. But it was after dark in a sprawling, crime ridden district, and residents did not open their doors for any reason. By sunrise the next morning, they were exhausted, hungry, and bewildered. Three times they approached men leaving for work and were told to get lost before they could explain their circumstances. No one wanted to have anything to do with them. Finally, they met an elderly, wrinkled woman who stepped out of her house to throw a pan full of water into the dirt street.

"Please help us. We escaped from kidnappers and don't know where we are," Daniel told her.

Sofia Garcia looked at the boys through cataract-filled eyes. "You look like one of my sons many years ago." She put her hand up to touch Mario's face, and the boy shrank back in fear. "Are you hungry?" she asked.

"Oh, yes," Daniel said.

They followed Mrs. Garcia into her small house and nearly collapsed on an old couch as she prepared tortillas, rice, and beans. The boys ate ravenously, barely chewing the food as they wolfed it down. She smiled, showing a mouth empty of teeth.

***

Bruno de la Garza telephoned the boys' mother, Bianca Pacheco, that morning before returning to the safe house in the Neza district.

"Listen, bitch. I've got your sons. Get a lot of money together, and you'll get them back in one piece," he said, and hung up. Satisfied that the kidnap negotiations had begun, he drove back, parked, and hiked up the hill to the dilapidated building.

The three young men stood rigid, eyes wide and mouths open as their boss approached. "Well, how did the first night go?" Bruno asked.

Paco fell to his knees, hands clasped in front of him. "I'm sorry, boss. Forgive me. It'll never happen again. I'm so sorry!"

"What happened?" he growled.

"He was drunk and left the door unlocked. The kids ran off," Pepe said in a worried voice.

Bruno made a rumbling sound like an angry animal, pulled out a revolver, and walked over to Paco.

"Please, no. Have mercy," Paco cried out.

De la Garza's eyes were mere slits as he pulled the trigger, and the slug tore through Paco's head. The shot echoed in the quiet of the early morning. The other two young kidnappers were frozen in place.

"They can't have gotten far. No one would take them in at night. Drive your bike around and ask if anyone has seen them. Get moving," he told the two snatchers.

Pedro and Pepe nearly tripped over each other as they ran down the hill to their motorbike. They drove off to the distinctive pinging sound of the small motor.

***

The twins' grandfather was Diego Santana, one of the richest men in Spain. He controlled a worldwide commercial contracting company that primarily built highways and commercial high rise buildings. His daughter, Bianca Pacheco, called her father shortly after the kidnapping occurred. Santana contacted Mark Danforth at California Fidelity, and Danforth phoned Tom Bradshaw. Tom was at the Pacheco home within two hours and set up recorders and the other necessary equipment to monitor all incoming calls. He was outside the home checking wiring and a new antenna when the first call came in from Bruno de la Garza.

"Don't worry about me missing the first call. The kidnapper was just letting you know that he has the boys. I'll be here for the future calls," Tom assured her.

Bianca was a beautiful brunette with a cascading mane of raven hair pulled back from her face but flowing down on her shoulders. Her honey-colored, almond-shaped eyes and creamy skin boosted her allure and contributed to her attractiveness.

At first, Tom was all business when he talked to her about her sons. But even the anxiety and stress of the kidnapping did not lessen her desirability. She kept her worry and uneasiness under control and listened attentively to every recommendation he made. Her violet eyes seemed to soak up the information. Tom forced himself to remain business-like even though her perfume was intoxicating.

"The boys are the sons of my first husband, Damon Rios, who was killed in a small plane crash. Within two years, I married Salvador Pacheco, who was my husband's best friend. He was very attentive to the boys, and I thought he'd make a great father," she said in an uncertain, anxious voice. "But that was not to be."

"You don't have to tell me anything of a personal nature unless you really want to," Tom said.

"There's something about you, Tom, that makes me feel I can trust you," she said.

Their eyes met and held. Bradshaw knew from past experiences that wives were often very emotional when a husband or son had been kidnapped. They were vulnerable and often looked at a negotiator as being a savior. Thus far in his career, he had been able to conduct himself in a professional manner, no matter what circumstances arose.

"I'll always be straightforward and honest with you," Bradshaw said.

"Salvador is an entrepreneurial type, always putting together mergers and sales of businesses. His company is here in Mexico City, but he spends very little time here.

It was silly to move here from Spain, but I did it thinking the boys would benefit from being around Salvador."

"Apparently, it didn't work out?" Tom asked.

"No. We very seldom see him. He spends most of his time in Europe. I also didn't realize he had a gambling habit. Lately, he's been borrowing from my father to cover his gambling losses."

"When you called him today about the kidnapping, how did he respond?" Tom asked.

"He said he would catch a flight from Paris to fly here, but I haven't heard anything more from him. My father is urging me to divorce him, but I don't know what effect that will have on Mario and Daniel, especially after this ordeal."

"They'll get through it. They're young. I promise you, I'll get them back," he told her.

She walked over to him, put her hands on his chest, and looked into his eyes. "I believe you."

Bradshaw was only human. He took her in his arms and held her for what seemed like an eternity. He felt her shiver. Tom's body was rigid with emotion, and his resolve to remain neutral and steadfast to negotiation principles was suddenly up in the air.

Her cell phone rang, shattering the intimacy of the moment.

"Both your cell phone and the house phone are hooked into the recorder. Give it to me if it's the kidnapper," he said. Tom turned on the recording device. The call was from her maid, who said she'd be late to work.

CHAPTER 14

Daniel and Mario were identical twins with brown curly hair and brown eyes, tall for their age, and very slender. They played baseball and soccer daily and had insatiable appetites, which translated into a high level of athleticism. The boys left Sofia Garcia's house and headed south along a road that she said would take them to a gas station, where someone would have a phone. Twice they talked to men they met, asking to make a cell phone call. However, most people in these slums couldn't afford phones. All of the ramshackle, dilapidated buildings were grey or rust covered. The residents could not afford paint.

Twice they heard the pinging made by the kidnappers' motorbike. They hid and watched the bike drive by, the two snatchers looking in every direction.

"What are we going to do?" Mario asked. "They'll find us."

"No, they won't," his brother said. "They don't know where we are. Let's keep going."

They saw the gas station ahead of them, and Daniel stopped and watched for a while until he was satisfied that the hunters were not there. They cautiously approached the old building with two gas pumps outside. As soon as a pickup departed, they ran to the building and were met by a heavyset attendant.

"We escaped from kidnappers. Can we use your phone to call my mother?" Daniel asked.

Manuel Ayala's eyes narrowed as he looked the boys up and down. "Those are nice jackets you're wearing. They'd fit my boys nicely," he said, a smirk on his face.

"Take your jacket off," Daniel told his brother.

"But I'll be cold," Mario complained.

"Just do it," his brother ordered.

They quickly pulled them off and handed them to Ayala. The attendant saw the gold chain with a crucifix around Daniel's neck. "Take off the gold chain," he ordered. Daniel frowned but did as he was instructed. "What's the phone number?" Ayala asked.

Ayala held his cell phone in the air, trying to get reception. He turned in a circle until faint reception registered on the face of the cell phone. He called the number, and Bianca answered. Ayala handed the telephone to Daniel.

"Mom. Is that you?" he asked.

Bianca cried out. "Are you all right?"

"We escaped from the kidnappers and are calling from a gas station. Can you come and get us?"

Tom came on the line. "Daniel, my name is Tom, and I'm hired to bring you home safely. What are the cross streets near the service station?"

Daniel looked at Ayala. "What are the cross streets here?"

"Guadalupe and Hidalgo in the Nez."

Daniel gave the information to Tom. "They're hunting us. I've seen them driving by on a motorbike," he said.

"Listen, Daniel. I'm coming to get you and your brother. I'll be driving a dark grey Chevrolet Tahoe. Do you know what the vehicle looks like?"

"Yes. I see them at the school all the time."

"Hide near the gas station until I get there. Don't talk to anyone. It'll be about an hour before I get there. Do you understand everything I've told you?"

"Yes. Can I talk with Mom again?"

"Only for a moment. I have to get started, and you boys need to hide. Do you understand?"

"Yes."

He handed the phone to Bianca, and she trembled as she talked with her son again.

"I have to give the phone back, Mom," he told her. "I love you."

Bianca broke down crying, no longer able to maintain a calm demeanor. Tom put his arms around her and let her sob for a few moments. "I've got to leave now. It's a long drive into the slums."

She looked up at him. "I'm coming with you."

"That's not a good idea. I don't know what I'll run into. It's no place for a woman like you."

"Tom, I'm going with you. Those boys mean more to me than life itself." Her beautiful, tear-filled violet eyes reflected determination. "Let me change my clothes before we go," she said.

Bradshaw waited for her in the SUV, and five minutes later, they were off. Bianca was quiet most of the trip, events churning in her mind and fear choking her. Traffic was heavy at first and then thinned out as they entered the Nez. The Tahoe's GPS took them in a roundabout fashion on the few roads that could handle a large vehicle.

"There it is up ahead," Tom said. The Tahoe crept forward slowly as Tom scrutinized the few people walking on the dirt paths. They all looked poor and afraid. He stopped in front of the gas station, and they both exited.

"Daniel, Mario," she called out.

The boys came running up the street just as the first shots were fired, striking the SUV's windshield and shattering the glass. Tom and Bianca ran towards the boys, each grabbing one and darting down a narrow path between shacks, then zigzagging among the buildings until they were out of breath.

"What's happening, Mom? Why are they shooting at us?" Mario whimpered.

"They were trying to hit me. They thought I had a gun," Tom told the boys.

"What should we do?" Bianca asked, gasping for breath.

"We'll keep going deeper into the slums and find a place to hide. Then I'll think of some way we can get out of here," Tom replied. He held his cell phone in the air but got no reception.

***

"You dumb son-of-a-bitch, why did you shoot?" Bruno yelled at Pepe. "I told you I would shoot first. Now they're off and running, and we have to chase them. Get on your motorbike and go after them."

"What if they shoot at us, boss?" Pepe said in an alarmed voice.

"They don't have weapons, or they would have shot back at us. Get going, goddamn it."

Pepe and Pedro shoved their revolvers under their belts, jumped on the motorbike, and slowly rode after the fleeing group. Bruno de la Garza went behind one of the dilapidated buildings and climbed aboard a motorcycle, circled the gas station, and rode down one of the paths between the hovels.

***

After fleeing for nearly a quarter of a mile, Tom saw a shack with a door hanging open. He directed Bianca and her sons to the small hut, checked the interior, and found it empty except for trash. They went inside, Bradshaw closed the door, and they sat down.

"Mother, this place stinks," Mario said.

"We need a place to catch our breath and rest for a few minutes," Tom told the boy.

In the distance, they heard the ping, ping of the motorbike.

"Two of the kidnappers ride on that bike! It makes that pinging sound all the time," Daniel explained.

The pinging sound drew closer until it was immediately in front of the small building. Tom peered out through a crack in the wall and noted that the young snatchers were in their late teens or early twenties.

Bradshaw conversed with the boys and their mother in low tones for fifteen minutes, answering a variety of questions about the kidnapping business and why people could be so cruel to one another. The boys said they were cold, so Tom lay down on an old blanket and took the boys under his arms. Bianca covered them with Tom's coat and lay down next to them. The boys were asleep within minutes.

"You're a good man, Tom," she told him. "You're risking your life for people you don't even know."

Tom sighed. "I get so involved in the negotiation business that sometimes I forget about everything else. Bringing them back alive is the goal."

"Were you always like this?" she asked. "I mean, caring for others."

"No. In Afghanistan, I killed men who were trying to kill me. It made me see the futility of war in general and what it does to a person. I had the opportunity to join a negotiations team, and I took it. I became pretty good at it, and it just carried over into civilian life as a business."

Bianca was quiet for a moment. "Have you ever been married?"

Tom smiled in the dim light coming through a rear window. "I've come close a few times, but my being gone from the United States for long periods of time ultimately led to the demise of the relationships."

"I see," she said.

"Bianca, I have to ask you this. Did you talk with anyone by telephone before we drove to the Neza?"

"My husband called," she said quietly.

"Did you tell him where we were going to find the boys?"

She made a strange sound and then began weeping softly. "Yes. He wanted to know the exact location, and I told him."

Now Tom was silent as he thought about how to tell her the gut-wrenching truth. "The kidnappers were waiting for us. It was a set-up, and your husband was the only person who knew the exact location."

She pulled a handkerchief from her coat and dried her eyes. "I never thought he could do anything like that. How could a man sacrifice his children?"

"If he had heavy gambling debts, people might be after him. Ransom money could be a way of solving his problem," he said quietly.

Tom stood up, trying not to wake the boys. Bianca stood up and put her arms around his waist. They kissed for what seemed like an eternity to Tom. She moaned as he enveloped her in his arms.

"I don't know how to describe what I'm feeling. It's electrifying," he found himself saying. As usual, Tom was a sucker for a beautiful woman in distress.

"I trust you, Tom, and I want to be with you," Bianca said softly.

Tom heard the pinging of the motorbike in the distance and listened as it grew louder. "I have an idea. If it doesn't work out, I want the three of you to stay here in the building until nightfall. Then try to find someone with a telephone."

Bradshaw walked outside and searched until he found a long board. In the distance, he could just see the motorbike with two men aboard coming in his direction. He walked across the street and stood in the shadows as the snatchers rode slowly down the street. When they were abreast of him, he stepped out and swung the board. It smacked into the driver, and both kidnappers tumbled off the bike.

In a split second, Tom jumped on the driver, smashed him in the face with his fist, and pulled the snatcher's revolver from his belt. Pepe was on the ground behind Pedro and was pulling out his revolver when Tom fired. The slug tore into his shoulder, and he began screaming and thrashing around in the dirt. Bradshaw walked over to him and grabbed his revolver off the ground.

He walked back to Pedro, who was groaning, grabbed him by the shoulders, and began shaking him. "What is your boss's name?" he growled.

"You bastard!" Pedro shouted.

Tom grabbed him by the hair and put his knee on the young man's chest. He shoved the barrel of the gun in his mouth and cocked it. Pedro's eyes were wide, and his face turned white as his teeth grabbed the barrel.

"Wait," he cried out in a muffled voice.

"What is his name? This is your last chance," Bradshaw told him as he withdrew the barrel.

"Bruno de la Garza. Please don't kill me," he begged.

"Where is he now?"

"I don't know. He was riding around on a motorcycle looking for all of you."

"Your buddy's bleeding pretty badly. See if you can wrap his wound," Tom ordered.

Pedro's eyes opened wide again. "Don't leave us here. If Bruno finds us, he'll shoot us both."

"If you survive, choose another line of work. You punks are not good kidnappers." Pepe began moaning, blood gushing from his wound. Tom grabbed Pedro by his dirty T-shirt and pulled him over to the wounded youth. "See if you can help him."

Tom walked over to the building where Bianca and the boys were hiding. "We can go now."

Both boys were hugging their mother. Bianca looked terrified and clutched her sons. "Are you sure?"

"Yes. I'm sorry you had to see and hear what went on. We need to get going," Tom said in a calm voice.

They walked outside and saw Pedro trying to wrap his companion's wound. The group moved swiftly down the street, heading back in the direction they'd come from. Mario was sniffling. His brother looked at Tom with admiration.

"Are we going to be okay now?" Daniel asked.

"I think so. We'll head back to the car. If it's drivable, we'll get going. If not, I'll get the gas station owner to let me use his telephone," Tom replied.

"He took our jackets and my gold crucifix on a gold chain. Can we get them back?" Daniel asked.

Tom looked at Bianca and smiled. "You've got one tough son here."

"He's always been the leader and decision maker. Mario is very sensitive and caring. The two are very different but have always been inseparable," she said.

"Yes, we'll try to get them back," Tom said, looking at Daniel.

Twenty minutes later, they could see the gas station in the distance. What looked like a swarm of humanity was all over the Tahoe as they neared the SUV. Tom shook his head in disbelief as he viewed what had been a nearly new vehicle. All four tires were missing, and the car seats had disappeared, as well as the SUV doors. The bumpers had been removed, the sun roof was gone, and the front hood had disappeared. An open shell remained where the motor once proudly shined.

"Sweet Jesus," Tom commented. "It's as if locusts descended on the Tahoe."

A motorcycle rounded the corner a block away and headed towards them at a high rate of speed.

"Get inside," Tom ordered.

Bianca and her sons ran inside the small building. Bruno de la Garza held the motorcycle handle with one hand as he started firing his pistol with the other. Tom raised his revolver and fired four quick rounds. One found its mark, breaking the kidnapper's collar bone. He yelled as the motorcycle crashed into a small gully behind the building opposite the gas station. The heavy cycle pinned de la Garza to the ground, and he struggled to pull himself out from under the metal bike.

"I'll kill you, you son-of-a-bitch," he growled. The gang leader made loud cries and yells as he attempted to extricate himself from under the heavy bike.

"Did Salvador Pacheco phone you with information about where we'd be?" Tom asked.

"Up yours, you asshole," Bruno bellowed. "I'll be out of jail quickly and will come after you. I'm going to cut you in small pieces, very slowly."

Tom jumped down in the gully and jammed his foot onto de la Garza's shoulder, causing him to bellow like a bull.

"Answer my question. Did Salvador Pacheco call you?"

"What if he did? Who gives a shit now? He said I could screw her all I wanted."

Tom looked down at the bull-like man, blood covering his bald head, eyes glaring hatred as he spit out teeth.

"You're through," Tom said, a note of finality in his voice.

"You haven't got the guts. You're soft. You don't have that killer instinct, you prick," de la Garza growled.

A shot rang out, and Tom slowly climbed out of the gully and walked across the street. The gas station attendant, Manuel Ayala, stared at Tom, an expression of intense dislike on his face.

"Give me your phone. I want to call the police," Tom said.

"It'll cost you a hundred bucks," Ayala said in a nasty voice and reached under the counter.

Tom slammed his revolver down on the counter. "Give me your phone and take your hand out from under the counter. If you pull a gun, I'll blow you away."

Ayala's eyes flickered momentarily. Then he removed his

hand from under the counter. The attendant gave Tom a nasty look as he placed his cell phone on the counter.

Bradshaw picked it up. "Come out from behind the counter and walk out into the street with me. Now!" he ordered.

Reluctantly, Ayala complied. Tom held up the phone and walked in a circle, trying to find reception. One bar showed faintly. He remembered key phone numbers, and one was that of Assistant Police Chief Franco Gomez. Bradshaw punched in the number, and it rang twice before Gomez answered. Tom explained about the kidnapping, the boys' escape, and the fact that they needed help now. He gave Chief Gomez the cross streets, and the police official said officers would arrive within fifteen minutes.

Bradshaw and Ayala walked back inside.

"He's wearing my gold crucifix," Daniel told Tom.

"Take it off and give it back to the boy," Tom ordered.

"That was payment for using my phone," Ayala growled.

"Take it off, or I'll tear it off you," Tom said in an angry voice.

Ayala reluctantly complied and handed the gold neckless to Daniel. Mario stood motionless, arms around his mother while the scenario unfolded.

Within five minutes, the scavengers returned and began prying and pounding apart the aluminum and steel body parts. By the time two squad cars pulled up, sirens blaring and lights flashing, the vehicle was little more than a skeleton.

"Are you Mr. Bradshaw?" a thin lieutenant asked.

"Call me, Tom. Am I ever glad to see you guys."

Bianca put her hand over her mouth as tears ran down her cheeks. Her sons wrapped their arms around their mother as they realized the ordeal was over.

"I knew we could do it, Mom. I knew it," Daniel said excitedly.

Tom explained what had occurred over the past two days

and pointed across the street. "There's a dead man, Bruno de la Garza, in the gully over there. He was the head of the kidnapping gang."

The lieutenant looked surprised. "He was wanted for murder and kidnapping. You did everyone a favor."

Bianca sat in the back of a squad car with a son on each side of her as Tom gave the details about the kidnapping and escape to the police. Two more police cars arrived. The scene took on a carnival-like atmosphere as people formed a large circle around the gas station. Street vendors appeared, selling food and drinks to the bystanders.

Tom walked over to the squad car holding Bianca and the boys. "I'm through here. Do you want me to accompany you back to your home?"

"Yes. Please come with us. I'd feel better if you were there with us," Bianca said.

She and the children were transferred to a large Chevrolet Suburban and sat in the back seat. Tom sat in front where he could talk with them. The third row of seats was occupied by two additional uniformed officers.

"Well, I'll be damned," one of the officers said. "There must be a dozen men carrying away that old carcass of a car."

CHAPTER 15

When they arrived at the sprawling Spanish style home in a gated community, Daniel was ready to kick a soccer ball around in the huge backyard. Mario, however, clutched his mother's hand and did not want to leave her side. Their cook, a heavyset woman in her late fifties, prepared the boys a mini-feast in the kitchen, and they began devouring the food.

"Try to get both boys into therapy as quickly as possible," Tom told her. "It won't take Daniel long to get back to normal. Mario will need more help."

"I talked with my father, and he's flying here tomorrow from Spain. I know he'll want to do a quick turnaround and return to Madrid. We'll return with him," she said, a sad tone to her voice. "Is there any chance you could accompany us for a vacation?"

"Not right away, but that sounds like a great idea," he replied.

They looked at each other, longing in their eyes. Tom had known the raven-haired beauty for only a short time, but he was captivated. Her pecan-shaped violet eyes cast a spell that was incredibly difficult for him to avoid. For some inexplicable reason, Crystal Henderson had temporarily vanished from his mind.

Following dinner, the exhausted twins took showers and went to the bedroom they shared together. Bianca talked with them for a few minutes before they fell asleep. She returned to the living room where Tom was relaxing, and they briefly talked about the boys. Bianca then went to the master suite, showered, and returned in a short blue skirt and white blouse that immediately caught Tom's attention. Her long legs and nineteen-inch waist were mind-bending to Bradshaw, who often was captivated by beautiful women.

He stood up, walked over to her, and began kissing her passionately. She put her arms around his neck and was breathing hard as they kissed. Suddenly she jerked away and cried out, eyes wide and a look of terror on her face.

Her husband, Salvador Pacheco, had entered the living room and stood staring at the pair. His dark blue suit looked as if it had been slept in, and his white shirt was drenched in sweat. The once dapper Mexican businessman had red circles under his eyes, his hair was hanging over his forehead, and he appeared to be drunk.

Caught off guard, Tom stood still as Bianca pulled away from him and walked over to her husband. "You coward. How could you ever come around me and the boys again after what you've done? I despise you!"

"It didn't take you long to find another man," he said. His speech was slurred, and he was barely able to remain upright.

Tom walked over to Salvador, grabbed him by the arm, and threw him face down on the floor. He searched the much smaller man as he squirmed on the floor. Bradshaw pulled a small revolver from Pacheco's suit coat pocket, then flipped him over on his back.

"I need the gun. They're after me," he yelled. He flailed around until he was on his hands and knees. "I owe everyone money. You're my last chance, Bianca."

"How could you have my sons kidnapped? You are a

terrible person," she said loudly.

"It wasn't supposed to be like that. They told me the boys would be kept in a guest house, watching television and eating cookies. It would only be for a day or two," he croaked, his voice nearly gone.

"You have no morals. I wish you were dead," she cried out.

"I have huge gambling debts, and your father cut me off. Please give me money, or they'll kill me," he whined.

Bianca was speechless. She stared at the once proud man, now reduced to sniveling beggar status. "I hope they kill you," she said.

"We had good times together. Remember? My gambling just got out of hand. Have mercy," he pleaded as he began crying.

Bianca's head dropped to her chest. "What should I do, Tom?"

"I'll take care of it," he replied. Bradshaw grabbed Pacheco by the collar and pulled him to his feet. "How did you get here?"

"I took a cab. When he stopped for a red light near here, I got out and ran. I don't have any money."

"This is a gated community. How did you get by the security guards?" Tom asked.

"They know me."

"Did you use a key to the house to get in?"

"Yeah."

"Give it to me," Tom ordered.

Salvador was shaking as he pulled out a key ring and pointed to the house key. Tom removed it and handed the key ring back to Pacheco.

"It's time for us to go," Bradshaw announced.

Pacheco looked bewildered. "Wait a minute. I need money," he said, and glanced at Bianca.

Tom shook his head no. He grabbed Salvador by the arm and marched him towards the front door. "I'll be back in a few minutes," he told Bianca.

Bradshaw pushed Pacheco into the passenger seat, slammed the door, walked around to the Cadillac's driver side, and got in.

"Where are you taking me?" Salvador whined.

"To the police station. You can tell them about your involvement with Bruno de la Garza."

Pacheco's eyes widened. "Oh, no. He'd kill me if I mentioned his name."

Tom's eyes were mere slits as he looked at the shipwreck of a man sitting next to him. "You don't need to worry about that. I killed de la Garza."

Suddenly, fear made Salvador's mouth fall open. "You're not going to kill me, are you?"

"No."

They drove in silence for ten minutes, Salvador suddenly fearful of the man sitting next to him. A half block from the police station, Tom pulled the Cadillac over to the curb. He removed the bullets from Pacheco's revolver and handed the gun to him. Then he handed him one bullet.

"Use it," he said in a determined voice.

***

Bianca was anxiously waiting when Tom returned. She raced across the living room and threw her arms around him. She was shaking but kissed him passionately, gripping him as tightly as she could, not wanting to let go. Tom was mesmerized by the beautiful brunette. All thoughts of keeping a professional demeanor went out the window as he enveloped her in his arms. She quickly led him to the sprawling master suite, and they were making love within minutes.

When they finally rested in each other's arms, she told him, "I'm not expecting any commitment from you. I'm just terribly attracted to you and want to be with you."

"I feel the same way towards you, Bianca. I can't fly back

to Spain with you right now. But I'll join you soon," he promised.

They finally fell asleep in the early morning hours. Both were exhausted but very happy. At seven, they were awakened by knocking on the master suite door.

"Mom," Mario called out. "It's time for breakfast."

Bianca sat upright in the bed. "The boys. I forgot about the boys."

Tom jumped out of bed, grabbed his clothes, and moved swiftly into the master bathroom. Bianca put on a robe and went to the door. "Has Carla arrived yet to make breakfast?" she asked the two boys who were standing side by side, looking at her expectantly.

"She's making breakfast now. Where's Tom?" Daniel asked.

"He'll join us for breakfast in a few minutes. Tell Carla to cook enough for all four of us."

The boys headed down the hallway. Ten minutes later, they were all in the kitchen, sitting around the breakfast table, enjoying a huge breakfast. The boys had multiple questions about their abduction and their freedom. Bradshaw assured them that they were safe and nothing would ever happen to them again. Daniel looked pleased, while Mario appeared skeptical.

"Your grandfather arrives today from Spain, and we'll be flying back with him to Madrid today or tomorrow," she told the twins.

"Is it a vacation?" Daniel asked.

"No. We're going to live in Spain. Is that all right?" she asked.

"I guess so," Daniel replied. "What about Salvador?"

Bianca had already decided she would be straightforward with her sons. "It just hasn't worked out between us. When we return to Spain, I'll file for divorce. You won't see him again."

"We never see him anyway," Mario pointed out.

Tom and Bianca glanced at each other with questioning

looks. The boys then started talking about their favorite soccer players. Bianca exhaled sharply, relieved that the subject of divorce did not bother the boys.

The cook had gone out to the front drive and brought back the morning paper. Carla had a worried expression on her face as she handed the newspaper to her employer. Bianca glanced at the front page and choked on her coffee. The lead story was about the killing of Bruno de la Garza, a notorious Mexican criminal, who looked even uglier in the death photo.

The news story related the facts about the shooting and abduction of Daniel and Mario Rios from in front of the Chapultepec College Preparatory Academy by the de la Garza gang. It told about the twin's escape and how a kidnap negotiator had killed de la Garza during the final confrontation that led to the boys' ultimate freedom. The negotiator was not identified.

Tom glanced at the article and winced. He motioned for Bianca to join him, and they walked out of the kitchen.

"What am I to do? I don't want the children involved with the press," she said in a worried voice.

"Call your father and find out when he will land. Tell him you want to shield the children from a circus-like atmosphere that could damage them emotionally. Right now, they're safe in a gated community," Tom said.

Bianca called her father, Diego Santana, and learned that he was two hours from landing at the Mexico City Airport. He fired questions in rapid succession, wanting to know all of the details about the kidnapping, the escape, and the final confrontation. Finally, she broke into the constant stream of questions.

"Father, listen to me. The kidnapping was featured on the front page of today's newspaper. I don't want Mario and Daniel to be grilled by the press before we leave for Madrid. What are your suggestions?" she asked.

Santana was quiet for a few moments. "Pack a few suitcases. Then drive to the private jet departure gates at the airport. I'll call ahead and see to it that you're immediately taken to the VIP waiting lounge. No one will bother you there."

"When will we depart?" Bianca asked.

"The Cessna will be serviced and refueled immediately. Then we'll take off. Hopefully, the boys will be shielded from the paparazzi." Santana said.

"Okay, Dad. I'll get started packing. I love you," she said.

"Wait. Wait. I have many more questions for you."

"We'll talk at the airport. Bye."

Bianca stared at Tom, realizing regretfully that their time together was drawing to a close. She told him what her father said, and Bradshaw nodded his head in agreement. Bianca told the boys to go to their rooms and each pack a suitcase. She and Tom went to the master bedroom while she packed. Tears spilled down her cheeks as she finished packing.

"Please come with us. I don't want to lose you," she said in a soft, caring voice.

"I feel the same way. But I have business commitments," he lamented.

"Think about it on our ride to the airport?" she said, assuming he would be accompanying them.

Minutes later, a guard at the front gate phoned the house. Bianca took the call and suddenly looked alarmed. "Oh, no. The paparazzi have arrived. There's TV trucks and reporters at the front gate."

Tom thought for a few moments. "Whose old pickup is parked at the side of the house?"

"It belongs to the gardener," she said.

Fifteen minutes later, Bianca's Cadillac exited through the front gate at a high rate of speed. Many of the TV and news reporters jumped in their vehicles and gave chase. The old pickup drove slowly through the security gate and headed towards the airport. Tom took off the gardener's straw hat, and Bianca and the twins sat up in their seats.

"That was fun, Mom," Daniel said.

Even Mario was excited. "Can we do it again?"

The drive to the airport was uneventful. Guards checked the old pickup carefully, not understanding what the jalopy was doing at the private jet departure gates. Tom parked it between a Maserati and a Ferrari, laughing at the odd looks he received. Bradshaw had not been able to change clothes for several days during the kidnapping and escape scenario. His suit was torn, dirty, and looked as if it had been slept in, which it had.

After tipping him handsomely, an airport employee went to the mezzanine that held numerous stores in the main airport. He returned with a grey leisure suit that had airport logos on the jacket and pants. Tom changed, and Bianca and her sons laughed at his new identity.

"Are you ready to gas up the plane?" Bianca asked, and laughed.

An hour later, the Cessna 560 landed. Her father, Diego Santana, nearly ran down the portable stairs to the runway apron. His daughter and grandsons threw their arms around him. A teary reunion took several minutes. Santana was short, bald, and had a white moustache. His body was rotund, and he walked on plump legs that moved surprisingly fast.

"Is this an airport employee?" he asked as he glanced at Tom.

Bianca laughed. "No, this man is Tom Bradshaw, who saved me and your grandsons."

Santana moved quickly to Bradshaw and encased him in a bear hug that took Tom's breath away. "Thank you. I'm indebted to you forever," he said.

They went to a large VIP room in the waiting area, and Santana gave orders to bring an array of food and toys for Mario and Daniel. At first, the airport employees appeared reluctant. But he gave each man one hundred American dollars, and suddenly they were in high gear filling the orders.

"It'll be an hour or longer before the plane is carefully inspected, gassed up, and ready for the return flight. We won't leave until I'm sure everything is in top shape. The return flight should take about nine hours. We'll be flying just under the speed of sound," Santana said. He signaled for an employee, and one came on the run. "Take the boys on a tour outside. Show them some of the aircraft up close," he instructed.

Once the three of them were alone, Bradshaw launched into a long explanation about the kidnapping, the escape by the boys, their phone call to their mother, and the trap that was sprung once he and Bianca arrived at the gas station.

"Bianca told me the only person she talked with about the location was her husband," Santana emphasized. His expression was one of anger and hatred.

"He admitted to us that he tipped off Bruno de la Garza. He needed the money and didn't want the hostages to escape." Tom pointed out.

"Mother of God! How could that miserable excuse for a man deliver Daniel and Mario to the kidnappers?" Santana bellowed.

Without answering, Tom continued with his review of the events, wanting to complete his explanation. He recounted how Bianca and the boys hid with him in an abandoned hut, his knocking the young kidnappers from the motorbike and wounding one of them. Then he told about the final confrontation with de la Garza and shooting him when he was in the gully.

Santana was on the edge of his seat, staring at Bradshaw as the story played out. "I don't know what to say to you, Tom. Words fail me."

Tom smiled. "Thanks is good enough. I got the boys back, and that feeling is terrific. It's what negotiators live for."

"Any idea where my son-in-law is?" Santana said as the cold look of hatred returned to his face.

"I took a revolver away from him at the house yesterday.

I gave it back to him after I drove him away from Bianca's home and handed him one bullet. I told him to use it," Tom said.

Santana's eyes narrowed. "I was going to send men to find him."

"I don't think you'll have to. There's men trying to find him. When they do, his chances of survival are non-existent," Tom pointed out.

Bianca stared out the window, deep in thought. When the men finished their conversation regarding Salvador Pacheco, she looked at her father. "I care for Tom very much. I've asked him to come to Spain with us. He needs a vacation."

Santana's eyes widened, and his mouth fell open. "What?"

"You've told the story many times about how you fell in love with Mother the first time you met her. Now I know what you mean," she said in a calm voice.

Her father appeared stunned by the revelation. Finally, he shook his head yes, and looked from one to the other. "It's true. I knew it the first time I saw her."

"Are you all right with him coming with us to Spain?" she asked.

Santana looked bewildered. "Tom, what do you say?"

Bradshaw had been waiting for the right time to repeat his claim that he had pressing business in Mexico City and really could not join them. Instead, he found himself saying, "I do care a great deal for your daughter, but I —"

"Wonderful!" Santana said in an exuberant voice. He reached out and clasped Tom in a bear hug again. "I couldn't be happier."

"I'm so thrilled," Bianca cried out.

A half hour later, Tom found himself climbing the portable stairs into the Cessna, a look of disbelief on his face. "What am I doing?" he muttered to himself.

The ultra-glamorous interior of the plane featured warm cream and light honey tones for the color palette. Large, luxurious, light tan seats were spread throughout the cabin that could seat eighteen people. A glamorous leather sofa with lacquered wood veneer detailing was opposite the dining area.

Circular faux skylights added an abundance of light. A faux fireplace in the wall opposite the eating area show-cased shimmering life-like flames and crackling embers. The overall effect was a cozy, relaxing atmosphere.

Santana proudly showed Tom around. "All of the chairs can lay flat for sleeping during long flights. There's high speed Internet, and you can use your mobile phone to call anywhere in the world. The bathroom has a double-size shower and heated marble floors."

The three adults chatted for nearly an hour before Santana excused himself to catch a nap in the far corner of the cabin on one of the plush leather chairs that lay back. Mario and Daniel played a variety of games on the dining room table until their mother made them lie down and rest. They were asleep almost immediately. The chef, who doubled as host on the flights, busied himself in the kitchen preparing the next meal.

Tom and Bianca were alone and moved to the plush leather couch so they could be near each other.

"I'm not asking for any kind of a commitment from you," she said softly. "It will be nice to be with you under normal circumstances so we can see how well things play out. Who knows, maybe I'll tire of you," she said, and laughed.

Tom grinned and then laughed. "You know I wasn't planning on coming with you. But I do need a vacation, and there's no one I'd rather spend it with than you."

"How long can you stay?"

"Two weeks. Maybe a little longer."

"Come here. I want to show you something," she told him and gave Tom a sly look.

He followed her to the rear of the plane. She opened a door, revealing a single bed in a very small compartment. "If someone is ill, she can lie down here away from the other passengers."

Tom grinned. "This is small."

They entered and locked the door. Tom took her in his arms and began kissing her passionately. Bianca's desire was as strong as Tom's, and her intense emotional excitement matched his. She was quickly out of her skirt and blouse. However, he got his foot caught in the leisure suit, stumbled, and fell onto the bed. Bianca laughed and pulled them off his legs.

CHAPTER 16

An hour later, Tom sat in a corner of the Cessna and made three phone calls that he was not looking forward to. The first was to his boss, Mark Danforth, in Los Angeles.

"Hi, Mark. I'll bet you'll want more of an update than that brief phone call I made to you."

"Yes, you're right. Are you sure you're okay, no bullet holes or anything?"

"Not a scratch," Tom replied. He went through the entire scenario involving the twins and their mother, ending with the revelation that the boys' stepfather was responsible for the final confrontation.

"What was his name again?"

"Salvador Pacheco."

"I didn't see anything in the latest Mexico City newspaper stories about him. I subscribe online to all the large papers," Danforth noted.

"Let me know if his name pops up," Tom said.

"Are you coming into the office today?" Mark asked.

"No. I'm heading for Spain in a Cessna."

"Dream on. Are you in Los Angeles?" Danforth asked.

"I really am flying over the Atlantic headed for Spain. Diego Santana asked me if I would accompany his daughter and grandsons back to Spain, and I agreed."

Danforth was quiet for a moment as he read between the lines. "Are you involved with his daughter?"

"Well, maybe a little," Tom replied.

"Jesus, Tom. If there's a skirt around, you'll head for it like a retriever. I thought you had a girlfriend in San Francisco."

Tom hesitated. "Well, maybe yes or maybe no. I haven't talked with her for a couple of weeks."

Mark chuckled. "Out of sight, out of mind. Are you a little remiss about keeping her happy?"

"You could say that."

"Well, you need a vacation after this last fiasco. You're lucky to be alive. How long will you be gone?"

"I'm committed for two weeks or less if there's an emergency."

"I know you'll keep Santana happy and put a smile on his daughter's face. Of course, they don't know yet about your famous disappearing act," Mark said, and laughed.

"Up yours, Mark."

The second call was to his father. His earlier call to Douglas Bradshaw was hit and miss when it came to details. Tom had told his Dad that two boys had escaped from kidnappers, and he helped their mother locate and retrieve the twins. His father answered his cell phone, an angry tone to his voice.

"I had a newspaper friend of mine make inquiries in Mexico City. You didn't tell me half of what happened or that you'd killed the gang leader."

"Oh. Well, I didn't want to worry you, Dad."

"I just don't understand you, Tom. You take so many unnecessary risks. I'm afraid you're going to end up dead, and I'll have to fly down there and claim the body."

"I'm sorry, Dad."

"You're supposed to be a negotiator. That's your job title. Please leave the Lone Ranger stuff to police or security officers.

You're really beginning to worry me," his father said. "You're rushing to your downfall."

"I'll take fewer risks in the future, Dad. I promise."

"Where are you calling from?"

"I'm in a Cessna flying to Spain. The boys' grandfather invited me to Madrid for a vacation, and I accepted. I'll be gone about two weeks before I return to Los Angeles," Tom explained.

Douglas was quite for a moment. "The newspapers in Mexico City said the boys' mother was a former beauty queen. Are you involved with her?"

"Maybe a little bit,"

"My God, Tom. What about Crystal?" Douglas asked. "Does she even know what took place?"

"No. I was going to call her as soon as we finish talking."

"We talk with her frequently because she's helping Marilyn with interior design ideas. Marilyn says Crystal can sense that your relationship is not progressing forward. I don't know what to tell her, and I feel bad for her," Douglas said, a note of sorrow in his voice.

"I never misled her. She knew that I spend two-thirds of every month out of the country."

"You've got to stop playing with women's emotions. This will be the third woman you've grievously harmed. It's deplorable," Douglas emphasized.

Tom had never been reprimanded by his father in such a harsh manner, and he suddenly felt guilty. Several moments passed without either man speaking. Tom exhaled sharply. "You're right, Dad. I realize I haven't been as forthcoming as I should be with women I care about. I'll try not to make that mistake again."

"I love you, son, and I'm very proud of you and your accomplishments. I don't want our conversation to end on a bad note. So, try to do better with the ladies, and for God's sake, be careful. That's all I ask," the elder Bradshaw said.

"I will, I promise. I love you too, Dad."

Tom sat in the plush, honey-colored leather chair, dreading to make the third call to Crystal Henderson, the vivacious young blonde he'd met in Mexico City. Now his feelings were jumbled. He cared for her, but not enough to commit to a long-term emotional relationship. Tom had no idea what he was going to say to her as he placed the call.

"Hello, Tom," she said in a subdued voice.

"Hi. I'm sorry I haven't called lately. I really have no good excuse."

"I talked with Marilyn today, and she told me what your father found out about the latest kidnapping in Mexico City," Crystal said.

"I got through it without a scratch."

"I'll be honest with you, Tom. I don't want to continue in a relationship where you're continually placing your life at risk. I think we should part company as friends and call it a day. We had fun, but I think we should end it," she said in a dejected voice.

Bradshaw was stunned. No woman had ever thoroughly dumped him in a short space of time, and it hurt.

"I don't know what to say," he replied.

"Something nice would have been appropriate. But I think you're probably relieved. And I can move on with my life with my pride intact," she said.

"Jesus Christ, I feel like a real bastard."

"You should. But that's beside the point. Let's face it, you just don't want to commit. And I'm through being treated like a plaything you can occasionally meet with and enjoy."

"I don't mean to treat you that way."

"Maybe the glamour of your job will wear thin. But until it does, you'll go on playing a role you enjoy and expecting those around you to accept it. Goodbye, Tom," she said, and ended the call.

Bradshaw was at a loss for words, and his emotions were jagged. The chef on the Cessna approached and asked if he would like a snack or a drink. Tom looked up, not really seeing the man, then dropped his head without replying. For the next few minutes, he stared out the window at the clouds far below. Bianca approached and sat on the edge of his padded chair.

"Are you all right?" she asked, her violet eyes showing deep concern.

He didn't know what to say. Then Tom decided that a half truth was better than the full truth. "I'll be okay. My dad doesn't want me to continue in this line of work. He says it's too dangerous, and I take too many chances."

Bianca thought for a moment. "My sons and I were caught up in a terrible situation. If it weren't for your fast action, we all might be captives right now or worse. You're a good man, Tom. Don't let anyone tell you differently."

Tom smiled, moved by her kind words. The impact of his father's condemnation, and the abrupt ending of his relationship with Crystal Henderson, were suddenly lessened by having her near him.

***

Diego Santana's estate in Madrid was a spectacular four-acre botanical garden surrounding an eight thousand square foot rambling mansion. The grounds included a man-made stream and waterfalls that meandered through the tall trees and jungle-like grounds. The estate was filled with dozens of varieties of fruit trees, rose bushes, ferns, bamboo trees, and wild strawberries. A focal point was a thousand year old olive tree.

The interior of the seven-bedroom, eight-bathroom house was unique. The four major living rooms had floor to ceiling windows and partial glass ceilings that looked out into the botanical gardens, creating an atmosphere of pure relaxation.

"We do a lot of entertaining," said Santana's wife, Maria.

She proudly led Tom through the colorful mansion,

showcasing terracotta and marble floors, red travertine marble walls, and artwork from around the world. Then she took him along the winding outside paths so they could view and listen to more than a dozen varieties of birds.

Tom's lodging was a separate guest house the size of a small home. "The boys will be continually running about, and they do make noise," she told him. "This should give you some privacy."

Maria was in her early sixties but still was a very attractive woman. Tom was able to imagine what Bianca would look like when she reached that age, and he liked what he saw.

"Your home is exquisite," Tom told her. "Honestly, I've never seen anything quite like this property and house. You must be very proud."

They walked and talked for nearly an hour, giving Maria ample time to study Tom, his mannerisms and his personality. She already knew from the way Bianca looked at Tom that her daughter was very much in love with the handsome American. What she saw was a friendly, kind, and very polite young man. She liked him but found it hard to imagine the other side of his personality because violence was foreign to her.

Bianca had taken her sons to therapy sessions, leaving Diego and Maria to entertain Tom. The patriarch invited Tom into his mammoth office, and they chatted about business.

"Are you planning on leaving the negotiation business?" Diego asked.

"Soon, probably. But there's some business I have to attend to first. My dad is particularly insistent that I go into business in Los Angeles. I'm thinking that international business negotiations and acquisitions would be a field I'd like to explore."

Santana smiled. "I've mentioned to you that most of my business now is in the United States due to the economic slowdown in Europe. I'd certainly like you to join my company. I could use a good American negotiator."

"I appreciate the offer, but I'm not an engineer," Tom pointed out.

"Engineers do the work, and we put together the numbers. Then we make our presentations. It's a bidding game. We win some, and we lose some. But equally important is the impression the negotiator makes with city, county, and state officials who have to approve the projects in the United States," Diego said.

Tom was no fool. He could feel Santana trying to lasso him with a velvet noose.

"I appreciate the offer, and I'll certainly think about it," Bradshaw said.

"Wonderful!" Diego exclaimed. The rotund grandfather's eyes sparkled at the thought of having Tom as his new son-in-law. Then his eyes narrowed, and his face hardened. "There's another thing we need to talk about."

"What is it?"

"Salvador Pacheco is dead. I just received word from Mexico City that his badly beaten body was found on the street. I don't want to tell Bianca and the boys right now since this is sort of a vacation for everyone," Diego said.

Tom nodded his head. "I understand. His fate was sealed a long time ago. A gambling addiction will kill you."

Their eyes locked, and Tom could see and feel the toughness in Santana. Diego suddenly reverted to the role of jovial patriarch. "I have a surprise for you. I've made reservations for you, Bianca, and the boys at the Ibiza Grand Hotel for a week. Have you ever been there?"

Tom could feel the velvet noose settling on his shoulders, but at this point, he didn't care. "No, I haven't, but I've heard a lot about it."

"It's a fantastic island with powder-white beaches and sparkling blue water. This hotel has the best sea views, beachside restaurants, and a superb spa. What do you say?"

Tom raised his hands and surrendered. "That surrounds

terrific. When do we leave?"

"Day after tomorrow. There's a suite with two bedrooms, plus an adjoining suite. Have fun," he said, and smiled.

***

The flight from Madrid to the island of Ibiza was an hour and ten minutes. The beach-side hotel had sweeping views of the Mediterranean. Both suites had terraces that opened to the sea. The Ibiza Grand Hotel was family friendly, with a kids club that had daily activities, a game room, and an arcade.

Tom spent part of each day involved in water sports with Daniel and Mario while Bianca enjoyed the world-class spa. They did surfing, snorkeling, paddle boarding, jet skiing, and sailing. The twins had never-ending energy levels and voracious appetites that continually refueled their desire for more activities.

"I'm exhausted and can't keep up with nine-year-olds. I'm amazed at their high energy levels," Tom said. He and Bianca were sitting in comfortable chairs on the terrace, watching the twins swimming in the surf.

"You're not as young as you used to be," she said, and laughed. "The boys are crazy about you. They've never had a man in their lives like you."

"What did the therapist say?"

"They only visited her once before we came here. She said Daniel will quickly snap out of it. It will take Mario longer because he's so sensitive. But she recommended that Daniel continue with sessions so that Mario doesn't think he's being treated any different than his brother."

"Good. What about you?" Tom asked.

Bianca stared at the ocean. "I went through some bad times before the kidnapping. My husband was killed, Salvador turned out to be a mistake, and our move to Mexico City was a complete disaster. So I've dealt with some major problems. The kidnapping is still fresh in my mind, but being with you has been wonderful. I'll probably do a couple of sessions after you leave, but I'm fine."

"I care about you a great deal, more than any woman I've ever met. I—"

"I'm not asking for a commitment," she repeated. "In fact, I believe we both need to think about our relationship once you return to Los Angeles. Distancing ourselves from one another might be a good idea."

Tom nodded his head in agreement.

The boys were running through the sand towards the terrace.

"When do we eat?" Mario asked.

CHAPTER 17

Tom took a cab from LAX to his condo and was unlocking his front door when he heard a voice from his past that sent cold chills up his spine.

"Young man, may I have a minute of your time?"

Wide-eyed, he turned and stared at the prim and proper grey-haired lady who walked swiftly up to him. "Mrs. Fairchild. How are you?"

"Not so good. The door to my master bedroom keeps sticking. It's very annoying. Could you take a look at it?"

"Have you called the handyman?"

"That man is not to be trusted. He came out to fix a leaking faucet and charged me two hundred and sixty dollars. I told him that was robbery, and we got in a terrible quarrel. After arguing for what seemed like an hour, he took my offer of one hundred and sixty dollars and left. He had the audacity to tell me not to call him again."

Tom turned his head, tried to muffle a laugh, opened his door, and shoved a new suitcase inside. "Give me a minute." He looked around the condo, found everything in order, and took a deep breath as he walked outside. "Now, let's look at your sticking door."

They walked next door to her condo, and she showed him

the door that was sticking. Tom opened and closed it several times, and it did stick near the bottom.

"I could sand it a little and see if that solves the problem."

"Whatever you say."

Tom brought back sandpaper and worked on the door for several minutes. It did no good. He closed the door and inspected the rectangular opening, which appeared to be slightly out of alignment. There was space between the door and the door frame at the top but none at the bottom.

"The door opening isn't completely rectangular. Sometimes, over the years, a house will settle slightly, creating problems like this. You'll need a carpenter to come and give you his opinion on what should be done," Tom told her.

"That's not very encouraging."

"I'm not a carpenter."

Vivian Fairchild looked at Tom with suspicious eyes. "You've scraped paint off the door. What are you going to do about it?"

"Now wait a minute Mrs. Fairchild."

"I can't have a door looking like it needs paint at the bottom. You need to do something, young man."

Tom began breathing hard when he remembered he had original cans of paint in his pantry. He retrieved the can of door paint, opened it with a screwdriver, and used a small brush to coat the side of the door.

"This will need to dry for several hours before you close the door," he advised her.

Mrs. Fairchild bent over until her nose was almost touching the side of the door. "This isn't an exact color match. Can't you do better?"

Tom let out a growling sound.

"Are you feeling ill? If you are, please vacate the premises. I don't want to catch anything," she told him.

"Mrs. Fairchild, the paint color on the door changes with

age. The paint in the can is the original color. There's bound to be a slight difference."

"Will the door still stick?"

"Yes. You'll need a carpenter to take care of the problem. I'll go online and come back with the names and phone numbers of local carpenters. Then you can call and hire one."

"I can do that," she said in an unpleasant voice.

Tom looked surprised. "I thought you said you didn't know how to use a computer."

She gave him a devious look. "There's one more thing you can do for me. The air intake in the ceiling makes a terrible noise when I turn on the air conditioning. Can you take a look at it?"

"Oh," Tom groaned.

He returned to his condo, grabbed a short stepladder and his spare AC filter, and returned. He mounted the ladder, unscrewed the bolts, and lowered the metal louvered cover. A huge cloud of dirt plummeted downward, covering his face and chest and the walls and floor.

"My God, what have you done?" Mrs. Fairchild shouted.

Tom was choking, coughing, and missed the last step as he came down off the ladder. He fell backwards, kicked the small ladder down the hall, and then rolled on the floor. The air filter with a large hole in it fell to the floor, bringing down another load of dirt.

"You're making a total mess of my home. What is wrong with you?" she cried out.

Tom sat up, his green eyes peering out from a grey face. "I need a shower," he croaked as he stumbled toward the front door. He stayed in the shower for fifteen minutes before he dressed in a polo shirt and shorts and walked back to the Fairchild condo.

"It's about time," she announced.

"Do you have a vacuum?" he asked.

"Yes, but I don't want to fill it full of this dirt."

Tom trudged to his condo and returned with his vacuum.

He cleaned the air intake area, then began working over the floor. But the walls and the off-white tile retained a light coating of grey. He put a new air filter in place and closed the metal cover.

"Whatever you do, don't turn on the AC until a heating and air conditioning company has inspected the unit. The noise you hear probably means the unit is malfunctioning and will need to be repaired," he warned her.

"What about the walls and the floor? You've done a shoddy cleaning job," she said.

"Have your housekeeper try to wash the walls and floor. You may have to have the walls painted," he advised.

"And who is going to pay for that?" she barked. "You made this mess."

Tom grunted, picked up the vacuum, and walked to the front door. "I'll have the walls painted if they need it and pay for it. I've used the same painter for years."

"What about the air conditioning? I don't know if it works or not."

"Go online, pick out an air conditioning and heating company, and have them come out for a total inspection. Whatever you do, don't turn it on," he cautioned her.

"Maybe I won't have to go to that expense," she snapped. "I won't know unless I try."

Tom's eyes opened wide as she reached for the thermostat.

"No," he yelled.

The AC unit made a grinding, growling sound as it tried to function, followed by a loud popping sound and a muffled explosion. Then there was silence. Tom and Mrs. Fairchild stared at each other.

"I warned you," Tom said in a loud voice. He turned and exited the condo, a big smile on his face.

"Young man, this is all your fault. You'll be hearing from my lawyer," she yelled after him.

***

Bradshaw walked into Ike's Sand and Surf just off the Santa Monica beach and stood there, genuinely shocked at the size of the surfboarding store. Three different rooms were filled with surfboards and men's and women's clothing, double racked to the ceiling.

"Tom, you son-of-a-bitch, how in the hell are you?" Ike Chambers yelled. He came rushing over, engulfed Tom in a bear hug, and nearly lifted him off the floor. "Like what you see?"

"I'm amazed. I haven't been here since you expanded. Jesus, you did a great job," Tom told his army buddy from Afghanistan days.

"I got professional help in organizing everything. The store is super commercialized and colorful," Ike pointed out.

Chambers had long blond hair, a muscular physique, a ruddy complexion, and bright blue eyes. Ike had been Tom's best friend before the negotiating business separated them.

Tom watched the large number of patrons milling around, checking out the latest in surf brands and styles and an entire room filled with short boards, fun boards, and long boards. Six friendly staff members, all UCLA and Southern Cal students, were happily tending to store goers' needs.

"Are you still giving private surfing lessons to all the young ladies?" Tom asked.

"Well, I'm more selective now. I'm a businessman working eight hours a day, sometimes seven days a week. The sweet young things who I give lessons to have to have long, shapely legs, great asses, and tits to write home about," Ike said as he began laughing. Tom joined in.

Ike took him through the store, showing him how displays were organized to catch customers' eyes. "Is it always this busy?" Tom asked.

"Pretty much so. There's no specific season for surfing. People of all ages do it year round. You just have to be friendly, helpful, and knowledgeable, and you can sell a lot of merchandise.

Plus, we really push our surfboarding lessons, which bring in a lot of bucks," Chambers said.

"And you've got free parking. That's almost unheard of here near the beach," Tom noted.

"Yeah, I got the neighbor to share his parking lot with me."

"I didn't notice. What kind of business is it?" Tom asked.

Ike began laughing, displaying large white teeth. "Erectile dysfunction."

Tom bent over laughing. "You're shitting me."

"I swear to God, I'm not. His business has increased by one-third since he opened up his lot to surfers. Everyone wants to surf with a stiff dick, and you can walk next door and get it straightened out," he said, grinning.

"I'm really glad you've become so successful," Tom said, still laughing.

"I couldn't have done it without you, old buddy."

Tom had provided the seed money for Ike's first surf store. It had taken off, and his business had done nothing but expand since. Ike paid Tom back in half the time they thought it would take, and he was well on his way to making big bucks.

"I've got to go. Got a meeting with my merchandising people. How about meeting me at Charlie's Swinging Bar down the street after I close at 8 p.m.? The chicks are fantastic," Ike maintained.

"I'll be there," Tom promised.

***

Charlie's featured a local band called the Wild Child, and the music was loud and raging, almost ear shattering in its unrestrained, pounding rhythm. Ike walked slowly from one end of the nightclub to the other, introducing Tom to what seemed like a never ending collection of college girls. Most were customers at his surfboarding store.

Ike ordered drinks. "You're going to love this new drink. It's a collection of six different rums. There's nothing quite like it," he yelled in Tom's ear. The drinks came, and Tom reluctantly took a sip. It took his breath away.

"You know I'm not good with hard liquor," he shouted. "I'm strictly a beer man."

"Take a really big swallow. It'll change your mind," Ike bellowed.

Tom did as instructed, and suddenly he felt almost detached from the noise and pounding music. A short while later, he found himself in a booth with a beautiful redhead perched on his lap. They tried to talk, but Tom only heard every other word. She ran her fingers through his curly dark hair, and a silly grin appeared on his face. After the second drink, his field of vision gradually diminished until it seemed as if he was looking through two small holes.

Much later, Ike half carried him out to the car. Tom's words were unintelligible as he waved goodbye to no one in particular.

***

There was a pounding on the door that continued until Tom awoke, his head beating like a drum. He stared at the ceiling, not comprehending where he was. Tom propped himself up on his elbows and looked around. Lying next to him on the bed was an obese redhead, about sixty years old.

Bradshaw stifled a scream as he sat up, eyes wide and mouth open. His hangover was fierce, and his terrified expression signaled panic. Suddenly, the redhead's arm slapped him on the stomach. "Was it as good for you as it was for me?" she asked in a deep guttural voice.

The slap triggered a jump off the bed. Tom landed on his feet and headed for the door, forgetting that he was dressed only in boxer shorts. He tried to pull the door open, but it was stuck as if someone was holding it shut from the other side. Tom gave a gigantic pull, and the door flew open, knocking him back onto the floor.

Bradshaw quickly was on his hands and knees. He stared

at his buddy, Ike, standing in the doorway laughing, holding Tom's shoes in one hand and his pants in the other. "April Fool, buddy! Got you," Ike yelled, and began laughing hysterically.

"I'll kill you, Ike. You son-of-a-bitch," Tom shouted as he ran down the hallway after his close friend, who was known for his practical jokes.

CHAPTER 18

Carol and Rodrigo Rojas had just finished dropping off their three children at a private school not far from their home in a middle-income neighborhood west of downtown Mexico City. An SUV cut in front of their vehicle, causing Rodrigo to jam on the brakes. An old Chevrolet came up behind them and smashed into the rear of their Nisson Altima. Men wearing ski masks jumped out of both vehicles and used tire irons to smash in the windows of their car.

"Stop! What are you doing?" Rodrigo yelled.

He was clubbed in the head with a revolver, and his semi-conscious body was dragged out of the car and over to a Honda SUV. Carol fought her attackers, scratching at their faces, yelling and kicking. She was thrown on the ground, and her hands and legs were wrapped in duct tape. Then, unceremoniously, she was dumped in the drainage channel beside the road. Before driving away, a kidnapper dropped a piece of paper on top of her.

Carol struggled to get to her feet, then hopped up the incline and waited for the first car to come along. It stopped, and a woman got out and ran over to her.

"My husband has just been kidnapped. Please help me," she told the middle-aged Mexican woman.

The rescuer and her husband removed the duct tape and

volunteered to take Carol to her home. Carol almost forgot to retrieve the note, which read, "We will be calling your cell phone with the amount of money we want in exchange for releasing your husband."

Carol Evans had met Rodrigo Rojas fifteen years earlier in New York while attending a national real estate convention. Their attraction to one another was immediate, and they were married a year later. Carol took several trips to Mexico City with Rodrigo and fell in love with the city. She was enthusiastic about changing countries.

Both were real estate brokers. Rodrigo had a number of income producing homes and also handled management for owners who wanted to lease out their houses and condos but not get involved in the monetary aspects of the business.

Business flourished, and so did their family. They now had children, twelve, seven, and six. Carol and Rodrigo made a nice income from their real estate business but were not wealthy. Neither were their parents.

Carol was a strong, tough lady endowed with perseverance and drive, plus the ability to analyze all aspects of business in depth. All these character traits were about to be tested in ways she never dreamed possible.

She immediately called her best friend, Maria Trevino, explained what happened, and asked who she should contact about the kidnapping.

"Don't call the local police. Often the cops are working with organized crime, drug cartels, and kidnapping gangs," Maria warned. "I think the Mexican attorney general's office has a kidnapping department or something along that line."

"All right, I'll try that idea," Carol said, her voice cracking.

"Do you want me to come over?"

"Please. I'd appreciate it," Carol responded.

Fifteen minutes later Maria arrived, and they both hugged each other and cried. But Carol knew she had to be strong for her children, and this was one of the few times she let her emotions rule. She was thirty-nine, had dark brown curly hair, a lovely figure, and exceptionally large blue eyes that were constantly analyzing people and events as they transpired.

"Did you have any luck at the attorney general's office?" Maria asked.

"They referred me to the federal police, but that agency has not gotten back to me. I tried the FBI, but they said they could not be of assistance unless requested by the host country. There's a lot of red tape involved even when a man's life is at stake," Carol said in a bitter tone of voice.

The Mexican Federal Agency of Investigations called an hour later. The lady on the other end of the line was very sympathetic, and said they would send a man out immediately.

When she picked up her children from school, Carol was relatively quiet, mainly answering yes or no to a multitude of questions from the kids. After they entered their home, she took them into the living room and tried to explain to them the concept of stealing daddies for money. Her youngest daughter, Camila, ran upstairs and got her piggy bank.

The following day a young man, who appeared to be in his early twenties, arrived chewing gum and wearing a baseball cap. He read instructions from a notebook and smiled politely. After writing down all the facts, he said he would stay as long as the family needed his advice. Carol took him to a guest bedroom at the rear of the home and said he could stay there.

Three days later, Carol received the first phone call from her husband's abductors.

"We want eight million dollars, American, for the release of your husband," the voice on the other end of the line said in a gruff voice.

Carol was astounded and speechless for a few moments. "We don't have a lot of money," she finally replied.

"The Rojas family does. Get it from them," the snatcher

said, and hung up.

The kidnappers mistakenly believed Rodrigo was a member of the Rojas family that owned hundreds of gas stations throughout Mexico. He wasn't.

Five days later, the kidnapper called again. "Did you contact the Rojas family? Are they getting the money?"

"Listen. You've made a mistake. My husband is not related to the Rojas family that owns the chain of gas stations."

"You're lying to me, Carol. I think we need to teach you a lesson," the gravelly voice said loudly. Then, he hung up.

Rodrigo Rojas was tall and thin, very handsome, had expressive eyes, and weighed one hundred and sixty pounds. The kidnappers did not like Carol's response and decided to work on Rodrigo. They beat and kicked him, began starving him, and stuffed him into a cramped wooden box with built-in speakers that blared non-stop music to keep him awake.

Rodrigo was forced to write down all of what occurred and begged his wife to save his life. The letter arrived a week later, and Carol began taking tranquilizers.

The next telephone conversation was similar to the previous one. She acknowledged receiving the letter but told the gang member that they had little money and were not members of the Rojas family that owned the gas stations.

"We only have thirty-five thousand in our bank accounts. You can have all of it," she told him.

"You're lying to me, Carol," he growled, and hung up.

The beatings and torture continued. So did the pleading letters from her husband. The young negotiator recommended that she should read only enough to verify Rodrigo's handwriting, then stop. He would read them for information. She agreed.

Maria Trevino was her only visitor. Carol had stopped communicating with her friends, fearful that the kidnapping might negatively affect their real estate business, which was the family's only source of income. Carol's main goal was to keep the cash flow coming in order to provide her children with an uninterrupted lifestyle. The kids were prohibited from discussing the abduction with anyone.

As the weeks rolled by, Carol ate less and less, existing only on juices, herbal tea, and chicken broth. She lost her nice figure, and her large, beautiful blue eyes began to look out of place in a gaunt face with dark circles around the eyes.

"It's time we had a talk," Maria told her friend. "You need to begin doing the things you did on a day-to-day basis before the kidnapping. If you don't, you're not going to make it through this ordeal. Your body is slowly disintegrating."

Carol stared at her best friend. "I'm constantly thinking about Rodrigo. Where is he sleeping? Does he have a pillow and blanket? Is he in a box all day and night? I can't sleep or keep my focus. I'm falling apart."

"You're an extremely strong woman, Carol. So start acting like the woman I've always known and loved. Go to your office on a daily basis and get involved actively in your business. Show these bastards that they're not going beat you into the ground," Maria emphasized.

The verbal slap in the face worked, and Carol suddenly became angry. Her blue eyes opened wide, and rage replaced fear.

"You're right, Maria. Who in the hell do these people think they are? What right do they have to torture my husband, terrify my family, and demand our money? I'm through being a shivering, sniffling housewife."

Carol reverted back to doing the things she did when she led a normal life. She began celebrating birthdays and holidays, went to the spa and fitness center twice weekly, and spent time each day at their real estate office.

She knew she was being spied on. Carol became aware of a dirt bike that often followed her car. An old blue Ford often parked near her office and near the school. The occupant was dressed in khaki clothing, just like the kidnappers had worn.

Anger had taken a firm hold on the spirited woman. She would stare back at the kidnappers until they looked away.

Rodrigo's weekly letters became more intense and desperate. One letter indicated he was never taken out of the box except to relieve himself in a small bucket. Another letter said his beatings had been upped to twice per day. Then, a blood-covered letter arrived in which he said he had been shot in the left leg. Two weeks later, another letter came saying the abductors had shot him in the left arm. Photos copied from a computer and mailed to her showed bullet holes in his arm and leg.

Just when Carol didn't think conditions could get worse, the phone calls began.

"How is it possible that you've done nothing? You're going to let them kill me so you can keep our money for yourself. You're such a bitch. I can't believe you'd be so selfish," Rodrigo blurted out.

Carol could tell he was reading the condemnation. Rodrigo sounded unconvincing as if his lines were scripted.

"I love you with all my heart," she told him.

"I love you, too," said Rodrigo as he began crying.

The phone call abruptly ended, and a feeling of deep depression swept over Carol. "How could something so terrible happen to such a fine man?" she said to herself. She broke down crying as a feeling of despair exploded her defiant confidence.

The young negotiator staying in her home told Carol that her waging psychological warfare with the kidnappers might be having a negative effect. Staring down the kidnappers and showing disdain for their surveillance techniques could anger them more, he said. Carol replied that the kidnappers had been starving and torturing her husband for three months.

"The only thing worse would be if they killed him," she pointed out. "I don't think that will happen. They want money. At least I can show them my disdain, a symbol that they can't control me or frighten me into submission."

"Suit yourself," said Felipe Alvarado, as he gave her a doubtful look.

Alvarado was twenty-two and looked sixteen and did everything by the book. He'd joined the federal investigation agency after graduating from the National Autonomous University of Mexico a year earlier. Although he had no formal police training, he did have a family with political connections. Therefore, he was immediately hired and underwent a year of training in police procedures and kidnapping response techniques. This was his first assignment. Carol liked Felipe, but the agency he worked for was woefully understaffed, and he was given no support.

Maria Trevino told Carol about a very effective insurance company negotiator who had been successful in freeing the son of a wealthy owner of shopping centers. Maria's mother was related to the owner's wife. Women talked even when they were sworn to secrecy.

Tom Bradshaw was surprised when his phone rang, and Carol Rojas introduced herself. She explained the situation regarding her husband and how the snatch had deteriorated to a point that they were torturing him.

"Carol, I can't work outside the scope of my company, California Fidelity. I'm bound by contractual obligations and can't do work for other companies or civilians," he explained.

"Won't you at least meet with me and talk? After all, we are both Americans," she said, acting as if she was crying.

Tom was still a soft touch for a damsel in distress. He took a deep breath and exhaled sharply. "Okay. I'll meet with you. Do you know where the downtown Hilton Hotel is located?"

"Yes. I've been there several times over the years."

"Go to the parking garage entrance and show identification. I'll have left word for the guards to allow you to enter and park."

They set a meeting time for the following day, and he

gave her his suite number. Carol arrived promptly on time. They exchanged pleasantries and moved to his office. Tom saw a haggard woman with dark circles under her eyes. She had lost a lot of weight, and her dress hung on a much smaller body now. But her large blue eyes showed intensity and dedication to finding a solution to her problem, he thought.

Tom questioned her at length and was surprised to learn that the kidnappers were following her and using intimidation tactics.

"That rarely happens. Normally, negotiations are done on the phone in very quick conversations," he noted.

"The man on the motorbike followed me all the way to the hotel. Almost every day, the old blue Ford follows me to the school and then to my office," Carol said.

Tom was silent for a few moments. "I have a good friend on the police force, Assistant Chief Franco Gomez. I'll call him and see if he'll meet with us."

"Is he honest?" she asked.

"Yes. And, I'm told it's the main reason he's not a police chief in another city. During interviews, he emphasizes that he doesn't take money from criminals and drug cartel operators and will investigate anyone who does. That usually ends his chance at becoming a police chief anywhere in Mexico."

Bradshaw telephoned Gomez and briefly explained the circumstances concerning the Rojas kidnapping and the fact that the gang members were continually following Carol, trying to intimidate her. Gomez agreed to meet with them in Bradshaw's suite in one hour.

Gomez knocked on the door and was greeted warmly by Bradshaw. The police officer was dressed in a dark blue suit, blue and yellow striped tie, and a white shirt. Gomez was tall, athletic, had a large head and a neatly trimmed moustache. His dark, penetrating eyes and no nonsense demeanor signaled a toughness in the man that many of his peers felt threatened by, especially if they were not totally honest.

He saw in Carol, a woman who was undergoing a terrible, never-ending ordeal but still was strong and committed in her quest to save her husband. She went through the entire kidnapping scenario, the threatening phone calls, and blood-stained letters from her husband, and constantly being followed.

"It's very strange that they would allow themselves to be seen by you. Normally kidnappers will go out of their way to prevent being identified," the assistant chief said.

Carol appeared perplexed. "I can't really identify them. They're average looking young men with shaggy dark hair and bearded faces. If you were to put them in a lineup, I probably couldn't identify them."

"What about this negotiator that the state police sent over? Do you trust him? Has he been of help?" Gomez asked.

"He's young, inexperienced, and tries hard to help. I think he's honest but doesn't get much support from his office. Felipe Alvarado has almost become part of the family, like another son," Carol said, and managed a slight smile.

The assistant chief's eyes never wavered as he studied the woman seated across from him. "This is what we're going to do," he said emphatically. "We're going to grab both the bike rider and the man in the old blue Ford. Everything will have to be done quickly so we can find out where your husband is being held and rescue him before the kidnappers realize they've been compromised."

"Do you think they'll give you that information?" she asked.

The assistant chief's eyes took on a hard, merciless look. "Believe me, they will tell me everything I want to know." Gomez took notes during the next few minutes as he questioned Carol. "It's best that we do this quickly. We'll go after the kidnappers tomorrow morning when you leave to take your children to school. Just act as normal as possible."

Carol's blue eyes were as large as huge gemstones the size of eggs. "Are you serious? I probably won't sleep a wink all night."

Tom had been silent during the question and answer period but now was curious. "Chief, why do you think the kidnappers are acting in such a bold manner? I deal with gangs on a regular basis. Normally they never want anyone to see them."

"There's been a lot of questionable activities in that police division west of downtown where these kidnappers are operating. Some police officers are being investigated by our Internal Affairs Squad," Gomez related. Their eyes met and held, and Bradshaw got the message.

CHAPTER 19

The following day Carol pulled out of her driveway with her three children in the car and began the five minute drive to their school. Her palms were sweaty, and she had a death grip on the steering wheel. As usual, the motorbike pulled in behind her for the short trip to the award-winning school. It suddenly sped up, passed her, and then slowed down, forcing her to jam on the brakes. Next, it did a sliding U-turn and sped by her in the opposite direction, only to repeat the maneuver and begin following her as usual.

Coming up behind them was a fast moving motorcycle. When it came abreast of the motorbike, the driver pulled a club into view and smashed the kidnapper across the side of the head. It sent the motorbike flying into a gully alongside the road, flipping the driver on his back. His helmet came off, and he dizzily lifted himself on his elbows, not knowing what happened.

Carol slowed down to a crawl in her car, finding it difficult to believe what she was seeing in her rearview mirror. A black Buick sedan came into view behind her. It stopped, and two men grabbed the young kidnapper and threw him into the back seat of the car. Then it made a U-turn and disappeared into the distance.

"My God!" she exclaimed.

"What just happened, Mama?" her youngest daughter

asked.

She found it difficult to contain a small smile. "One down and one to go," she said quietly.

"What do you mean, Mama?" Camila asked.

"Nothing, dear. We'll be at school in a couple of minutes."

She slowed down, not knowing what to expect and not wanting to expose the children to any type of danger.

The old blue Ford was parked in its usual spot close to where Carol would have to unload the children. The young kidnapper was looking at the pretty mothers and paid no attention to the two men approaching his car from the rear. The man walking forward on the driver's side suddenly swung a tire iron and shattered the window glass. It literally covered the young Mexican in glass shards, and he screamed loudly. The man walking on the passenger side pulled the door open and waited to see if additional assistance was needed.

The police officer with the tire iron reached in and grabbed the gang member by the throat then pulled him out of the vehicle. Much of the glass dropped down his shirt and inside his pants. The pieces of glass tore into his skin, causing the snatcher to scream. A black Chevrolet SUV halted alongside the Ford. The kidnapper was forced into the back seat, continuing to holler as the glass cut deeper into his stomach and legs.

Women and children were running in every direction as pandemonium set in.

"Emiliano, go into the school and tell them that there's been a police arrest," Assistant Police Chief Franco Gomez ordered. "Tell them there's no risk to the children."

The SUV drove away. However, it took some time for the officers to clear away enough glass from the driver's seat of the Ford to make it drivable and move it off the school grounds.

A mile from the school, the black SUV pulled off on a side road and parked in a stand of trees. Gomez got out, opened the door, pulled the snatcher out, and stood him up against the vehicle. The kidnapper's mouth was wide open as he howled in pain.

"I'm going to ask you questions, and you're going to answer them. Understand?" he said, and hit the young man in the crotch with his revolver. The gang member screamed louder. "Where is Rodrigo Rojas being held?"

"I don't know," the kidnapper cried out.

Gomez grabbed him by the throat and hit him in the crotch a second time. He yelled even louder.

"On Bonita Street, a block from the Catholic Church. I don't know its address. I can take you there," he gasped. "Don't hit me again, please."

"Who's the leader of the kidnapping gang?"

The young man began crying. "He'll kill me if I tell you."

"I can keep smashing you until the glass cuts your dick off. Now, what's his name?" Gomez growled.

"Mario Lobos," he said, amidst sniffling and gurgling.

Gomez grabbed him by the hair with his left hand and slapped him gently on the cheek with the other hand. "Good boy. Now that wasn't hard, was it? What's your name?"

"Chuco Rivas."

"Okay, Chuco. Where's Mario Lobos's headquarters. Where do you meet with him?"

"The All Saints Bar," he said, his voice cracking.

The chief smiled. "I could never figure out that name. Who would ever name a bar All Saints, especially in that shit hole of a neighborhood? How many men are in your kidnapping gang?"

Chuco Rivas looked disheartened and was about to cry again.

"None of that now. I don't want to have to swat you in the balls again," said Gomez as he lifted his arm.

Chuco's eyes widened in fear. "No. No. There's five, including Lobos."

"Give me the names of the other three."

"Hugo Perez, Mateo Reyes, and Carlito Ortiz. Don't tell them I gave up their names," Chuco whined.

"How many are guarding Rodrigo Rojas?"

"Just Mateo. He's real nervous and always walks around carrying a pistol or an automatic rifle."

"Who was on the motorbike?"

"Hugo."

"Why did Mario Lobos try intimidating Carol Rojas?"

"Because she's a member of a rich Rojas family and wasn't trying hard enough to come up with the money," he said, and began moaning. "I'm starting to hurt real bad. I need a doctor."

***

Hugo Perez was dizzy, groggy, and couldn't comprehend what had happened to him. Knocked from the motorbike, the young Mexican was quickly grabbed by two police officers and taken to a police SUV. Assistant Chief Gomez had given orders that he was to be questioned quickly so that there would be nothing to hinder a speedy rescue of Rodrigo Rojas.

Police Captain Eduardo Desoto began by asking Perez where Rojas was being held.

"Screw you. You ain't getting nothing from me," he said loudly. "I want a lawyer."

"Hold him against the hood of the car," Desoto told his officers.

Perez struggled and cried out as he was pinned to the vehicle. Desoto seized his right hand and grabbed the middle finger, which he bent backwards until it snapped and was pointing in the opposite direction. The gang member screamed loudly and began crying when he glanced at his finger.

"Don't.... No more!" he yelled.

"Where are you holding Rojas? Answer me, or I'll break another finger," the police captain growled.

"On Bonita Street. Oh, God, what have you done to my finger?"

Desoto quickly asked the same questions that Gomez had asked Chuco. He received the same answers and called his boss. The police officials compared notes and decided to head directly to Bonita Street.

"How did you get the information out of Perez?" the assistant chief asked.

"We played the finger game and he quickly gave up all the information."

"How many fingers did it take?" Gomez asked and chuckled.

"Just one. This guy was easy."

"Well, put it back in place and let's get started to Bonita Street."

"Just a second," Desoto replied, and put his phone down.

He grabbed Perez's arm, took the broken finger, and forced it back to its normal position, then smacked it hard with his fist to make sure it stayed in place. Perez screamed even louder than the first time.

Desoto picked up the cell phone and told Gomez, "It's fixed."

***

The caravan of police vehicles stopped in the parking lot of a Catholic Church less than a block from the small house that Rivas and Perez identified as the kidnappers' holding cell for victims. The old home was a two bedroom, one bath, tile-roofed stucco house that had seen better days. Paint was long gone, and the stucco was peeling off.

Mario Lobos had killed the owner in a dispute over money and taken possession. No one objected. The one attribute that stood out was a two-car attached garage. The kidnapping gang leader was able to transport victims to the home, drive inside the garage, and transfer them to the interior of the home without being seen.

Assistant Chief Franco Gomez had eight hand-picked

officers in the small strike force. Two cops took positions at the rear, one on each side of the house, and two moved to the front door along with the assistant chief. Captain Desoto and another officer stayed in the two SUVs at the church along with the two young prisoners.

The cops were dressed in dark blue fatigues, bulletproof vests, and helmets. They carried Glock pistols and semi-automatic rifles.

Assistant Chief Gomez tried the handle on the door. It was locked. The officer carrying a hand-held battering ram approached and swung the steel weapon. It crashed into the door handle, and the door splintered and sprang inward.

Mateo Reyes was watching television in the small living room and jumped in the air. He grabbed his semi-automatic rifle and sprayed the front door opening with bullets.

"Cover your ears," Gomez yelled.

He pulled the pin on a stun grenade and tossed it inside. There was a loud explosion and a blinding flash that caused temporary blindness if you were within five feet of the weapon.

Reyes was in a rear corner of the room. His ears felt like they exploded, and he was virtually blind, but the gang member kept firing towards the front door. An officer rushed in and sprayed the interior of the room with bullets from his semi-automatic rifle just as Reyes ran out the back door. He was met with rifle fire from two officers and plowed face-first into the ground, dead.

The strike force quickly searched the small home and located no one else but found a large box in the middle of one of the bedrooms. Gomez opened the lock, raised the top, and looked down at a small man in a fetal position.

"Are you alive?" he asked.

"Yes," came a faint reply.

"Let me help you out of there. We are Mexico City police officers, and you are now free, Mr. Rojas. We're going to take you home," the assistant chief told him.

Rojas began crying, and his whole body quivered. "My wife.... My wife can't see me like this. I know I look horrible."

"There's a police substation on the way back to your home. You can shower there, and we'll find some clean clothes for you," Gomez told him.

With an officer on each side supporting him, Rodrigo Rojas walked out of the building, taking his first few steps in four months. "I almost forgot what it's like to walk," he said quietly, then began crying again.

***

Showered, shaved, and wearing oversized clothing, Rodrigo Rojas was driven to his home and helped out of the car. Carol looked out the front window at a man she did not recognize. Most of his hair on top had fallen out, and the remainder had turned grey. His face was emaciated, his cheeks sunken, with dark circles under his lifeless eyes and deep lines in his forehead. He was supported by an officer on each side but was barely able to walk. Rodrigo looked like an eighty-year-old clinging to life. His weight had dropped from one hundred and sixty pounds down to eighty pounds on a skeleton-like physique.

Carol looked through the window at his fragile body, his weary face, his lack of hair, and almost broke down crying, but knew she had to be strong.

"Go to your rooms, kids. I'll call you to come down in a few minutes," she told the three children. They reluctantly did as they were instructed.

Rodrigo came through the doorway. "I love you," he said in a soft voice. "I've been thinking about your strawberry pancakes for months. I'm so hungry."

She was careful not to squeeze him too hard, afraid she might hurt him. Carol thanked the police officers, and they departed. After they talked for a few minutes, she brought him his cowboy hat and favorite bandana so he would look a little more like himself.

Carol walked to the children's bedrooms. "Daddy's here, but he's changed a lot. He doesn't look at all like he used to. He's very thin and has lost a lot of hair. He's very weak and fragile, so don't pounce on him. Okay?"

The children were somewhat timid as they walked over to their father seated on an overstuffed chair. They took turns embracing Rodrigo with the care children use around an old person.

Carol went into the kitchen and made a large batch of strawberry pancakes for the entire family.

CHAPTER 20

The All Saints Bar had the prime location in an L-shaped strip center in a sleazy neighborhood of slum housing. It was the corner business and had street entrances on both Guerrero and Santana Streets, where the strip center made a right turn. There was a run-down dollar store on one side and a small café on the other side. Patrons could also enter from the rear parking lot if they dared to leave their cars unattended.

The booze parlor had a long wooden bar along one wall, four pool tables, and two dozen tables and chairs. A small bandstand took up a corner of the tavern. Young women in tight, short skirts circulated among the patrons, showing off their wares and quoting prices. Cocktail waitresses were continually busy serving drinks during afternoon and evening hours. The upstairs was the private office and living quarters of the owner.

Mario Lobos had paid the previous owner forty percent more than the tavern was worth in order to purchase fifty percent ownership. The original owner was thrilled with the deal until Lobos put a revolver in his mouth and pulled the trigger. Now the kidnapping gang leader owned one hundred percent.

Lobos was short, fat, and balding in front. He wore a long pigtail down his back. His eyebrows were wide and dark, as was his moustache. His piercing dark brown eyes analyzed every person who appeared in front of him, looking for ways to coerce, threaten, and intimidate. Mario was a true psychopath who had no remorse and enjoyed the thrill of killing.

The beer parlor/cocktail lounge brought in a healthy income from booze and prostitution. But Lobos enjoyed kidnapping more because he could inflict great pain on the victims. Hearing a man scream brought a smile to his fat lips that looked as if he'd overdosed on Botox.

Today he was angry and frustrated. He'd continually tried to reach his kidnapping gang members by telephone but kept getting voice mail or no response from the three snatchers, Hugo Perez, Chuco Rivas, and Mateo Reyes. He called from his second floor office to the bar downstairs, and ordered the bartender to send Carlito Ortiz to his office.

Ortiz quickly arrived, although he was half drunk and it was only 1 p.m., Carlito tried to emulate his boss but couldn't quite get the job done. He wasn't as rotund as Lobos, his ponytail was not as long, his eyebrows were thin, and he had a difficult time growing any moustache of substance. Lobos enjoyed the comical impersonation and was flattered.

"I haven't been able to reach any of our gang. Did you talk with them this morning?" Lobos asked.

"I didn't try. Do you want me to drive over to the safe house and check on things?" he asked.

"Yeah, do that," Lobos responded.

Carlito exited the rear of the tavern and climbed in his old Chevy Cruz. Fifteen minutes later, he drove up to the old house and parked in the driveway. He couldn't believe what he was seeing. The front door was gone, and bullet holes were in the walls around the front entrance. Through the hole in the front, it looked as if a bomb had gone off. He looked around furtively. It looked deserted, so Carlito exited his vehicle and walked cautiously into the home.

"Mateo! Are you here?" he called out.

"Who are you looking for?" Captain Eduardo Desoto said in a loud voice.

Desoto had been wounded in the right leg. His wound was bandaged, and he volunteered to stay behind in case any snatchers showed up.

Carlito literally jumped in the air, startled by the voice from within. He reached for a pistol under his shirt.

"Don't do that, or I'll blow your head off," Desoto warned him.

The kidnapper raised his hands, eyes wide, a shocked look on his face. "I was just driving by."

"Come in here," Desoto demanded.

Carlito slowly walked through the rubble until the two men faced each other. Desoto's Glock pistol was pointing at his head.

"Where is your boss, Mario Lobos?"

"I don't know what you're talking about," Carlito responded, fear in his voice.

The captain slowly limped over to Carlito and smashed him alongside the head with his revolver. The kidnapper dropped to the floor, and Desoto disarmed him.

"I'm going to ask you one more time. Where is Mario Lobos?"

"He'll kill me if I tell you," he whined.

Desoto kicked him in the face, causing Carlito to fall on his back, moaning.

The cop jammed his pistol in the young snatcher's mouth. "Tell me, or I'll put an end to you right now," he growled.

All fight left the kidnapper, and his eyes looked like goose eggs as he sucked on the barrel of the Glock. He let out a terrified scream, and Desoto removed the pistol from his mouth.

"He's at the club, upstairs in his office. He can't locate anyone and sent me to find out what happened. Please don't kill me," Carlito pleaded.

The captain pulled out his cell phone, called Assistant Chief Franco Gomez, and relayed the information.

"We're about to go in. Take that little asshole to the substation and book him on kidnapping charges," Gomez said.

"I'll hate to miss the action," Desoto said.

"I could get you a set of crutches, and you could lead the assault," Gomez said, laughing.

"Very funny, boss."

***

Assistant Chief Gomez assembled his crew of six men three blocks from the bar. He had a picture of Mario Lobos sent to their iPhones.

"This is the guy we're after when we go in. We aren't looking for anyone else. Chances are he'll be upstairs, and we'll have to go up and get him. He's a real psycho, so shoot first, and we'll ask questions later," said Gomez.

He stationed one cop in front and one in back of the tavern. The remaining four officers and Gomez entered the bar from the rear parking lot and spread out. The afternoon activity was in full swing, with loud music playing from the jukebox. Men were drinking, laughing, and fondling the hookers. Two of the four pool tables were in use. The patrons stopped what they were doing and stared at the police officers dressed in dark blue clothing, bulletproof vests, and hard helmets.

One of the two bartenders started the afternoon's activities by pulling a shotgun from under the bar. A police officer fired, striking him in the left shoulder, causing him to fall down behind the bar.

Pandemonium broke loose. Hookers and barmaids began screaming, men were running in every direction, several tables were knocked over, and many of the patrons ran out the front and rear entrances. There was no sign of Mario Lobos.

Gomez and two officers began climbing the stairs to Lobos's office and living quarters just as the gang leader opened the door and looked out. Lobos and Gomez stared at each other for a moment. Lobos fired his revolver, and the bullet whizzed by Gomez's ear. The fat man ran back to a couch and grabbed a naked whore who had been auditioning for a job. He put his arm around her waist and pulled the screaming woman in front of him as a shield.

"I'm going to use a stun grenade, so cover your ears," Gomez yelled at the officers near him at the top of the stairs.

The assistant chief pulled the pin on an M84 stun grenade. He kicked the door inward at the top of the stairs and tossed the stun grenade inside. The officers covered their ears as the grenade exploded, emitting a powerful bang.

The hooker went limp, and Lobos threw her aside. He was practically blind as he began firing his revolver at the front door. Lobos was disoriented, confused, and had lost coordination and balance. He kept pulling the trigger on his empty revolver as he swayed from side to side, waiting for the haze to clear.

Gomez peered into the room and saw the fat gang leader continue to pull the trigger on his empty gun. He entered and walked over to Lobos.

"Greetings from Rodrigo Rojas and his family," Gomez said.

"What? I can't hear you," Lobos shouted.

Gomez raised his Glock pistol and shot Lobos between the eyes. The gang leader was propelled backwards and flopped on his back, dead.

"Grab the whore and take her downstairs," he told a policeman who came rushing inside the room.

He turned and walked to the top of the stairs just as a patron pulled a pistol and fired at one of the cops, striking him in the arm. The unfortunate drunk then was riddled with bullets. As he fell, he fired in the air. His shot brought down a chandelier, which created a fire in the center of the tavern. Gomez and his men ushered the remaining drunks and patrons outside as the building went up in flames. Within minutes, the entire central portion of the strip center was ablaze.

"The All Saints Bar is gone. I'm sure the local clergy won't mind," Gomez said to the officers standing near him watching the fire.

***

Local television stations and newspapers featured the demise of the Lobos kidnapping gang as their top story for the next two days. Pictures of the kidnapping headquarters going up in flames and the bullet-ridden safe house made for exciting photos and TV coverage. The amazing rescue of Rodrigo Rojas was tempered somewhat because Carol Rojas would not let her husband be interviewed.

Mexico City Police Chief Hugo Escobedo and Assistant Chief Franco Gomez were pictured together smiling and chatting. Gomez gave extensive credit to Escobedo for his leadership in seeking out and destroying criminal gangs. The Mexico City Police Chief was basking in praise and admiration from Mexico's top politicians, including the president of Mexico.

Shunted aside and never mentioned when the accolades were handed out was Deputy Police Chief Luis Romero, whose district the destruction of the Lobos kidnapping gang took place in. Romero was Escobedo's nephew, and he had made it up through the ranks at supersonic speed.

Romero had a long neck and a prominent Adam's apple that bobbed up and down when he was anxious or under stress, which was most of the time. His long, thin face and beak-like nose added to the incongruous assortment of facial features.

Two days after the successful assault and firefight, the three men met in Escobedo's office at Romero's request. As soon as they were seated in leather chairs, Romero began a tirade, denouncing Gomez's actions.

"This all happened in my district, and you never contacted me. You never got me involved. Why?" Romero asked loudly.

Gomez stared at the man with the chicken-like neck, his Adam's apple bobbing and eyes blinking.

"You're a deputy chief, and you work for me," the assistant chief said in a firm voice. "I don't answer to you. You answer to me. Let's get that straight before we begin."

Romeo looked at his uncle, his expression indicating he wanted help. The police chief was non-committal as he looked from one officer to the other.

"Why didn't you contact me and let me lead the assault?" Romero said. "You owe me an explanation."

"The group of men you have around you is not trustworthy. Mario Lobos and his men would have disappeared before you arrived," Gomez said in a matter-of-fact voice.

"That's absurd!" Romero yelled, nearly jumping out of his chair.

"Your group leaks like a sieve. Why didn't you take action against Mario Lobos a long time ago? That psychopath has killed and tortured many men."

Romero's Adam's apple was working overtime as he tried to formulate an answer. "He was a confidential informant."

Gomez laughed, and the police chief managed to hold back a smile.

"He was guilty of more crimes than I can count," Gomez said.

Romero was suddenly uneasy and anxious. "Did you question him before he died? What did he have to say?"

"He wasn't very talkative. He took a bullet between the eyes during the attack on his headquarters."

"How did you find out about the gang members following Carol Evans?" the police chief asked, entering the conversation for the first time.

"A kidnap and ransom negotiator contacted us with the information. We took it from there," Gomez replied.

Romero sat up straight in his chair. "Was it that bastard,

Tom Bradshaw?"

"That's the man. He's the best in the business," Gomez pointed out.

Romero grimaced. "He was responsible for the death of my police captain, Rodrigo Castio. We never could discover who murdered him. I think Bradshaw did."

Gomez shook his head from side to side. "You need to get a grip on reality. Tom has been responsible for freeing dozens of kidnap victims. He's no murderer. Castio was taking money from the drug cartel and from kidnappers, our investigation revealed. One of those people killed him."

Romero jumped to his feet and looked directly at the police chief. "He's making false allegations about me and my division. Do something about it."

Chief Escobedo believed that the meeting had gone on long enough, and his nephew was getting pummeled. "Calm down, Luis. I thought this meeting might bring the two of you closer together, but I was mistaken. So, we're done here."

The tall police chief had thick white hair combed back on the sides and in front. The impression he manifested was of a strong, experienced decision maker. In reality, Escobedo seldom knew what to do as crime escalated throughout Mexico City. But he was an effective politician who frequently did favors for those in high places, which solidified his position.

As Gomez and Romero walked down a long hallway outside the chief's office, Gomez suddenly grabbed Romero by his chicken neck and threw him up against the wall. "If anything happens to Tom Bradshaw, and I mean anything, I'll immediately come after you, and you'll join Mario Lobos in the great hereafter. Do you understand me?" Gomez growled.

Romero sounded as if he was gargling. "Yes. Don't hurt me," he said in a garbled voice.

CHAPTER 21

A month later, Tom had completed another successful kidnapping negotiation. He safely brought back the owner of a men's upscale clothing store chain with stores in twenty locations throughout Mexico. The ransom paid was five-hundred-thousand American dollars. The amount demanded initially was five million.

Now he was preparing to land at the Madrid airport, and the craving to wrap his arms around Bianca Rios was overpowering. This was the second time he had flown to see her in Spain since he'd rescued the beautiful brunette and her twin sons, Daniel and Mario. Her father, Diego Santana, continued his pursuit of Tom in a very easy going, casual manner. He'd point out that Tom could work from Los Angeles as he negotiated large highway construction and road rebuilding contracts, plus high rise construction throughout the southwest United States.

It wasn't exactly the international business venture Tom was looking for, but he realized it would give him much needed experience from an entry level standpoint. Little by little, Diego Santana was tightening the velvet noose.

Tom disembarked, passed through security, and was met by the ravishing beauty with the almond-shaped, violet eyes. Her perfume was overpowering as he took her in his arms, kissed her passionately, and felt her body move against his.

Bianca smiled at him. "I'm alone. Perhaps we can make a detour to the Rio Hotel before going to my parents' house."

Bradshaw was breathing hard. "That would be wonderful," he said, grinning.

They spent the next two hours in a lavish hotel suite, making love, laughing, and thoroughly enjoying the splendor of the occasion. Tom knew he was in love, and Bianca never tried to hide her loving feelings.

Tom called a cab, and they took the taxi to the entrance of the Santana mansion, surrounded by a botanical garden. Parked across the street from the gated entrance was a grey Chevrolet Malibu. Bradshaw glanced at the driver and saw that he had a scar down the left side of his face. The Spaniard quickly looked away. Suddenly, Tom was uneasy.

Bianca raised a hand-held clicker, and the tall, iron gates slid open. The car made its way along a wide brick driveway to the stately home. Once inside, Tom was met by two raucous nine-year-old twin boys, Daniel and Mario, who wanted to pull him outside to play soccer.

He promised to do so later, and the boys ran outside to play. Tom spent the next half hour chatting with Diego and Maria Santana. Bianca only occasionally would inject her thoughts into the conversation, preferring to watch.

"Diego, there was a man with a scar down the side of his face sitting in a car opposite your gated entrance. Have you seen him there before?" Tom asked.

The short, rotund man with a white moustache and a shiny bald head thought for a couple of moments. "No, not that I can remember."

"I've seen him a couple of times," Maria said. "Once at the shopping mall and another time at the spa."

Tom sat up quickly in his comfortable leather chair, alarm registering on his face. "How long ago did these sightings take place?"

Now Maria looked worried. "During the past couple of weeks."

"My wife was guarded by Eduardo Vargas, who's been with me for almost ten years," Diego pointed out.

"Not during the past few trips," Maria said. "Bruno Cabazos was driving me."

Diego picked up his cell phone, hit two numbers, and waited. "Eduardo, come into the main living room."

Two minutes later, a tall, thin Spaniard with large dark eyes entered. "How can I help you, boss?"

"I thought you were taking Maria on her shopping trips and to the spa," Diego said.

"I usually do, boss, but Bruno said he had things to do in town. He volunteered to take Mrs. Santana. I didn't think there was anything wrong with him escorting her," he explained.

"Bruno is very nice," Maria interjected.

"How long has he been working for you?" Tom asked.

"About a year. I have extensive background checks made on all security personnel. He came with glowing recommendations and passed a lie detector test," Diego said.

"I like him," Maria pointed out.

"Are you armed?" Tom asked.

"Sure. Always, why?" Eduardo asked.

Bradshaw explained about Maria seeing a man with a scar on his face on two occasions. Eduardo shook his head back and forth and said he couldn't positively remember seeing such a person, but he did see the car.

Bianca sat still in her chair as the blood drained from her face. The kidnapping of her sons was still fresh in her mind. Tom walked over to her and put his hand on her shoulder. "It'll be all right. Nothing is going to happen to your mother."

Tom's demeanor changed dramatically. His face took on a hard expression as his eyes narrowed, and his body language indicated he was ready to do battle. His personal charm disappeared, and his mouth was drawn into a hard, grim line.

"Eduardo, get the boys and take them upstairs with the women," Tom ordered.

Vargas looked at his employer. "Is this what you want?"

"Do as he says," Diego said emphatically.

As the women left the room with Eduardo Vargas, Tom looked at Diego. "Do you have a weapon?"

"I have a .357 magnum revolver in my desk," Diego replied, looking somewhat perplexed.

"Let's go get it," Tom said. He had an appearance of calm sureness as he handed out orders.

They walked to his office, and Diego opened his top desk drawer and pulled out a Smith & Wesson revolver. "I'm trying to remember where I put the bullets. Because of the grandkids, I don't keep it loaded." He searched around on his bookcase and found the cartridges in a small bowl on the top shelf.

Tom loaded the weapon. "Let's go out to the guest house. You can call Bruno Cabazos from there."

Diego looked worried. "There isn't going to be any shooting, is there?"

Tom lied. "Absolutely not. I'm just going to question him about the man with the scar. Did he see him or not?"

The men walked along a brick path to the guest house. Tom entered, followed by Diego. Santana was sweating, and his bald head glistened. He swallowed with difficulty as he hit the numbers on his cell phone that dialed up Bruno. "Come to the guest house. I want to talk to you."

Several minutes later, Bruno appeared, and his face froze when he looked at Tom. Bruno was an average looking man, slightly less than six feet in height, clean shaven, and with small dark eyes that continually shifted about. The one physical attribute that stood out was his body-builder physique, indicating long hours in the fitness center.

"Come in and sit down, Bruno," Diego said, and motioned for him to sit on a couch opposite two overstuffed chairs occupied by Tom and himself. Bruno reluctantly complied, his posture indicating uneasiness.

"You've traded assignments with Eduardo and have driven Mrs. Santana on several shopping trips and to the spa. Why?" Tom asked.

"I don't take orders from you. Mr. Santana is my employer," he said gruffly, not making eye contact with Tom.

"Answer his questions," Diego ordered in a gruff voice.

Bruno glanced at the door as if he wanted to leave. "I have friends that I wanted to visit," he said. Bruno's eyes began blinking rapidly, and he touched his hand to his mouth, then rubbed his chin.

"There's been a grey Chevy Malibu parked on the other side of the street opposite the entrance to the Santana mansion. Have you noticed it or the man in the driver's seat? He has a long scar running down his left cheek," said Tom.

Bruno glanced upward and to the right before he spoke. "I've never noticed it."

"Have you ever seen the man with the scar down the left side of his face?" Tom asked.

"No," said Bruno, tilting his head backward.

"Mrs. Santana says she has seen the man with the scar in the mall and near her spa. Have you?" Tom asked, never taking his eyes off Bruno's face.

The bodyguard put his hand on his head and stroked the hair down in back. "I don't remember seeing him." Bruno's feet were pointing towards Diego while he answered Tom's questions.

"The Chevy Malibu frequently parks in the same general area outside the gates. You must have seen it," Tom emphasized.

Bruno's eyes continued blinking rapidly. "How do you know that?"

"The ground is littered with cigarette butts," Tom said,

guessing that the driver smoked.

"Well, I might have seen it. Who knows?" said Bruno. He began breathing hard, his chest heaving. He looked at Tom with hatred in his small eyes that were now slits. Bruno reached inside his coat, and Tom pulled his revolver from between the seat cushion and the arm of the chair.

"I'll blow your brains out if you touch your weapon," Tom warned him, pointing the magnum at his face.

Tom slowly rose from his seat, took one step, and jammed the gun in Bruno's chest. The bodyguard took a deep breath and froze. Tom disarmed him and returned to his chair.

Diego looked amazed, eyes wide and mouth slightly ajar. The patriarch of the Santana family suddenly was angry. "Why? I pay you well to take care of my family, and you betray me. You miserable son-of-a-bitch."

"You fat bastard," Bruno blurted out. "You live like a king. I have to live from paycheck to paycheck. I want more out of life."

"I should kill you myself," Santana shouted as he jumped out of his chair.

"Diego!" Tom said loudly. "Let me handle this."

Santana sat back down, making noises as his labored breathing continued.

"Bruno, you're after money. How much will it take to give us the information we need?" Tom asked.

Bruno continued breathing hard and was silent for several seconds. Then he gasped and exhaled sharply. "One hundred thousand American dollars," he blurted out in an angry voice. "That's just a small portion of what I would have received if we had snatched your wife."

Diego choked and coughed, and his face turned red.

"All right, here's the deal. You'll continue in your present position, driving a woman who looks like Mrs. Santana to the mall and to the spa. You'll know when it's time for the snatch.

Everyone involved will be nervous and anxious. I take it that this is your first kidnapping involvement?"

"Yes," Bruno said quietly. "What about my money?"

"When the kidnapping goes down, all of the snatchers will either be killed or captured. That's when you'll be paid the one hundred thousand dollars. Your alternative is to refuse to cooperate. Diego Santana then will determine your fate. If you run, I'm sure he'll send mercenaries to find you," Tom emphasized.

Bruno looked at Diego and saw that the patriarch's eyes were angry, almost menacing. "Okay. I'll do it. But you have to promise to pay me."

Tom lied. "Absolutely. Now, what do you know about the ring leader?"

"I met him twice. On the second occasion, he offered me one million dollars to gather information about Mrs. Santana's movements and make it easier to snatch her," Bruno replied. "I don't know his real name. He goes by the nickname Hunter."

"Describe him," Tom said.

"He's a big man, powerfully built body, dark hair with grey along the temples, probably ex-military. His eyes are dark and friendly one moment and menacing the next. You'd never want to cross him, that's for sure."

"What nationality is he?" Tom asked.

"He doesn't have much of an accent, but I think he's an American. It's the way he carries himself."

"The man with the scar. What's his name?"

"Damon Valverde."

"What does Valverde say about the gang leader?"

"I meet with Valverde each time I take Mrs. Santana on her errands. He passes the information along to Hunter," Bruno replied. "I heard him on the phone talking and laughing with Hunter the other day. Valverde told him not to forget that he wanted a Lamborghini or a Ferrari as a bonus when this snatch was done."

"So, he's a regular gang member?" Tom asked.

"Yeah."

"What does that make you? You're not invited to join the gang. It would make it simple for Hunter to shoot you between the eyes rather than pay you one million dollars once the snatch is completed. Also, you're a loose end that could be quickly eliminated," Tom pointed out.

The reality of the statements struck Bruno like a club. He groaned, his head dropped down on his chest, and his whole body indicated defeat. "I don't want to die," he said in a garbled voice.

"You're not going to. You're going to live and walk away with money," Tom assured him. "Just keep performing in the same way. Obviously, a female bodyguard will take the place of Mrs. Santana as we move forward. She'll dress and walk like Mrs. Santana. Valverde won't know the difference."

CHAPTER 22

The Spa and Wellness Clinic of Spain was a four-story circular building, with each story encircled with gleaming white exteriors and floor to ceiling windows set back from the futuristic wraparound pools and terraces on each level. This favorite retreat of top athletes and high-powered executives also catered to the wives of wealthy businessmen, including Maria Santana.

Upon arrival, she was met by two in-house specialists that catered to her every whim and need. She could enjoy a hot stone massage, four-hand massage, or receive a unique treatment from the extract of sheep embryos. This mecca of wellness was brimming with healthful amenities, including hydro-massage tubs and aromatherapy steam showers.

Gourmet kitchens turned out the latest in healthful cuisine, complete with a private chef. The spa's programing included brain training and live blood analysis, should you be so inclined. Maria loved the on-site facials, yoga, meditation, fitness instruction, and a wide variety of salon services. The spa had become the highlight of Maria's week.

"Jesus, this looks like a spaceship ready to take off," Tom commented.

Tom, Diego Santana, and Bruno Cabazos got out of Diego's Escalade. It was immediately whisked away by a valet parking attendant. They walked up a porcelain stairway and through the massive glass and gleaming silver front doors. Diego told the concierge that his wife wanted him to look over the spa with the intent that he join her on her weekly wellness sojourns.

They toured the futuristic building for the next half hour. Diego looked with wonder at the infinity-edged pools that curved around each floor, giving swimmers and bathers dramatic views of the city and its parks. Tom saw virtually none of the amenities as his mind focused on how and where the kidnappers would attempt to snatch Maria. Bruno was just along for the ride, a sour expression on his face.

The three men concluded their visit and walked out to the landing above the porcelain stairs. Diego gave the valet a parking ticket, and they waited for the Escalade.

"They'll make the attempted snatch as Maria exits the car and prepares to walk up the stairs when she arrives. Inside, there are just too many employees and security personnel. A lot of different things could go wrong," Tom explained.

"What about as she exits the spa?" Diego asked. "Couldn't they try it then?"

"As she arrives, it's an exact point in time and an exact spot. The moment at which she departs is not really known for sure. And the kidnappers outside the spa would have to wait, unobserved, for an extended period of time. That's not a good idea," Tom replied.

Diego looked at Tom and saw an entirely different young man than the American he'd come to like and trust. Gone was the affable demeanor, the friendly smile, and the pleasant dialog. Instead, his eyes were intense, his body language that of a man ready to attack, and he was focused on planning a response to the coming snatch attempt. His lips were clenched together, and Tom's eyes were mere slits as the Escalade headed for their next stop, The Madrid Exotic Car Company.

Diego Santana told Tom that his friends all frequented the

exotic car firm when they were looking for a prestigious ride. He had been there twice looking at a red Ferrari, but his wife talked him out of the purchase. She told him he was too old to be driving a car that took off like a missile.

He remembered the owner, Jack Riley, who fit the description of Hunter, the gang leader described by Bruno. Now the turncoat bodyguard would get his chance to positively identify Riley as being the gang leader.

The Escalade pulled up in front of the dealership that was a solid, floor to ceiling continuation of windows for half a block. Tom got out and walked in the front entrance. He was amazed at the blaze of overhead lights that filled the warehouse-sized showroom with lighting that equaled bright sunlight. Highlighted was a maze of brightly colored, extremely expensive automobiles, including Maserati, Rolls Royce, Lamborghini, Bentley, and Ferrari. It looked as if a bag of multi-colored gumdrops had spilled from a sack.

The lights reflected brightly off seven rows of exotic cars, parked ten in a row, end to end. The super expensive autos were every color of the rainbow, and the overall effect was breathtaking. Customers walked with salespeople examining vehicles that were mostly one owner cars imported from the United States.

Tom was met by a bald-headed, clean shaven salesman, whose head resembled an egg. Alberto Hidalgo discussed a variety of cars with Tom. Bradshaw said he was most interested in acquiring a Lamborghini, and they looked at three before Jack Riley appeared and introduced himself.

"You're an American, I can tell," the six-foot, five-inch owner said in English, and smiled.

"I was just going to say the same thing about you," Tom said.

"I'm from New York originally. How about you?" Riley asked, his dark eyes probing.

"Los Angeles. But I'm about to marry a woman from

Madrid. I'll need a fancy car here to go with a new condo. We'll be going back and forth a lot," Tom replied, letting the story flow forward.

"Well, that's terrific. What line of work are you in?" Riley asked as he attempted to qualify Tom.

"Oil. My family's been in the oil business for many years," Tom replied.

Jack Riley was dressed in a well-tailored grey suit that went perfectly with his dark hair and grey streaks along the temples. His dark eyes were penetrating yet friendly as he continued to size up his quarry.

"How did you end up in Spain?" Tom asked.

"I was in the army for a while. A buddy's family was in the luxury car business in New York. When I got out, I went to work for the family. And ultimately, I ended up here. The tax situation is good in Spain," Riley explained.

In reality, once Riley learned the business, he began stealing every luxury car he could lay his hands on. The VIN numbers would be changed and the cars painted before they were shipped to Europe. The return on investment was huge. He also gained complete financial information on his clients. Thus began his kidnapping business that brought him even more rewards with less work involved.

Bradshaw and Riley talked cars for the next fifteen minutes. Tom's favorite as they moved around the showroom floor was a Lamborghini Aventador SVJ convertible in matte bronze. Tom found himself falling in love with the car, almost forgetting what he was there for. Riley coaxed him to take it for a spin. Tom wanted to, his palms itching with desire, but there was work to be done.

"It sells for about $520,000 new. This one's a year old, and I'll sell it to you for $400,000, just because we're both from the USA," Riley said in his closing sales pitch.

Tom exhaled sharply. "Let me think about it for a day.

I'll come back tomorrow when I have more time and take it for a ride."

They moved towards the front door together. Riley opened it for him, and they both stepped outside.

"Is that your white Escalade Platinum?" Riley asked.

"No, it belongs to my fiancée's father. You can see the chauffeur in the driver's seat," Tom replied.

"They sell for about $95,000 new. That's last year's model. Tell him I'll give him $80,000 cash if he wants to unload it," Riley said.

They shook hands, and Tom promised to return the following day. He got in the passenger side and waved before he shut the door. Riley waved back.

Bradshaw turned in the seat. "Well?" he asked.

"That's him, all right," Bruno replied. "Could he see me through the back seat windows?"

"No. They're so dark I couldn't see anyone in the back seat."

Bruno exhaled loudly. "Where do I go now?"

"You've got an apartment, don't you? We'll drop you off. Scarface will be in contact with you. Just go through the normal routine when he calls. Let us know immediately," Tom said.

Bruno put Tom's cell phone number in his phone. Diego sat in the back seat, not saying anything, but his questioning look was met with a steady gaze from Tom that told him to remain quiet. They dropped the turncoat at his apartment and continued back to the mansion.

Once they were inside, Santana exploded. "Goddamn it, Tom, we can't trust him. And I sure as hell don't want to pay him a hundred thousand dollars for betraying my family. I want to kill the son-of-a-bitch."

"Calm down, Diego. I know what I'm doing. Bruno knows that Jack Riley is going to kill him, so he'll help us. He has visions of big money coming from you. That's enough to keep him in line. When it's over, I'll give him enough money to leave Spain. That's all he'll get," Bradshaw explained.

The short, bald-headed patriarch was upset, eyes wide and breathing hard. "I'm so worried about Maria, Bianca, and the grandkids that I can't think straight."

Tom walked up to him and put his hands on Diego's shoulders. "Trust me. I'll see to it that nothing happens to them."

They walked into Diego's office. "What do you want me to do?" Just tell me, for Christ's sake," Santana said loudly.

The two men sat down on a couch. "I'm going to contact a friend of mine, Charlie Sanders, who owns a highly specialized security firm called Royal Blue. We served together in Afghanistan. Within a few days, a squad of men will arrive. They're top level security personnel, elite agents with extensive military backgrounds. Immediately they'll assess the situation and come up with a plan to counteract the kidnappers."

Diego looked at Tom as if he was crazy. "What are you talking about? This isn't a war zone. This is my family."

Bradshaw did not say anything, giving Santana an opportunity to rant. The rotund husband and father jumped up from his seat and walked nervously back and forth, throwing out question after question, not waiting for an answer. Finally, he walked back to the couch and slumped down. He had a pleading look on his face. "Just tell me what to do. I trust you."

"It's going to be expensive to bring in an elite team. Are you ready for a big bill?"

Tom asked.

"Of course. I'll pay any amount of money to get this over with," Santana replied. "But can't we just call the police and let them handle it now that we know who the leader is?"

"It wouldn't do any good. Riley would deny any knowledge of a pending kidnapping. Bruno can't substantiate his claim that Riley is the leader. Scarface would disappear. The investigation by police would go nowhere. Then, six months or a year from now, they might snatch Maria," Tom explained.

"Oh, God," Diego moaned. His head fell to his chest.

"Police have to play by the rules. Private security firms don't. That's why we need highly trained professionals on our side. After carefully assessing the situation, they'll snap into action when the kidnapping begins. Does this make sense to you, Diego?" Tom asked.

Stress and anxiety had caught up with the businessman. He stared at Tom out of half-closed eyes, breathing hard, unable to focus. "I'll do whatever you say," he mumbled.

Charlie Sanders' number was in Tom's phone, and he immediately dialed it. The receptionist who answered transferred the call to Sanders' office. His private secretary asked several questions before she was satisfied that they were friends, then put him on hold.

"Hey, buddy. It's been a long time since I talked with you. Are you still in the insurance negotiation business?" Charlie asked in an upbeat voice when he came on the phone.

"I sure am, most of the time in Mexico City. It's a hot bed for kidnappings."

"My firm provides premium bodyguard services for executives around the globe. A lot of them are in Mexico," Charlie pointed out.

"I'm calling in regards to a planned kidnapping of a business owner's wife in Madrid. I'll need your help ASAP. I'm dating his daughter."

"I'm not pressed for time, so give me the facts," Sanders said.

Tom laid out all the facts in the case during the next ten minutes of questions and answers. Charlie quickly digested the information.

"I understand. You need one of my elite teams to come in, study the situation, and plan an immediate response. These guys love firefights, so it should be interesting."

"How many men will you send, and what's the time frame for arrival?" Bradshaw asked.

"I'll send a Latin American ten-man team. Spanish is their native language. They should arrive from Columbia tomorrow or the next day. The group just finished a job in Bogota," Charlie explained. "Does your girlfriend's father understand that the cost is high?"

"How much?"

"Fifteen hundred per man per day plus expenses. When he hears the price, it should make his dick shrivel up. But you need immediate help, and I can provide it."

"He doesn't care what it costs as long as you nail these assholes before they snatch his wife," Tom pointed out.

Diego nodded his head up and down, thereby agreeing to an open-ended price.

"You said you needed a woman to masquerade as the wife. One of the men coming to you is short, thin, and can easily assume the identity of a woman. He's played that part before."

"You know what you're doing. How large is your company now?" Tom asked.

"I've got about seven thousand personnel under contract. We're one of the eight contractors recruited to replace U. S. forces in Iraq. I have nearly two thousand men protecting non-military supply convoys there," Charlie said.

"I had no idea you were that large," Tom said, a note of surprise in his voice.

"Hell, we're small potatoes compared to private armies like G4S. They have about 625,000 employees worldwide. That makes G4S the second largest private employer in the world behind Wal-Mart."

"Do you have a specialty?" Tom asked.

"Anything and everything you want protected. We also have about two thousand men protecting key oil pipelines and other assets in Iraq. Another thousand are in the Republic of

Congo for security at major iron ore and oil and gas projects. We're also very active in other parts of Africa, eastern Europe, and especially Latin America."

"Where do you get all of your security personnel?"

"There's an unlimited supply of ex-military men with significant prior experience around the world. I hire them, train them in a variety of other protocols, including risk assessments, logistics, and bodyguard training. In your case, it's emergency response," Charlie said.

"Who will be in charge of this guns for hire team?" Tom asked.

"Angel Mendoza. Believe me, he's anything but an angel. He's tough, smart, and loves firefights. Angel fought the drug cartels in Columbia for many years. To him, going after bad guys is a stimulating way of life," Sanders noted.

Bradshaw and Sanders exchanged cell phone numbers and agreed to talk the following day. When Tom hung up, his eyes shifted to a very nervous Spanish patriarch.

"It'll be a ten-man team, arriving tomorrow or the next day," he told Santana.

Diego groaned with relief, and his body relaxed. "I'm so happy to hear that help is on the way."

CHAPTER 23

Tom met Angel Mendoza and his men as they disembarked from an Air Europe flight at the Madrid airport. They were dressed in casual clothing, but they all looked like battle-hardened, ex-military men, which they were. They took a shuttle bus to the hotel. Tom sat with Mendoza, which gave them time to discuss the coming events.

Angel Mendoza's face was ruddy, lined with creases across his forehead, and he had a predator's eyes, dark and foreboding. He listened attentively to everything Tom knew about the pending abduction.

"You've done your homework. My men and I will begin assessing everything from the travel routes to the anticipated kidnap location at the spa," Angel explained. "I haven't been involved with striking kidnappers as they commit a snatch. Usually, we track them down after the kidnapping and attempt to rescue the victim."

"I was lucky in being able to put together most of the pieces," Tom said.

"Let's look at some of the key players again," Angel stated.

They discussed Bruno Cabazos, the turncoat bodyguard, and his willingness to stay involved, even though his life was in danger.

"More than anything else, he wants money," Tom pointed out. "We've promised him one hundred thousand dollars."

"Do you think he'll follow through at the end?" Angel asked, his eyes showing doubt.

"Yes. My gut feeling is that money overrides fear in his case."

"Damon Valverde, or Scarface as he's called, keeps in phone contact with Bruno. This is when Bruno should be able to recognize when the real snatch will take place and contact you. Is that correct?" Angel asked.

"That's right."

Angel thought for a few moments. "What about the gang leader, Jack Riley? Do you think he'll actually participate in the kidnapping?"

"No. He selects the target, then lets his men do the leg work. I can't imagine him getting his hands dirty. He dresses in thousand dollar suits and Italian leather shoes. This is the lifestyle he enjoys," Tom explained. "But he's ex-military, and looks like he could be as deadly as a rattlesnake."

"Where do you think he'll be when the snatch takes place?"

"Probably in his office above the showroom at the exotic car dealership," Tom said.

Angel nodded his head in agreement. "Seems likely. I'll get started tomorrow driving over the projected route to the spa. My men will participate in the analysis. Can you get me a mini-bus that will hold a dozen or more men?"

"Sure. I'll have it delivered to the hotel tonight."

***

Tom arrived back at the mansion and was immediately met by Diego Santana, who pummeled him with questions. Tom answered them in a calm voice, reassuring Diego that everything was moving forward according to plan.

Bradshaw felt the full weight of his responsibilities. He had learned to live with major decisions, not easily but gracefully. The worst part of making life and death decisions was the loneliness that prevented comradeship. The decisions were his and his alone. Everyone else had a role to play.

In a very real sense, his word became the truth, made so by his singular decision making. He operated unaided, with the final responsibility being his. The moment had come when his deepest inner qualities would be revealed as he made the decision to move forward with the firefight. His self-assurance had grown enormously since he joined California Fidelity's kidnap and ransom division. His successes were constant and frequent.

"Are you sure these men know what they're doing?" Diego asked.

"They've been involved in numerous kidnap scenarios in Central America and have been very successful," Tom pointed out. "But, it's very expensive. You'll be charged fifteen hundred American dollars per day, per man, plus expenses."

Diego's eyes opened wide as he did the math. "Why, that's over a hundred thousand dollars per week."

"They're expensive, but what kind of a price are you willing to put on your wife's safety in the future?"

Santana stared at Bradshaw for a few moments. "Her safety is priceless. I hope they kill every last one of those bastards."

They talked for a few more minutes. Then, Tom sent Diego to bring his wife to Santana's office. Maria entered, appearing fragile and afraid. Dark half-circles surrounded her eyes. She sat down on the couch, her hands clasped tightly together and her back rigid.

Tom sat down on the couch next to her and took her hands in his. "You don't have to be afraid about what is going to take place. You are not in harm's way and never will be. The main objective is to capture the gang members and their leader so that all future threats will be eliminated."

"I haven't been sleeping well. What is happening to our society that we have to be fearful about leaving the house? First, they went after our grandsons, and now me. Will we ever feel safe again?" she said in a trembling voice.

"Of course you will. Once this threat is eliminated, you and your family will return to leading a normal lifestyle," Tom assured her. "I'm sure your belief and trust in God contributed to your grandsons' safe return and to our ability to identify the Spanish kidnappers before they could strike," Tom said in a sincere voice.

A look of relief came over her face, and she groaned softly. "I pray several times a day. Our Heavenly Father has heard my prayers."

Tom played the God theme as if he was playing a fine-tuned violin. "I'm sure he has heard your prayers. Everyone is safe, and this troubled period will pass. God reaches out to help those in need."

Maria raised Tom's hand and kissed it. "You have become an inspiration to our family. I thank God that he brought you to us."

Now Tom was feeling benevolent to a point that tears came to his eyes. "I hope you are feeling better," he said.

"Oh, yes. I feel so much better. Thank you, Tom, for being so understanding and gracious."

Diego was transfixed, staring at Tom and his wife, wondering how Bradshaw knew to play the religious theme. Even Santana's urge to kill had been quieted, temporarily. Maria and Tom talked for a while longer, and then she left the room to find Bianca.

Tom walked to the main living room after he and Diego finished conversing. The beautiful brunette met him there. She wore a white silk blouse and a light purple and gold mini-skirt that accented her long, gorgeous legs. Bianca smiled as she came into his arms, her violet, almond-shaped eyes expectant as she passionately kissed him. She groaned softly, which sharply increased his level of passion. He held her tightly, his hands moving about her body, causing her to tremble.

"The boys are in school. Let's go to my room to talk," she said in a playfully mischievous voice.

Five minutes later, they were in bed. Tom's time with her had been limited during the past few days, as his attention was entirely on solving the imminent crisis. Now he released his passion, letting his intense emotional excitement run free, causing her to cry out. They climaxed, and he was content to hold her, smell her fragrance and feel her flesh. He was overcome with an intense love for the woman in his arms.

"Are you all right?" she asked.

"Couldn't be better. I just want to savor this moment."

"Me too."

A few minutes later, Tom rolled onto his back and sighed. "You're fantastic. Making love to you is just what I needed."

"I'm glad to be of service," she said, and smiled.

Tom laughed. "I love you, Bianca."

"And, I love you."

***

Two days later, he met with Angel Mendoza at The Bonita Hotel, where the squad of ten Latin American security personnel was staying.

"We've assessed the route taken by Mrs. Mendoza, the spa, and the exotic car dealership. We've reached a different conclusion about where the snatch might take place," Angel said.

"Really," Tom responded. "I'm all ears."

"The perfect spot to hit the Escalade probably would be on the narrow road leading from the mansion to the main highway. It has limited traffic and would be a perfect location to set up a quick roadblock," said Angel. His dark eyes were fixed on Tom, trying to read Bradshaw's response.

Tom thought for a few moments, then nodded yes. "I see your point. It's up to you to set up the response, so move forward as you see fit."

Angel appeared satisfied and surprised that Tom could be so easily influenced to change the game plan. "The spa location is loaded with cars and people. If it weren't so busy, it would be a great snatch location. Maybe they will choose that spot. In any event, we'll be ready to respond to either location," Angel explained.

"I trust your judgement, since you're in the firefight business," Tom replied.

"We also looked over the exotic car company location. A very tall American walked outside on two occasions and shook hands with prospective buyers. We assume this is Jack Riley."

"He's about six feet, five inches. Riley is the tallest man around," Tom pointed out.

"When the kidnapping goes down, and we hit them, he'll probably be warned. His vehicle is a red Ferrari parked in the rear parking lot. He'll probably make a run for it, and we can try to nail him then," Angel said.

"How did you find out about his vehicle?" Tom asked.

"I talked with one of the mechanics as he left work. A little money will buy almost anything."

The days of intense preparation work were over. The ensuing events were now in the hands of Royal Blue's experienced mercenaries. There was no external standard against which to measure the Latin American strike force's game plan. They would respond as the kidnapping unfolded. Angel had rented several SUVs that would be used as needed.

Tom's phone rang, and he answered. He asked a couple of questions and listened intently, then hung up.

"That was the turncoat, Bruno. He just received a call from Scarface wanting to know if Mrs. Santana was going to the spa on Wednesday. Bruno said she was scheduled that day. Scarface told Bruno to call before they left the home at the usual time, 10 a.m.," Tom explained.

Angel smiled, and his dark eyes were mere slits. "It sounds

like it's time to party."

***

A very short, thin mercenary, Carlito Sosa, was dressed in Maria Santana's clothing and wore a scarf over his head, tied under the chin. He walked to the Escalade, his gait identical to that of Mrs. Santana. Bruno Cabazos was in the driver's seat, nervous, his fingers tapping on the steering wheel. The Cadillac began its trip down the narrow road leading to the main highway.

A half mile from the highway, a panel truck pulled out, blocking the Escalade's forward progress. Three men jumped out and ran towards the Cadillac. Each carried a semi-automatic rifle.

Coming up behind the Escalade was an old red pickup. Two men exited and ran up to the rear of the Cadillac. Royal Blue's rented SUVs quickly joined the party, coming up behind the kidnappers' vehicles. The snatchers looked around in disbelief as the mercenaries jumped out of their SUVs and began firing. The kidnappers returned the fire, and the whole area erupted in non-stop gunfire. The noise became deafening, and the clash deadly.

One gang member at the front of the Escalade went down a bullet through his neck. Both kidnappers at the rear of the Cadillac were shot multiple times and fell on the dusty road. One remained alive and began yelling for help.

One of Angel's men at the rear of the confrontation was shot through the leg and went down. Bullets were flying in every direction. The Escalade's front windshield was blown inward, showering Bruno and Carlito Sosa with pieces of glass. Carlito scrunched under the dashboard. Bruno was lying in a fetal position on the front seat. Angel Mendoza was in the backseat. He opened the rear door and fired at the kidnappers.

The two remaining snatchers ran back to the panel truck, only to be met by more gunfire from the mercenaries. Both were hit, but one continued to shoot and wounded another of the Royal Blue attackers. He was quickly dispatched by heavy gunfire from the security professionals.

Scarface was in the panel truck and used his cell phone to call Jack Riley.

"It was a trap!" he shouted. "All of the men are dead or dying."

The line went dead immediately. Scarface moved forward into the driver's seat and stepped on the gas. His intent was to head forward at high speed and go around the vehicles as he tried to escape. The snatcher was met with heavy semi-automatic gunfire that blasted out the front windshield and turned his head and shoulders into a bloody mess.

Bruno Cabazos brushed off dozens of pieces of glass, then opened the driver's door, preparing to escape.

"Don't do that," Angel Mendoza said loudly. "I'll put a bullet through you if you try to run."

"I've done my job. I want my money," Bruno yelled.

"Take that up with Tom Bradshaw. Now shut up," Angel said as he ran towards his downed men.

He hurried over to help with first aid for his two wounded men and called 112, the equivalent of America's 911 emergency line. Then he called Tom and informed him that the attempted kidnapping was on the narrow road less than a mile from Santana's mansion.

"The snatchers are dead, and a couple of my men are wounded but will survive. I've already called 112 for emergency medical assistance. Have Santana call his friend in government and meet us here at the site. It's going to be a three-ring circus," Angel explained.

His next call was to his two men waiting at the rear of the exotic car dealership. "Jack Riley probably was warned. Get ready for a quick exit," Mendoza told his mercenaries.

The two wounded survivors of the kidnap gang were yelling out for assistance. Both had been disarmed, but no one paid any attention to their wounds. Satisfied that his men's wounds were not life threatening, Angel walked to one of the wounded kidnappers.

"No, don't," the snatcher yelled as Angel raised his pistol. "I'm a family man. I have kids." Angel put a bullet through his head, ending his pleading.

Then he walked to the remaining wounded kidnapper. "No," the gang member cried out as he attempted to crawl away from Mendoza. Angel put a bullet through the back of his head, ending the life of the last remaining kidnapper on site.

Ambulances arrived and transported the two wounded Royal Blue mercenaries to a nearby hospital. The site looked like a battlefield. Trucks and SUVs had been sprayed with semi-automatic gunfire. Dead bodies of five of the kidnappers lay scattered around the scene.

Local police and national police arrived at the same time as the TV trucks and newspaper reporters, who monitored the police radio frequencies. The scene was chaotic. Black uniformed national police and blue uniformed Madrid police swarmed around like ants on a hill, trying to grasp what had happened.

Angel Mendoza acted as spokesperson for Royal Blue and explained to the local and state police about the foiled kidnapping. They stared at him as if he was absolutely crazy.

CHAPTER 24

Royal Blue mercenaries, Arlo Castro and Antonio Falcon, were hiding behind an Audi Q7 located two cars away from Jack Riley's red Ferrari. Five minutes after the successful ambush of the kidnappers, Riley came out of the exotic car company, studied the parking lot, then descended the rear stairs from his office and hurried towards his sports car.

Both men raised up from crouching positions. "Riley, you're under arrest," Castro yelled out.

The gang leader came to an abrupt halt two car lengths from his Ferrari, a surprised look on his face. He pulled his revolver from a shoulder holster under his dark blue suit coat and fired at Castro, striking him in the left shoulder. At the same time, Castro fired his Glock pistol, the bullet striking the tall gang leader in the chest. Both men went down on the ground and continued to fire at one another. Another bullet struck Castro in the right arm.

Antonio Falcon ran forward using the Ferrari as a shield, then moved to where he and Riley were looking at each other.

"Screw you, asshole," Riley yelled as he tried to raise his revolver.

Falcon fired twice, one bullet striking Riley in the neck, the second hitting him in the side of the head, killing him. The mercenary then ran over to his companion and began first aid to stop the bleeding. He called 112 and informed the emergency personnel that one man was dead and another badly wounded at the exotic car company parking lot at the rear of the dealership.

Within minutes an ambulance arrived, the emergency personnel performed first aid, and Castro was off to the hospital. Falcon decided to stay in order to explain to the police what took place. Riley had been carrying a large duffel bag that now was lying next to his body. Falcon opened it, and his eyes widened. It was filled with American one hundred dollar bills. Later, police reported that it contained nearly two hundred thousand American dollars.

Employees at the dealership crowded at the window in the rear door, excited by the shooting but not wanting to go outside.

Falcon called Angel Mendoza and told him that Riley was dead and that Castro had been wounded twice and was on his way to the hospital. "He'll live. The wounds aren't life threatening, and Castro's as tough as shoe leather," he told his boss.

"I think we're about to be arrested listening to what the police are discussing," Mendoza replied. "It doesn't matter that we wiped out the kidnapping gang. We don't have permits for our weapons, so they're going to take us to jail."

"What do you want me to do? Stay here or fade into the background?" Falcon asked.

"It's up to you. I'd prefer that you stay and explain to the police that Riley was the head of the kidnapping gang. But, it's not imperative. If you want to head back to the hotel, it's okay by me," Angel said.

"I think I'll go to the hospital and see how Castro is doing. I've been in jail before, and I hated it," Falcon related. "I hear the sirens now."

Falcon drove away from the dealership just as police arrived, and employees poured out the rear door into the parking lot. Local police and national police ran in circles trying to locate

Riley's killers.

***

The small country road had turned into a parking lot filled with police cars and emergency medical services vehicles. All had lights flashing, creating a bizarre carnival-like atmosphere. Men and women from TV stations and the newspaper ran haphazardly throughout the crime scene. The five gang members' bodies had been covered with white sheets. The Royal Blue mercenaries were forced to sit in a group setting beside the road, awaiting their fate.

Entering the scene were Tom Bradshaw, Diego Santana, and the Deputy Minister of the Interior Emiliano Delarosa, whose department had authority over the national police. Local police were required to hand over all serious crime matters to the national police. Delarosa and Santana were good friends, and he and his wife attended many parties at the Santana mansion.

"Find the officer in charge and send him to me," Delarosa told a young national police officer, who had blocked their entrance into the crime scene.

"Who are you?" the officer said in an angry voice. "Can't you see we're busy, and this is a crime scene?"

"I'm Emiliano Delarosa, Deputy Minister of the Interior. Now get moving," he ordered.

The officer's eyes widened, then he turned and walked rapidly towards the group of Royal Blue mercenaries who were being interrogated by national police officers. He talked to Captain Rodrigo Gomez, and the two men walked back to Delarosa.

Delarosa was in his mid-fifties, distinguished looking with a full head of silver-grey hair, dark eyes, and a white moustache. Gomez was thirty-five, tall and thin and clean-shaven.

"The officer didn't recognize you, Deputy Minister. Would you like an update on what we've learned so far?" Captain Gomez asked.

"I know what happened. This gentleman is Diego Santana.

The kidnappers were after his wife. He hired the Royal Blue private security contractors to foil the kidnap attempt, which they did," Delarosa replied.

"None of these mercenaries have B licenses to carry a handgun. And as you know, semi-automatic rifles are strictly forbidden. I'm about to arrest all of them," Gomez explained.

"I'm taking over the crime scene," Delarosa said in a matter-of-fact voice. "None of the mercenaries are to be arrested. Continue with your interrogation until you feel you have all the facts for your report. Then release the men."

A perplexed expression passed over Captain Gomez's face. "I don't understand. All of these men have clearly violated our gun laws. How can we grant them immunity?"

In Spain, only eight thousand handgun licenses have been granted to people who are designated "at risk." Spain's population is forty-six million. Automatic weapons are strictly forbidden under any and all circumstances.

"These are special circumstances. I'll take full responsibility," Delarosa said in an authoritarian tone of voice.

Angel Mendoza had called Tom and told him that Jack Riley was dead, and one of the Royal Blue mercenaries was in the hospital. This information was passed on to the deputy minister of the interior.

Bradshaw turned to Delarosa. "Perhaps the captain should be informed that the gang leader, Jack Riley, was killed at his dealership," Tom said.

The captain's eyes opened wide. "Are you saying there's another dead man killed by Royal Blue security contractors?"

"That's right, Captain. You can add that to your report, too," Delarosa said.

***

Three hours later, Tom was in Diego's Lexus with the turncoat, Bruno Cabazos, as they headed for the Madrid airport. Bruno had made his full statement to the authorities about his involvement and his change of heart that led to the discovery of the kidnapping gang.

Bruno was depressed. His plan to get rich quick through the kidnapping had failed. His thought of making one hundred thousand dollars from Diego Santana had gone away, and in general, his self-esteem was in the toilet.

"I wasn't always like this, you know," he said in a dejected voice. "I was a personal trainer and a damn good one. Then I wanted to be a personal bodyguard. There was a lot of charisma attached. Well, we know how that turned out."

Bradshaw was driving and looked at Cabazos, seeing him as a real person rather than just a turncoat to be used and thrown away.

"Look on the bright side of things. You're the only member of the snatchers who is still alive. And you have ten thousand dollars to work with while you make a fresh start in Portugal," Tom pointed out.

"I wanted to start a fitness center. I know the business, my clients like me, and I can really help a lot of people live healthier lives. Ten thousand just isn't enough to lease a good property and buy the necessary equipment. All these exercise machines are expensive," Bruno said.

Tom didn't like the fact that he and Diego Santana had used Bruno and promised him money that they had no intention of paying him. It went against his code of ethics. Diego would only give Bruno five thousand dollars, so Tom kicked in five thousand of his own funds without telling Santana.

"Have you ever thought about partnering with someone who can provide the necessary funds to get the fitness center off the ground?" Tom asked.

"Who would help me? No one I know of. Those TV and newspaper reporters kept taking pictures of me. Tonight on television and tomorrow in the newspapers, I'll be labeled a scumbag traitor," he said in a sorrowful voice. "I guess I am."

Tom felt sorry for Bruno, a man corrupted by the thought of making a million dollars. More than one man's ethics and morals had been compromised by the thought of unscrupulous profits, he reasoned. Most never recovered.

"I'll help you out," Tom heard himself saying.

Bruno looked at Tom with skepticism. "Why would you do that?"

"I think you've learned a lesson about not getting caught up in promises of huge amounts of money," Tom replied. "When you get to Lisbon, get back to being a personnel trainer. Look for business opportunities."

"Then what?" Bruno asked.

"You have my phone number, and I'll give you my personal email. Contact me, and I'll review your ideas from a business perspective standpoint. If one looks good, I'll provide the financing and become your partner."

"You'd really do that?" Bruno asked, a note of hope in his voice.

"Sure. Everyone deserves a second chance."

Suddenly, Cabazos was talkative. They discussed training equipment, the effect various pieces of equipment had on the human body, and the Lisbon districts that would be best for a new fitness center. Tom drove up to the departure lanes at the airport, where Bruno got out and thanked him again.

Cabazos walked inside with a spring in his step that had been missing for some time. He checked in and decided to use the men's room before heading for the departure gate. Bruno walked down a long corridor to the restroom. A man walking behind him pulled out a pistol with a silencer and shot him through the back of the head. The assassin removed the ten thousand dollars from his coat pocket and walked away.

***

Tom drove back to the Santana mansion and was stopped by two new security guards at the entrance. He smiled as he produced identification. A call went to the main house, and Tom was verified as being a legitimate family friend. He drove the winding, narrow road to the home and parked in front.

Bradshaw recommended installing perimeter motion sensors around the entire acreage that activated lights and security cameras and fed directly into a monitoring room within the mansion. Diego had followed his recommendations, and also installed security cameras and lighting around the perimeter of the home and detached guest house. No one could approach the home at night without triggering one system or another.

Santana also increased the number of security guards, and they were active on the property day and night.

Tom walked into the main living room, where Diego awaited him. "I dropped Bruno off at the airport. He should be on his way to Lisbon."

Diego's expression was calculating, his eyes hooded. "I told you I wanted to get rid of him. He's part of the reason my wife's mental well-being is near the breaking point."

Tom was thinking about business in Los Angeles and Mexico City as he stared out the picture window at a magnificent display of flowers, shrubs, and trees. His mind was not fully on the conversation with Diego as he sat down on a couch. "He lived up to his agreement to lead the kidnappers into believing that the snatch was a sure thing. We got them all, including Jack Riley."

"There was no reason to let him live," Diego said in a hard voice.

Tom sat up straight, suddenly worried. "What do you mean?

"I mean that the son-of-a-bitch deserved to die," Diego said as he lit a cigar.

"What have you done?" Tom asked in a concerned voice.

"His life ended at the airport. I got back the five thousand I gave him. I suppose the other five thousand was from you," Diego said as he stared at Tom through a haze of cigar smoke.

A look of intense pain spread over Bradshaw's face. "Oh, no," he cried out as his head dropped to his chest. "Men can change. He wanted to make a fresh start. I even agreed to help him get started in business in Lisbon."

"Tom, sometimes you're too soft. He had to go," Diego said emphatically.

Bradshaw jumped up from the couch. "Who the hell do you think you are? You're not God! You can't kill people whenever you feel like it." Bradshaw put his hands on his hips and looked at the ceiling as if seeking help from on high.

"Calm down. You'll get over it," Diego said as he sat down in a large overstuffed chair.

"You let me drive him to the airport, and then you had him killed. I feel like I was partially responsible for his death." Tom groaned, his expression one of intense pain.

"It's over and done with, and I feel better. I didn't get where I am today by being soft," the patriarch said in a hard voice.

"You're a murderer, pure and simple," Tom growled. "I had no idea you were such a ruthless bastard."

"You can't talk to me like that. You're a guest in my home," Diego said in an angry voice.

"Not for long. I'm leaving as soon as I talk with Bianca. I wouldn't spend another night in a house with you, you miserable bastard."

Diego's eyes opened wide. "You're not going to tell her, are you? Think what it would do to Maria, Bianca, and the grandchildren."

"I love her, and I'd never lie to her. It's up to you to explain your lack of morals to her. I'm not going to protect you," Tom said in a menacing tone of voice.

Bianca moved towards the men from an entrance at the rear of the living room. Both men looked at her in amazement. They had been so engrossed in fighting that neither man noticed her.

"Father, I don't know what to say. I can't believe what I heard. You've always been such a good man towards your family," she said in a soft voice.

She continued walking until she stood in front of her father. Bianca stared into his eyes, trying to grasp the meaning of what she had heard. The short, rotund patriarch was momentarily speechless, then groaned and closed his eyes.

"I'm sorry," he said in a barely audible voice. "I don't want anything to come between us."

Bianca put her hands on his chest. "I'll pray for you," she said softly.

Her touch made Diego jerk and almost jump backwards. "Don't do anything that will break up our family. Please, Bianca," he pleaded.

"I must stay to give Mother support until she regains her mental fitness. That I will do because I love her so much."

"Oh, that's wonderful. I'll make it up to you, I swear," Diego blurted out.

She continued looking deeply into his eyes. "If you do anything to drive away the man I love, I'll take the boys, and you'll never see them or me again."

Sweat poured down Diego's face, his jowls and his lips quivered. "Please don't talk that way. I'll do anything you want."

"Go to church every day with me and pray for our heavenly Father to forgive you. I don't know that you dare go to confession," she said.

Tom was transfixed by the scene unfolding in front of him. He knew he should leave but felt mesmerized by the dialogue between father and daughter. He continued to stand motionless, rooted to the spot.

Bianca turned, walked over to Bradshaw, put her arm through his, and led him from the room. Diego stumbled as he attempted to sit on the couch and collapsed sideways onto the cushions.

"She'll forgive me. I know she will," he said aloud as his body assumed a fetal position.

CHAPTER 25

That same afternoon, Tom sat with Maria Santana, looking out the picture window as they talked about her grandsons, Daniel and Mario, and about Bianca. Maria was quite upbeat. There was no longer a threat to her life, her daughter had explained. The bad guys had gone away, and she was safe, Bianca told her. She was insulated in a magnificent cocoon of a home, away from the clamor and noise generated by the killing of the kidnapping gang.

"I was thinking that we all could go to the beach for a few days. Would you like that, Tom?" Maria asked.

"I would, but I can't. I'll be leaving tomorrow morning to fly back to Los Angeles. It's a business emergency, and I have to take care of it," he explained.

"Well, Diego has experienced many of those over the years. I understand. Will you come back soon?"

"As soon as I can, I promise," he said.

They chatted on a variety of subjects until she asked him about what was most important to her, Bianca.

"Forgive me for asking, but you're leaving. Will you and Bianca…?"

"I love Bianca, and she loves me. I'm sure we'll be together permanently in the not too distant future. But the timing isn't right at the moment," Tom hurriedly explained.

"Oh, I'm so happy to hear that. I've prayed that the two of you will spend your lives together. You're such a lovely couple," she said in a soft, loving voice.

Bradshaw felt a pang of regret about building up her hopes. The problem was Diego, who'd ordered a man to be killed without exhibiting any remorse.

An hour later, Tom and Bianca drove to the Hilton Hotel near the Madrid airport. They were chauffeured by Eduardo Vargas, the loyal bodyguard, who had just found out that Bruno Cabazos had been killed at the airport. Tom deflected his questions, saying that Bianca did not want to discuss the attempted kidnapping and its ramifications. Eduardo said he would return in the morning to pick up Bianca.

Tom paid for a suite, and the elevator whisked them to the futuristic set of rooms on the fourth floor. Maria stood in front of the floor to ceiling wall of glass, looking out on the surrounding green landscape. Tom joined her and put his arm around her.

"I don't know what to do about my father."

"I think it will take a while before we can come to any conclusions," Tom said.

"He's always been so good to me and the boys, and to my mother," Bianca pointed out. "Yet I heard him admit that he had Bruno killed."

"I know you must stay with your mother until she recovers from the shock. Therapy will help her get through it, I'm sure," he said. "Then you and the boys can come to Los Angeles for a vacation."

She smiled. "Maybe I'll just come alone."

"That would be good, too," Tom replied as he took the vivacious brunette in his arms.

***

Tom walked along the water's edge, the waves crashing and rolling around his bare feet. The flight from Madrid to Los Angeles had taken twelve hours. He was back in Santa Monica just before twilight and decided to take a long, leisurely walk along the Pacific Ocean.

His mind continually returned to the events in Madrid— his discovering the kidnapping plot, bringing in Royal Blue security forces to ambush the snatchers, and finding out that Diego Santana was a stone cold killer. Bradshaw wondered if Diego had also ordered the killing of Salvador Pacheco, Maria's second husband.

Revisiting the events, Tom knew the full weight of the decisions was his alone, and he believed he had made the right calls. He had taken decisive action without counsel and accepted the full weight and responsibility of his judgements. Bradshaw's experience in the K&R negotiation business over the past five years had brought him a great many triumphs. He had begun to accept them with pride that was not tainted by arrogance.

A succession of decisions, many being blind leaps in the dark, revealed his innermost character, which was based upon being honest, straightforward, and taking calculated risks. The triumph in Madrid that saved Maria Santana was shared by many, but his name was never mentioned at his request. He had called the shots from behind the scenes and felt pride in having made the right decisions.

But this feeling of success and pride could quickly be dumped in the toilet. Running towards him in the half-light was an older woman chasing her dog. The labradoodle had pulled the short leash from her hand and happily departed, bounding forward, playing in the surf and enjoying his freedom.

Tom watched the spirited, young, rust-colored dog happily enjoying his run. His sheep-like, curly hair was rising and falling as he galloped forward. Suddenly, Tom recognized the woman, his eyes opened wide, and a feeling of fear replaced his self-confidence.

"Young man. Stop my dog," the white-haired woman yelled.

"Mrs. Fairchild, is that you?" Tom asked

"Of course it's me. Now stop my dog."

Tom ran forward and tried to grab the labradoodle, but the dog easily made a quick cut to the left, then to the right and bypassed him.

"That was a half-hearted attempt," she said.

"I didn't know you owned a dog."

"Well, you do now. Are you going to catch him for me or not?'

"What's his name?" Tom asked.

As twilight turned to dusk, Vivian Fairchild's features took on a calculating, almost scheming look. "His name is Tom."

Bradshaw looked surprised. "You do know that my first name is Tom?"

"Of course. We've met several times. Now, are you going to catch him for me or not, young man?"

Tom turned, a pained expression on his face, and began running after the labradoodle. Tom, the dog, ran at a leisurely pace, enjoying every second of freedom. As soon as Tom, the man, got close, the dog speeded up. After five minutes of taunting, the dog abruptly abandoned his romp in the ocean and headed inland. Bradshaw groaned, gasping for breath, and followed. The dog soon reached Ocean Avenue.

"Oh, no!" Tom cried out, afraid the animal would be struck and killed if he tried to cross the busy thoroughfare.

But the labradoodle surprised him with his agility as he ran between cars at a fast pace and made it to the other side. Tom kept looking for enough space between cars to dart through. He made it to the center stripe, cars honking their horns and drivers swearing away from him. Tom shot forward, trying to time his sprint between cars, but one of his flip-flops came off, and he tripped. Bradshaw did a summersault, and a car had to jam on its brakes in order to avoid running him over.

"You drunken bum! Watch where you're going," the

driver yelled.

Tom managed to retrieve his flip-flop and made it to the other side of Ocean Avenue. His white cashmere polo shirt was ripped and soiled on the shoulder and back, and his brown shorts were ripped at the seat. Both legs and his left arm were skinned.

Man chasing dog continued through a commercial district, with the labradoodle stopping now and then to pee. Bradshaw began calling out the dog's name, but the rust-colored pooch paid no attention. Tom, the dog, turned a corner and ran behind some stores. Bradshaw followed, caught his foot, and rolled in the alley, nearly obliterating his white shirt and knocking over two garbage cans. It was dark as he began feeling around for his flip-flop.

Suddenly a flashlight was shined in his face. "Hold it right there, asshole, or I'll put a bullet through you," a night watchman yelled out.

Bradshaw was on his hands and knees, his eyes blinking from the bright light. "I'm looking for my dog, Tom. He got away and ran through here."

"Don't try to shit me. I know a homeless person trying to eat out of the garbage cans when I see one. Get your ass out of here."

Tom saw his flip-flop, grabbed it, and hobbled down the alley. He looked both ways at the next street and saw Tom, the dog, sitting and waiting, as if he was enjoying the game.

"Here, Tom. Good boy, come here," he said in a friendly voice as he advanced. Just as Tom was about to reach out for him, the labradoodle continued loping down the street, his namesake in pursuit.

The game continued as the two Toms entered a residential area. The dog ran between two houses, nose to the ground as he intermittently sprayed flowers, trees, and children's toys. Bradshaw was exhausted, hands on his hips, struggling to remain upright as he trudged along, calling Tom's name.

A woman looked out the window, saw Bradshaw in the light from the house, and called the police. Within five minutes, two cruisers were slowing driving through the neighborhood. The officers in one police car spotted Bradshaw and turned on their flashing lights. He turned and was met with a blinding light from two searchlights mounted on the cruiser.

A tall, uniformed officer walked up to him. "Have you got identification?"

"Sure. I'm running after the neighbor's dog that got away. I'm exhausted."

"You look like you've been rolling in the street," the cop said.

"I fell a couple of times."

The officer took his driver's license, then glanced at Tom. "You live at this address? These are multi-million dollar condos," the policeman said in a doubting voice.

"It's my dad's condo. I live there when I'm in town."

"What kind of a dog are you searching for?"

"A labradoodle, kind of rust colored," Tom replied.

"What's his name?"

"Tom."

The officer scratched his head. "Are you telling me you named your dog after yourself?"

"It's not my dog. I fell a couple of times while running. That's why I look kind of messy."

"You sure do."

The labradoodle walked into the light and up to the police officer. The cop scratched him behind the ears, eliciting a soft whine from the dog.

"That's the dog I've been trying to find. Don't let him get away," Tom said.

"Bill, bring me a piece of rope," the policeman told his partner.

Tom, the dog, and Tom, the man, sat together in the

backseat of the cruiser as it drove up to the condos. The officer walked with the two Toms to Vivian Fairchild's condo and rang the doorbell.

"Othello, where have you been?" Vivian said enthusiastically when she opened the door.

"You told me his name is Tom," Bradshaw said in a surprised voice.

"His middle name is Tom," she snapped.

"Dogs don't have middle names," Tom said in a disgusted voice.

"What happened to you, young man? You look like you've been rolling around in the street."

"I fell a couple times while chasing your dog."

"Well, don't come in the house. I don't want that dirt to get on my floors."

The patrolman stood to one side, amazed by the conversation. Without saying a word, he handed the rope to Vivian. She grabbed it.

"Come in, darling. You must have had a difficult evening."

She pulled the labradoodle inside and shut the door.

"Is she always like that?" the officer asked.

"Sometimes worse."

"What kind of a name is Othello?" the policeman asked.

Tom thought for a moment. "He was the title character in a Shakespearian tragedy."

"Be careful, or you could become a character in a Santa Monica tragedy," the officer said, and grinned.

Bradshaw thanked the officer for the ride home and spent the next twenty minutes in the shower washing away the grime and grit from the Santa Monica streets. He fell into bed exhausted and slept for nearly twelve hours. Tom had lunch at a beach-side café, enjoyed a long walk along the ocean, and visited his buddy, Ike Chambers. Ike tried unsuccessfully to get Tom to party with him that night.

CHAPTER 26

Tom and his boss, Mark Danforth, sat down in comfortable leather chairs in Danforth's office. They talked in depth about the Madrid kidnapping scenario. Tom had called him on three occasions while in Madrid, so Danforth already knew most of the particulars. Tom refrained from telling him about the killing engineered by Diego Santana.

"I'm glad you stayed out of the firefight. That must have been a real battle."

"There were dead kidnappers strewn about and vehicles shot to hell. Those Royal Blue guys are well trained mercenaries with a lot of military experience," Tom pointed out.

"I called the owner, Charlie Sanders, this morning. There's a gang that's been kidnapping a number of prominent business people in Rio. They're not too careful about concealing their identities. I put him in touch with a business association there. They may want to use his services," Mark explained.

"His men would be perfect for the job," Tom said

Danforth lit a cigar, and his red oval face and shiny bald spot were briefly clouded in smoke. His middle-aged spread around the waist was expanding as stress and tension mounted, Tom thought.

"There's another issue on my mind," Danforth said as he

blew a cloud of smoke to one side. "You're becoming too well known in Mexico City. It might just have a detrimental effect on your health."

Tom looked concerned. "Is there a specific threat?"

"No, just too much press. Part of being a good negotiator is working in anonymity. You do a great job, but it may be time for a change of scenery. Would you be agreeable to Rio de Janeiro or Buenos Aires?"

Tom thought for a moment. "I don't speak Portuguese, so that leaves out Brazil. Buenos Aires would be a possibility."

"It's on the ocean, it has fantastic nightlife, and is beautiful," Mark pointed out.

"I love Mexico City. It has everything, and the people are fantastic. Let me think about it. If at all possible, I still want to investigate and identify who's fingering the Mexico City bankers," Tom said.

"Take your time. I'm just thinking about your safety," Mark emphasized.

"I'll be ready to go back to work next week. I know that what you're saying makes sense. But I've made a lot of friends in Mexico City, and it's difficult to just leave," Tom pointed out.

***

Bradshaw lazily stretched out on his patio chaise lounge, half asleep when he heard a knock at the door. Tom got up, yawned, and walked slowly to the door. His eyes opened wide, and his back stiffened as he opened the door

Vivian Fairchild stood there, a frown on her face and her dog on a leash.

"Young man, I'd like you to look after Othello while I'm at the doctor's office."

Tom shook his head. "No way. Find someone else." He began to close the door.

"I haven't been feeling well. Surely you'd help a sick woman."

"Mrs. Fairchild, every time I try to help you, something bad happens. Just looking at you spells trouble. Don't you have another friend in the condo complex who can look after Othello?"

"No. You're my only friend here."

"Friend! You've got to be kidding. I don't think you even like me," Tom said loudly.

"I've decided to drop the name Othello and just call him Tom. Isn't he cute?"

The young, rust-colored labradoodle sat looking at Tom, tongue hanging out, expectant eyes radiating playfulness. Tom made eye contact with the pooch, and the dog knew he had him. He moved closer to Tom's feet, and Bradshaw reluctantly scratched him behind the ears. Othello's eyes lighted up, his tail wagged, and he licked Tom's hand.

"Well, how long are you going to be gone?" Tom asked.

Vivian sensed victory. "Not more than a couple of hours. He's been fed, and I walked him. He's housebroken, so there's no worry there. Just put down a pan of water for him to drink from."

Working in tandem, Vivian and Othello had snared the good-hearted young man, even though his face was clouded with skepticism.

"Okay, but make sure you come right back."

"Of course," she said softly as she handed the leash to Tom. Vivian turned and quickly headed for the elevator to the basement parking garage.

"Come on, Tom. I've got a tennis ball we can play with."

They played fetch the full length of the living room for fifteen minutes before Bradshaw opened the sliding glass doors to the large patio. Plexiglas fencing allowed for uninterrupted views of the ocean. The labradoodle went around the perimeter looking for a way out but found none. Tom stretched out again on the chaise lounge, and the happy dog jumped up and lay down in his lap.

His face looked into Bradshaw's. Tom petted him

continually until his eyes closed. As soon as he stopped, the doodle's eyes would pop open, and Tom would commence petting again. Soon a happy Tom Bradshaw was asleep, and so was the dog.

They both awoke to a knock on the door. Tom yawned, removed the dog from his stomach, and walked barefoot to the door. A young man was selling magazines at amazingly low prices, but Tom told him he wasn't interested.

Just as he moved to shut the door, the labradoodle flashed by him and out the door.

"Oh, no!" Tom cried out. He ran back inside, put on his athletic shoes, grabbed a baseball cap and dark glasses, and tore after the pooch. He knew the dog had gone down the stairs towards the ocean and could see the little ruffian frolicking at the water's edge. Tom ran up to within ten feet of little Tom before the labradoodle commenced running along the shoreline. The game was on, and little Tom loved it.

"Grab him," Tom called out several times to beachcombers, but no one attempted to nab the small dog.

Little Tom finally headed inland after running along the ocean for half a mile. He negotiated busy streets as if he was a professional athlete. Big Tom, on the other hand, got honked at and nearly hit on two occasions.

They entered a commercial district, and the labradoodle ran up to a young golden retriever. Instantaneously they were best friends. A middle-aged lady had the golden on a leash, which allowed Tom time to catch up and grab his dog by its collar. He picked up the labradoodle, walked into a convenience market, and bought a package of clothesline rope.

Tom actually enjoyed the exercise since he was wearing athletic shoes. He walked out of the store with little Tom on a makeshift leash and came face to face with an old man who angrily stared at the dog.

"There you are, you little bastard. When I get you home,

I'm going to beat you until you can't stand up," the grizzled old man yelled. His white hair was stringy and stuck out in every direction, his bulbous red nose and fat red lips both needed wiping, and his belly hung over an old belt that held up dirty, baggy blue jeans.

"Wait a minute. What makes you think this is your dog?" Tom asked.

"Look at the sniveling little bastard hiding behind your legs. He knows what he's got in store for him when I get him home — a beating he'll never forget. I'll teach him to run off."

Little Tom stuck his head out from between big Tom's legs and growled at the unkempt old man.

"See, the little shit knows what's in store for him."

Bradshaw surmised that the labradoodle probably did belong to the old man. "Do you have any proof this dog is yours?"

"He's got a chip in him, and I've got the paperwork showing vaccination, licensing, and a receipt for the two thousand I paid for him."

A startled look crossed Tom's face. "You paid two thousand dollars for a dog?"

"They ain't cheap."

Bradshaw looked down at the little rust-brown labradoodle, and the dog cocked his head and stared back at Tom. Tom was hooked. For some reason, love came easily to the big man, and little Tom was tap dancing on his heart.

"I'm not giving you this dog. Get that through your head," Tom warned.

"Why, you no good bastard," the old man shouted. He took a swing at Bradshaw, but Tom backed up, and he missed. Then he swung again with the same results. Now he stopped, hunched over from the exertion, the sound of a deflating balloon coming from his lungs.

"Listen. I'll pay you two thousand dollars if you have the documentation you claim."

The scraggly white hair hung down over his face as he gasped for breath. "Twenty-five hundred," he said in a garbled voice.

Bradshaw was angry. "Listen, old man, you'll take two thousand, or I'll walk away with the dog, and you'll get nothing. Understand?"

"Okay," the man said. He raised his head and looked through the white hair. His mouth was open, and Tom could see that most of his teeth were missing.

"There's a Wells Fargo branch a block from here. I'll meet you there in forty-five minutes. Have the documentation, and I'll give you cash," Tom promised.

"How do I know yer telling the truth?"

"I'll be there. Make sure you've got the papers." Bradshaw and little Tom walked away.

When they arrived back at the condo, Tom retrieved his Wells Fargo credit card and debit card. He put on a Tommy Bahamas sport shirt, brown slacks, and glove-leather loafers. Then he drove to the bank and pulled into the parking lot. The old man was already there and produced the papers. The dog's real name was Rusty.

They entered the bank. Tom used a debit card to withdraw two thousand dollars. "Here's a bill of sale for the dog that I drew up at my condo. Sign it, and the money's yours."

"I ain't signing no bill of sale."

"Then you're not getting any money," Tom said firmly.

The old man glowered at Tom. "If I had my way, I'd shoot that mutt."

"Sign it, or you get nothing," Tom ordered.

The disheveled, slovenly man grabbed the pen and paper and signed. Tom handed him the money.

"I hope that little bastard runs away from you. Then you'll be out two thousand dollars," he said as he walked unsteadily out the door.

Tom took a deep breath and exhaled sharply. He looked around and realized that every person in the bank was silent, watching the bizarre transaction. Bradshaw did a mock salute and exited the branch.

He drove back to the condo, opened the door carefully, and entered. Rusty came running, stood on his hind feet, and put his front feet on Tom's leg. Bradshaw picked him up and received several licks as thanks. They played fetch again until Tom was tired of throwing the tennis ball. He went into the master bedroom, lay down on the bed, and promptly dozed off with Rusty curled up against him.

Two hours later, he bought a retractable leash and a matching set of food and water bowls. He also purchased a new collar for Rusty, with his father's cell phone number as well as his own on the shiny disk that hung from the collar.

Bradshaw called his father, Douglas. "What time did you want me there for dinner tonight?" he asked.

"I think Marilyn wants to eat about six or six-thirty," Douglas replied.

"Sounds great. I'll have a surprise for you."

"You're getting married?"

"No."

"You're leaving California Fidelity?"

"Nope."

"You've become religious?"

Both men laughed.

"I'll see you at six."

Tom hung up and played with Rusty, paid some bills, and was preparing to take his labradoodle for another walk on the beach when there was a knock on the door. He hooked Rusty to the leash and answered the door.

"I see that you didn't let him get away," Vivian Fairchild said.

"You're late, Vivian, about four or five hours."

"Give me the dog," she said in an exasperated voice.

"You lied to me, Vivian. This is not your dog."

"He certainly is," she said indignantly.

"The labradoodle did get away from me. I chased him for a long time before I caught him. Then I bumped into the real owner. He had vaccination and license papers, as well as a receipt for his purchase. The dog's real name is Rusty," Tom said in an angry voice.

"Well, he's mine now. Give him to me," she snapped.

"No. I bought him from the real owner."

"He's still mine. You were just dog-sitting."

"I paid two thousand dollars for him and received a bill of sale," Tom said, and smiled.

"You're crazy. No one would pay two thousand dollars for a dog," Vivian said in a nasty voice.

Tom made a motion with his fingers as if beckoning. "If you want him, fork over two thousand dollars."

"I would be out of my mind to do such a thing," she said.

"You lied when you said Rusty was your dog," Tom pointed out. "Where did you get him?"

"I never said he was my dog. Keep the damn mutt," she said loudly as she turned and marched back to her condo.

During the exchange between Vivian and Tom, the pooch stood behind Bradshaw with his head peeking between his legs.

***

At exactly six, Tom rang the doorbell at Douglas and Marilyn's Brentwood home.

"Oh my goodness, what a beautiful little dog," Marilyn said when she answered the door. She kneeled down and began petting Rusty, who gave her several licks of appreciation.

They walked into the living room, where Tom's dad was mixing martinis. A surprised look crossed his face when he saw Rusty. "Where did you get the dog?"

"It's a long story, Dad."

Douglas watched Rusty walk around the room, smelling every piece of furniture. "Is he …?"

"Yes Dad, he's housebroken. This is kind of a bizarre story, so I'll run through it hitting the high points," Tom explained.

They sat and had drinks while Tom began talking about the odd chain of events that led up to Rusty being in the Bradshaw's home. The labradoodle sat on Marilyn's lap, thoroughly enjoying the petting, and repaid her with licks. Tom included all the details, which elicited laughter from the audience.

"You paid two thousand for this dog?" Douglas asked in an incredulous voice.

"I saw the receipt from the breeder. These labradoodles are expensive," Tom noted.

"He should have a gold sheen to his coat instead of the rust color," Douglas said.

Tom looked chagrined. "I really didn't have a choice. By that time, Rusty had a firm grip on my emotions, and I was committed to finding him a good home. I wasn't about to give him back to a man who would beat him."

"What are you going to do with him?" his father asked. "Your globe-trotting lifestyle doesn't lend itself to having a dog."

"I was wondering if you could make an inquiry at the hospital to see if one of your friends might take him. Most have homes and yards conducive to keeping dogs," Tom replied.

"Well, I suppose so," Douglas said.

Marilyn was quiet, petting the lap dog, who continued to look into her eyes and licked her hand.

"Do you have any ideas?" Douglas asked.

She slowly raised her gaze until she was looking into her husband's eyes. "We could try."

Douglas sat up straight. "Oh no. We agreed that with both of us working, there isn't time for a dog."

"I'm only working three days a week, Monday through Wednesday. We could have the housekeeper or the gardener let him out in the back yard on those days," Marilyn pointed out.

"Well...," said Douglas as he stared at Rusty.

"It wouldn't hurt to try. If it doesn't work out, I'm sure someone at the hospital will take him. He's such a nice, sweet animal," his wife said.

"Well...I suppose we could try," the defeated husband acknowledged.

Marilyn got up and took Rusty over to Douglas, and placed him in her husband's lap. Douglas scratched him behind the ears, and Rusty licked his hand. He smiled and began petting the labradoodle.

"I don't quite know how to describe his eyes. They're almost people eyes," said Douglas.

"I brought over new food and water bowls and a retractable leash. There's a bag of dog food in the car," Tom explained.

"I'll have to get a new tag for his collar and put my cell phone number on it," Douglas said as he petted Rusty.

"Your number is already on the current tag," Tom said, and grinned.

The elder Bradshaw's eyes opened wide. His wife laughed, and Douglas and Tom joined in. Rusty had a new home.

CHAPTER 27

Victor Chapa shook hands with Tom Bradshaw, and they sat down in leather chairs in the senior vice president's Banco Royale office. Bradshaw had successfully negotiated his kidnap release months earlier.

"Jesus, you've got a lot of security around you. I thought I'd never get through to your private office," Tom said, grinning.

"With the promotion I've been given, the president and board of directors want to make sure I don't get snatched again. I'm now overseeing and approving nearly all of the bank's major investments."

"Well, you're looking a lot younger and healthier," Tom commented.

Victor flashed a chagrined look at Tom. "My wife has me taking facial enhancement treatments. I admit it's removed a lot of aging spots and wrinkles, but I sure get a lot of kidding over it."

Tom laughed. "Keep it up, and you'll be a kid again."

They chatted for few minutes before Chapa got down to business. "I think I've got a line on one of the kidnappers who snatched me. He stuttered, not a lot, but enough that you realized he had a speech impediment."

"That's interesting," Tom said.

"I've talked to five of the kidnapped bankers who you successfully negotiated for their freedom. Two of them also remember a gang member who stuttered. One banker said he thought he heard a valet parking attendant with the same stutter at the hotel next to his bank branch. The bank puts up their important clients there."

Tom sat up in his chair. "He could have been checking out the banker's hours, whether or not he had a bodyguard, and if he would use the same vehicle each day."

"I discreetly inquired and found out he's no longer at that location. I didn't take it any farther until I had a chance to talk with you," Chapa explained.

"Good idea. Here's what I'd suggest. Find out how many banks are willing to pay to try and find out who's behind this coordinated kidnapping plot that targets Mexico City bankers. Ask them to split the costs," Tom recommended.

"Who would we use? Some local security company?" Victor asked.

"I wouldn't. You never know who's connected to who in this mixture of politics and government. You certainly don't want to contact the police department," Tom advised.

"I see your point. Do you have a company in mind?"

"Yes. Royal Blue, headquartered in London, hires mainly Latin Americans and offers immediate emergency response teams. They have a well-trained professional security workforce with a lot of previous army experience. Royal Blue would provide a top level security detail, reserved for the biggest names in business, to conduct the investigation. That means you and your banker associates," Tom said.

"What would it cost?"

"Charlie Sanders is a friend of mine and is the owner of Royal Blue. I just recommended that his company be used in Madrid. They broke up a kidnapping ring and killed all of the bad guys," Tom noted.

Chapa whistled. "I like the sound of that. I want every one of those bastards to pay for screwing up my life and the lives of my family members."

"I think Charlie will suggest using three or four of his men. The cost is fifteen hundred dollars American per day per man. They're expensive, but they're the best, and you never have to worry about leaks."

"I can get enough banks to participate, so the overall cost per bank will be reasonable. The bankers are beginning to really worry because so many of their top people have been snatched. It's like an epidemic," Chapa emphasized.

***

Angel Mendoza and two of his men began searching for the stuttering kidnapper by paying handsomely for any and all information. The Royal Blue guns-for-hire team traced him to another valet parking location. A banking vice president had been abducted from outside that branch.

They learned that his name was Fernando Garcia, and he had moved on again to another valet parking spot. This one was at a fashionable restaurant across the street from a First National Bank of Mexico branch. The information was passed on to Tom Bradshaw, who immediately contacted the bank's president and warned him about the probable kidnapping plot.

The bank branch was suddenly flooded with security personnel. Fernando Garcia left his latest valet parking job that same day. But Angel Mendoza previously had traced his movements to a Spanish style, red-tile roofed home in a modest, middle-income neighborhood. The house had a detached double garage in back, but Garcia parked his old Chevrolet Malibu in front.

"We need to take him alive," Angel told his mercenaries, Oscar Molina and Gabriel Colon. "If he comes out before dark, we'll follow him. If he's spending the night, we'll wake him up."

After dark, the three Royal Blue operatives moved

cautiously to the front door and heard Garcia talking on his cell phone.

"I don't know wha wha what happened, Carlos. The security men were everywhere. I told them I was le le leaving for an early lunch and came back to the house." Garcia paused while listening to his boss, then responded. "I'm sure that no one fo fo followed me. I've ta ta talked with the guys. They were all ready to do the snatch tomorrow, but I fig fig figured it's on hold for now." There was another pause in his conversation, then he said, "I didn't do anything wro wro wrong, boss, while I watched the banker."

The conversation ended. Garcia yelled, "Shit," and threw the phone onto a living room couch. He got a beer from the refrigerator, turned on the television, and began watching an old western movie.

Angel picked the lock with ease. The mercenaries waited until there was an eruption of gunfire in the western movie, opened the door, and quickly walked to the couch, where a surprised kidnapper looked up wide-eyed and frightened.

"Don't sha sha shoot," he pleaded.

They searched him and took a pistol from his pocket. Angel marched Garcia over to the kitchen table and made him sit down.

"I'm going to ask you questions. If you answer them, nothing will happen to you. If you don't, the evening could become very painful for you," Angel said.

"Go go go screw yourself," Garcia replied. "I want a lawyer."

Angel nodded at Oscar Molina, who handed his boss a large hammer. Molina and Gabriel Colon grabbed Garcia and forced his hand flat on the table. Angel struck the small finger on his right hand, smashing it flat. Garcia began screaming, and his body jumped around like a puppet on a string.

The Royal Blue leader put his arm around Garcia's neck

and twisted it until the gang member was looking into his eyes. "Are you ready to talk?"

Garcia began panting like a dog. "No no no more. I'll ta ta talk." Tears were running down his cheeks, and his face was twisted from the pain.

The mercenaries learned the names of the other three kidnappers. But the leader, Carlos, was known to his men only by that name. Carlos provided telephones to the gang members so he could contact them. But they were unable to call him because the cell phone he always used was a prepaid burner phone that was thrown away when he completed calls to his gang members.

The gang leader provided names, photos, and locations of bank branches to his men, who then monitored bankers' arrival and departure times, whether or not they had security escorts, and parking locations for their autos. Carlos placed a great deal of emphasis on bankers' punctuality, which factored into capture equations. Garcia was the most reliable snatcher and therefore received the most reconnaissance jobs.

Garcia's finger was bandaged, and he was taken on a car ride to identify the housing locations used by the other gang members. Two were living in slum housing, and the third was in a third-rate, broken down hotel.

The Royal Blue mercenaries decided to try and capture Rafael Perez, the snatcher living at the Bonita Vista Hotel, first. They walked into the dilapidated hotel with its dirty wood floors and flowered wall coverings that were beginning to peel. Garcia was to go up to Perez's room on the third floor with Angel and his men and knock on the door. Then the capture would ensue.

The four men headed for the stairs just as Perez started down the last flight of stairs to the lobby. Fernando Garcia's eyes opened wide. "Ra ra ra...," he stuttered but never completed the word, Rafael.

Perez immediately recognized that Garcia was accompanied by undercover police or security forces. The tall, thin kidnapper pulled a revolver from under his dirty T-shirt and began firing, then turned and ran back up the staircase. Fernando Garcia was accidentally wounded in the right arm. Garcia howled loudly, now having two wounds in the right arm and right hand.

Angel returned the fire but missed as Rafael Perez disappeared down the second floor hallway. The guns-for-hire leader and his two men ran up the stairs and were cautious as they moved down the corridor. People stuck their heads out of the rooms and quickly pulled back inside when they saw men with guns.

Perez exited onto the rear fire escape stairs, quickly made it down to the back alley, and disappeared into the poverty-stricken neighborhood. Convinced that they'd lost him, the hunters returned to the hotel lobby.

Garcia was crying out and yelling as he was hustled into an SUV and taken to an emergency services facility. Money changed hands, and his arm wound was treated and bandaged. No police report would be made.

"On to the next," Angel told Garcia.

"No no no," he pleaded.

"It's all right, Fernando. We'll drive up to the house. You can stay in the car and signal us if the right man comes to the door," Angel explained.

Garcia's expression was one of pure misery. "I do do do don't want to do this."

"Trust me, I'll take care of you. You've got nothing to worry about," Angel promised.

They entered the slums in a white Ford Explorer that looked out of place amid the shacks. Angel and his men ran up to the front door of the shanty, kicked in the front door, and ran inside. Two women began screaming, children began crying, and a dog attacked. They shot the German shepherd mix and pried Gabriel Colon's leg out of his mouth. Hector Zamora was nowhere to be found.

Then, the Royal Blue mercenaries got back in the SUV and headed down the garbage-strewn road to Jose Cantu's small house.

"We'll do this one differently. You guys stay on each side of the home out of sight. I'll walk up to the front door and try to find out if he's home," Angel told his men. "By the way, Gabriel, is your tetanus shot up to date?"

Colon groaned, more from exasperation than from pain. "Shit, I can't remember."

Angel made his way through a yard filled with trash to a front door that needed more than paint. Hunks of wood had been knocked out of the door that showed several colors of paint, one peeling on top of the other. He knocked.

"What do you want?" a voice growled from within.

"Fernando sent me."

"Bullshit. He wouldn't send you here," the voice yelled.

"You've won the lottery, you lucky devil," Angel said in a happy voice.

"Listen, asshole, get the hell out of here."

Angel remembered seeing lottery tickets strewn about the house where they had captured Garcia. "Don't you remember all those tickets you guys purchased? One of them was the big winner. You guys are all millionaires."

Jose Cantu jerked open the front door. "Really?"

"No, not really," Angel replied as he pointed his pistol at Cantu.

"You bastard," Cantu said and slammed the door just as Angel fired.

Another large piece of wood went flying off the front door. Angel grabbed the doorknob, but it wouldn't open. He fired two shots into the lock, then cautiously pushed the door inward. His men anxiously peered around the corners of the small home, then turned and ran to the rear of the house. There was no rear door.

"Where the hell did he go?" Angel said aloud.

A short while later, they found an escape tunnel in a bedroom closet. "Christ, I'll go," Angel said. He went head first down into the tunnel and wiggled along for ten minutes before coming out at the end of the property in a small wash. He stood up and yelled at his men, who came running.

"You look like a mole all covered with dirt," Oscar Molina told him.

***

Hours later, Carlos contacted his men by cell phone and made arrangements to meet them in a Mexico City warehouse district after dark. One by one, they warily approached the meeting spot. Carlos, dressed in a dark brown suit and matching striped tie, began quizzing his men.

"Rafael, are you sure Fernando was with the security people at the hotel?"

"I'm sure. He had a bandaged hand. They probably worked him over," Perez pointed out.

"You weren't at home, Hector. Was your family sure they were police officers?" Carlos asked.

"They were armed and wore blue uniforms. The dirty bastards killed my dog," Zamora said.

"Did the man at your door look like a cop?" Carlos asked Jose Cantu.

"Yeah. I only saw the one, but he was definitely a cop. He'd been to the house where we keep the kidnapped bankers. He knew we had lottery tickets laying all over the place. That's how he got me to open the door. He claimed we'd won the lottery," Cantu said in a disgusted voice.

The intelligent, sophisticated leader of the gang thought for a few moments. His pungent, spicy cologne filled the night air with a woody fragrance.

"I'm worried," Perez lamented. "We've all been in prison. If they know our names, they can get our mug shots. Police all over Mexico could begin hunting for us."

"You're the only one who can't be identified. Hell, we don't even know your real name," Zamora stressed.

"Is there someplace we can go until the heat is off?" Cantu asked.

"Yes, there is," Carlos said.

He turned to one side, drew his pistol with a silencer attached, and shot Cantu and Zamora in the face.

"No, don't," Perez pleaded just before Carlos shot him between the eyes.

Then Carlos moved to the bodies, shooting each man in the heart.

"Three down and one to go," Carlos said as he holstered his weapon and casually walked to his car.

CHAPTER 28

Tom and Angel were going over the details of the debacle and were brainstorming about their next step in trying to identify Carlos. The men were seated comfortably in the living room of Bradshaw's suite in the Hilton Hotel. Tom's phone rang, and he answered. Mexico City's Assistant Police Chief Franco Gomez was the caller.

"Those three members of the kidnapping gang that you identified have been found murdered," Gomez said. "They were executed, shot in the head and heart."

Tom jumped to his feet. "Jesus Christ."

"I've put Fernando Garcia in a maximum security jail. But that doesn't mean he's completely safe. If you put up enough money, any criminal in jail can be eliminated," Gomez emphasized.

"What do you suggest?" Tom asked in a worried tone of voice.

"Get him out of the country."

Tom ran his hand through his hair while he walked back and forth. "Give me a little time to talk to the group of bankers who are fronting the money for this investigation. I'll be back in touch with you today."

"All right. I'll make sure he stays alive," Gomez replied.

The call ended, and Bradshaw relayed the information to Angel Mendoza.

"Smart. He's eliminating everyone who can identify him. Those gang members may not know his real name, but they know what he looks like. He'll try hard to kill Fernando Garcia," Angel pointed out. "He the one remaining snatcher who can identify him."

Bradshaw called Victor Chapa, executive vice president of Banco Royal, who was the point man for the group of bankers paying for the investigation. He went over the facts to date, ending with the assassination of the three gang members. He then relayed the assistant police chief's recommendation.

"That Carlos is a vicious son-of-a-bitch. We really need to keep Fernando Garcia alive. Go ahead and ship him out of the country. We'll foot the bill," Chapa said.

Following the talk with Chapa, Tom and Angel discussed where to take Garcia.

"My first suggestion would be Bogota, Colombia. He'll think he's being taken to a comfortable, resort-like destination until we discover who Carlos really is. Actually, he will be transported to a jungle location far from any modern conveniences. It's where we train a lot of our people. No one will find him there, and he can't get out."

"Is it that remote?" Tom asked.

"Yup. You'd have to hack your way through the jungle to escape."

"Good luck with that," Tom said. "Let's do it."

***

An hour later, Tom was about to leave the suite when there was a knock on the door. Bradshaw opened it and looked startled.

Bianca stood there, stunning in a light blue silk dress that accented every curve of her body. Her violet eyes and cascading mane of dark hair enhanced her unforgettable allure. The high contrast of Bianca's white skin and gleaming black hair, plus her bold lip color and subtle eye makeup, contributed to her hyper-femininity. Tom felt instantaneous desire that quickly turned to lust.

"I never thought you'd ever come back to Mexico City," he said in a surprised voice.

"I didn't either, but I want to have a serious talk. So I made the decision to fly here," she explained.

She walked inside. Tom closed the door and reached forward to take her in his arms. Bianca put her hands on his chest to keep him at arms' length.

"Let's talk, Tom. If we are suddenly wrapped in each other's arms, my whole focus would be destroyed."

"All right. I'm listening," he said quietly.

Bianca walked to a blue and gold patterned couch and sat down. Tom sat down next to her, but not within touching distance.

"First of all, I want you to know that I love you and always will. What you've done for me and the boys and for my mother is so generous and wonderful that it's indescribable. Rescuing my sons was done without any thought to your own well-being. People just don't do those things. Kindness and caring are taking a beating in our society today."

Tom watched her talk and realized how much he loved her. He'd never met a woman with her combination of brains, beauty, and compassion.

"I appreciate all the kind words, but I sense that you're leading up to something," Tom said.

"Tom, my mother is not getting any better. She's concerned about my future. She's worried about Daniel and Mario. And you casting aside my father for being a terrible man has had a bad effect on her."

Tom frowned. "You know why I don't want to be around him. He murdered a man."

Bianca's small, slender jaw quivered slightly. "Mother doesn't know what the future has in store for you and me, and this worries her deeply. She wants stability back in our lives. Also, the twins keep asking me about when you will return. I have no answer. They need stability."

Tom reached out and touched her arm, causing Bianca to recoil slightly. He pulled his hand back. "I love you, Bianca, and I want to marry you. I've nearly wrapped up the investigation involving the kidnapping of numerous bankers. When this is concluded, I'll come to Spain, and we can be married."

"What about my father?"

"I'll treat him normally again."

"Will you, really? Tom, you have a tendency to cast people aside if they don't measure up to your standards of right and wrong, good and evil."

"I don't think that's...entirely accurate," he said in a soft voice as if trying not to be mean and overbearing.

"My father is a changed man. I made him promise to go to church with me every day. During the first week, he went grudgingly, just mouthing the prayers, not really feeling religious. Then he gradually changed. I could see the hurt in him, the desire to be a better man, and above all, he was seeking forgiveness."

Tom didn't know what to say. "That's remarkable," he finally replied.

"As far as I can tell, the only answer to all these family problems at home is to break off our relationship," she said. "I'll marry into one of the many upper class families that my parents continually socialize with. I'll pick someone who is kind, caring, and will make a good stepfather for my sons."

Tom looked shocked, eyes wide and mouth slightly open. "Oh, don't say that. We love each other."

"Yes, we do. But being around you is like being at the circus. You never know what act is coming next," Bianca said. "You live a bizarre life."

"That's not fair," Tom said, his voice sounding hollow.

"If I marry someone in Madrid, I think my mother's condition will stabilize, and her emotions will gradually return to normal. She'll begin thinking in the present and about the future, rather than about the past nightmares."

Tom felt as if he'd been clubbed over the head—his thoughts were jumbled, and momentarily he was filled with a feeling of emptiness. "I can change. You know I'm going to leave the kidnap negotiation business, and soon."

Her violet eyes bore into Tom. "You may think you want to, but you're hooked on the high it gives you. Each successful return of a kidnap victim enhances your desire for more. Your job has become an addiction."

Tom was breathing hard, and his expression was one of dismay. "I don't know who has put these ideas in your head. Perhaps it's a therapist, but the reasoning is not accurate. I started in this business because I really wanted to make amends for killing men in Afghanistan. Saving peoples' lives is my way of atoning for some of the bad things I did in the war."

Bianca stared into Tom's eyes. "You never told me that before."

"I haven't told anyone that. The past hurt never goes away, but it's not something I care to talk about. I feel it's my problem and mine alone," he emphasized.

She got up from the couch, slowly walked to the picture window, and looked out upon the high rise buildings and greenery. Bianca was lost in thought, not seeing the beauty in front of her.

Tom studied her, realizing she had matured a lot over the past few months. Bianca no longer was the beautiful, fragile woman who could not comprehend why bad things were happening to her children and to her mother. Now she had become the decision maker in her family and was plotting a course of action to bring them out of the throes of despair and depression.

Bianca turned and walked back to where Tom was sitting. She sat down on the edge of the couch, tears traveling down her cheeks.

"It's not easy for me to say goodbye. I love you, but there's no end in sight to your current quest. My family has immediate needs, and I intend to see that they're met, even if it breaks my heart," she said in a choking voice.

Tears welled up in Tom's eyes. "I'll marry you today."

"Oh, Tom. I would love to say yes. But it wouldn't change anything. It wouldn't resolve any of my family's problems. You would still be in Mexico City, and I would still be in Madrid." There was silence between them. Finally, Bianca arose from the couch. "I'm not going to rush into another relationship in Madrid. I've been married twice—both men are dead, and I'm not yet thirty. I'm not living in the past, but it's taught me that making the right decisions at the right times are all important."

"I don't know what else I can do to change your mind," Tom said.

She gazed at him, her resolve unfaltering. "You'll figure it out." Bianca walked towards the door. "Don't come with me, Tom. It would make it just that much more difficult to say goodbye."

***

Two days later, Tom had recovered sufficiently from Bianca's rejection of him to visit the downtown building housing The Mexico City Banking Association. The association was on the third floor of a nine story building ringed with outer windows around the suites on each floor. A large kiosk stood opposite the entrance on the first floor, and was occupied by a pretty young brunette in a red suit coat and matching skirt. Tom approached her and was met with a large smile and gleaming white teeth.

Suddenly, he stopped walking as a spicy, warm, rich scent reached his nostrils. His eyes opened wide as he remembered the cologne worn by Carlos in the run down hotel room where he transferred three million dollars to the kidnappers' offshore account.

"Are you all right, sir?" the young woman asked, concerned about the perplexed look on Tom's face.

"Can you smell the men's cologne hanging in the air?" he asked.

"Yes," she replied in a rather confused tone of voice.

"The man wearing it must have just walked by here. Do you remember him at all?"

"No, sir. There's a continual parade of men walking by and getting on the elevators," she responded.

"Oh. Well, thanks anyway." Tom turned and prepared to walk to the bank of elevators.

"I know the name of the cologne if that's what you're curious about," she said.

Bradshaw nearly jumped in the air. Wide-eyed, he returned to the kiosk. "Really!"

"My husband uses it now and then. It's called St. Johns Bay Rum Cologne. I bought him a bottle for Christmas. It's made on Saint Thomas Island in the U. S. Virgin Islands. I bought it on Amazon," she explained.

"My name is Tom Bradshaw. Here's my business card. If you ever come in contact with the man who wears St. Johns cologne, give me a call. But it has to be our secret. I think my wife has been around him too often," Tom said in a very quiet voice, almost whispering.

"Well, that explains it," she said, speaking in a low voice back to him.

"I'll see that you get a two hundred dollar gift card to your favorite restaurant if you can locate him for me."

"That sounds great," the pretty young woman said. "My nose will be on the lookout."

They chatted for a few minutes, and she introduced herself

as Samantha Rosario before Tom took the elevator to the third floor. He sniffed carefully, but no bay rum scent was evident.

He entered the association's suite of offices and told the receptionist he was there for an appointment with Association President Arturo Cervantes. Forty minutes later, he followed a secretary inside to Cervantes' private office.

"Sit down," Cervantes said after a brief handshake. "Why is it you're here?"

Bradshaw sensed that Cervantes had agreed to the meeting only because Victor Chapa had requested that he do so.

"Thanks for seeing me. I'm here because a large number of bankers have been kidnapped over the past two years in Mexico City. This is the only organization that all of them belong to," Tom explained.

Cervantes was tall for a Mexican, slightly over six feet, had a long thin face and small dark eyes. His black moustache and matching goatee blended with his dark suit and tie.

"You have the nerve to come here and accuse my organization of somehow being involved in the kidnappings? Are you crazy?" Cervantes blurted out.

"No, I'm not saying that," Tom replied.

"We carefully guard all the information in our files. If the kidnappers have acquired facts about certain bankers, it certainly didn't come from us." Cervantes growled.

Bradshaw decided to quit being nice and polite. "How would you know? Money can buy information from any organization, private or political, including yours."

Cervantes jumped up from behind his desk. "How dare you make accusations like that?!"

"I'm just gathering information."

"Well, gather it someplace else," Cervantes said loudly.

Tom stood up, preparing to leave. "One of the kidnappers was traced to this building."

Cervantes squinted, and his face jerked forward. "Where

did you obtain that information?"

"I'm not at liberty to say. But it's pretty evident that the leak is in your office, or your computer system has been hacked. Either way, the information came from here."

"That's crazy," Cervantes said. An alarmed look was frozen on his face.

"I'm a kidnap and ransom negotiator who's responsible for bringing most of these bankers back from the dark side of hell. I've been asked by a group of banks involved to try to gather as much information as possible," Tom explained.

"I don't have any information for you," Cervantes stated.

"When the case is broken, and the kidnappers are either killed or captured, I think you will be held accountable for refusing to help authorities," Bradshaw said in a hard voice.

Cervantes tripped over his chair and nearly fell. He stood up straight, smoothed his suit, and tried to look professional. "What is it you want?" he asked in a strained voice as he sat down.

"What is it exactly that your association does?" Tom asked.

Cervantes cleared his throat. "We represent the banking sector's general interests and provide communication between the banks."

Tom thought for a moment. "Then it's like our lobbyists in Washington, striving to present an industry in the most favorable light."

"Well, somewhat."

"How many members do you presently have?"

"About two thousand. Then there's another five hundred or so associates that don't have voting rights, nor do they have access to our computer files. People from industries like insurance, manufacturing, and so on are members," Cervantes replied. "We have gala events twice a year at major hotel convention centers that are well attended."

"Who has access to your computer system and the banking

representatives?" Tom asked.

"Every member can go online and contact other members. Many banks use it for job searches when they are hiring," Cervantes pointed out.

Tom groaned. "So kidnappers can gain just about any information they want if they use a banker's username and password."

"Well, I suppose so. I never thought of it that way," Cervantes said.

CHAPTER 29

Angelina Ramirez, the granddaughter of the richest man in Mexico, was anything but an Angel. She lost her virginity at fourteen and had sampled men of all shapes and sizes since that first encounter with a chauffeur on the backseat of her grandfather's Rolls Royce.

She now was a bombshell with large breasts, a nineteen-inch waist, and long, gorgeous legs. Her light brown eyes sparkled with mischief. Angelina had her pick of the boys at the university, where she was a freshman. She majored in young men, parties, and excitement. In her eyes, the world was a fantastic place in which to play and have fun and occasionally go to class.

Felix Ramirez implemented every recommendation Tom Bradshaw made pertaining to protecting his relatives from kidnappers. On campus, Angelina was protected by a high-level bodyguard who followed her discreetly wherever she went. Her attempts to seduce him thus far had been unsuccessful, but she continued to work on him.

Nights were party-time for Angelina, and the security detail was increased to two men who followed her every step. It was decided by the family that bodyguards would provide chauffeur service at night to keep the wild child, as Angelina was nicknamed, from totaling another sports car.

Angelina and four of her sorority sisters were riding in her grandfather's Cadillac Escalade, heading to the first of the lively nightclubs they would frequent that Saturday evening. Two bodyguards, Axel and Felipe, were in the front seat. The vivacious young women dressed in short mini-skirts and high heels were moving around on the second and third rows of seats like playful kittens.

Felix had given strict orders that no liquor was allowed in the Escalade. Angelina took a flask from her purse and passed it around among the girls. The giggling, laughing, and occasional shrieks got louder as the girls got an early buzz on.

Their first stop was at La Strada. The LED-lit entry staircase took them up to the first of four floors of uninterrupted classic Mexican pop songs intermixed with an occasional EDM or Pitbull banger. The DJ booth was raised and situated in front of a massive video wall that pulsed to the beat of the music. Disco balls synced up with the projectors and danced along with the videos on the screens.

A sparsely clad young man arrived inside a cake that sprang open as he delivered drinks to the delighted young ladies, whose fake IDs were done to perfection. They soon attracted a crowd of young men with chiseled jawlines and gym bodies, drawn by the magnetic allure of dense fragrances emanating from the young, sexy women. Soon they were all dancing, letting their emotions run free as testosterone ruled.

The bodyguards, Axel and Felipe, had a difficult time keeping up with Angelina, who danced on one floor and then moved up to the next. She would disappear among the crush of young people, only to reappear on a different part of the dance floor with a new dance partner. The security team split up, attempting to circle in different directions as it became more and more difficult to keep her in view.

An hour later, the inebriated women were off to another nightclub. Following was a carload of young men, equally tipsy.

They would stay for a half hour or forty-five minutes, then move on to the next nightclub.

When they reached PM Nights, the group took a glass-enclosed elevator to the third floor. Translucent tables changed colors, and the ceiling and walls were decked out with multi-colored LEDs that pulsated to an electronic music explosion. The music magic washed over the young people, creating constant dancing and champagne drinking.

"In the future, we need a couple more bodyguards," Axel told Felipe. "I'm exhausted just trying to keep up with Angelina. She can disappear faster than a loose dog."

"Yeah. If someone wanted to snatch her, this would be the ideal time. It's really difficult just keeping her in sight."

Angelina returned to the first floor and began dancing with a tall, very handsome young man, whose smile intrigued her. The light brown haired man pulled her up against him on the dance floor, and Angelina suddenly was filled with desire.

"Is there any place we can be alone?" he said.

"There might be down the hallway to the women's room. I have to go, anyway," she said, a come-hither expression on her face. She pulled away, made her way through the crowd, and walked down the corridor to the women's room. Minutes later, she exited, and the young man was waiting.

"We can go through here for privacy," he said as he kissed her passionately.

He opened the door, she walked through and suddenly stopped. "We're outside," she said. "I don't want to leave my friends."

The man grabbed her by the arm and began pulling her down the alley. "You're coming with me, bitch," he growled.

At the end of the alley, the headlights of a car went on, and the vehicle proceeded towards the pair.

"I'm not going anywhere with you," she yelled and kicked him in the groin.

The abductor doubled over in pain and cried out. Angelina pulled loose and turned around to run back inside just as Felipe opened the door.

"He tried to kidnap me," she said in an indignant voice.

Felipe bent over and pulled a pistol from an ankle holster. He also pushed Angelina behind him just as a shot was fired from the oncoming car. It ricocheted off the brick building, and the bodyguard returned the fire. His bullet went through the front windshield, and the car halted. The amorous snatcher hobbled, bent over towards the vehicle.

The bodyguard hurriedly pulled the girl back inside the nightclub just as his partner arrived.

"They tried to snatch her," Felipe said in a loud voice.

"I need to get back to the girls. They'll be wondering where I am," Angelina said in a nonchalant voice.

Felipe was on his cell phone asking for backup.

"The evening's over for you," Axel told her. "We'll stay inside the club until help arrives. Then we'll take you home."

"Oh, come on, Axel. There's still plenty of time left to party."

They walked through the crowd to the front door, and Angelina sent a bouncer to locate her companions. When they arrived, barely able to stand, she told them what had happened. One shrieked and began to cry. Another laughed loudly and clapped her hands with glee. The other two looked stunned.

Minutes later, four security men arrived, and a caravan of vehicles escorted Angelina back to her home. The mansion was ablaze with light, and security officers were everywhere. The story she told was somewhat different from actual events but close enough. Her parents praised her for her bravery. She smiled as she hugged her mother, thinking it had been great fun.

***

"I don't know what to do. I can't put a leash on her," a worried grandfather told Tom. "I'm open to ideas. Anything at this point. She's forever trying to ditch her bodyguards."

"She's high-spirited and has no sense of mortality," Tom noted.

They sat in Felix Ramirez's small, private office. "My son doesn't know what to do with Angelina, and his wife doesn't have a clue. They look to me to find an answer," he said in his low gravelly voice. "What about sending her to school somewhere else?"

"I'm afraid that wouldn't work. She'd be just as wild there, and you'd have no control." Tom replied.

"Yes, you're right," Felix admitted. His silver-grey hair hung down around his ears, and his large, very piercing eyes looked worried.

"I could try to frighten her. I can explain things that have happened to other kidnap victims that are difficult to imagine. It might catch her attention," Tom explained.

"Sure. I'm willing to try anything at this point. She's in the large conference room waiting for me to take her to lunch. She acquiesced to my request that she have lunch with me so we could talk. She probably looks at it as being penance."

Tom smiled. "I'm anxious to meet her."

"She's like a stick of dynamite waiting to go off. There's a sweet side to her also. She loves animals and has two dogs and two cats that her parents have now inherited since she's off to college."

The two men walked into the large conference room. Felix introduced them and told Angelina he would return following a conference call. On his way out, he turned on the intercom so he could listen from his office.

Angelina looked cute in a green mini-skirt and white blouse. The attire was as formal as she could find in her wardrobe. Her light brown hair fell to her shoulders in ringlets, and her smile revealed beautiful white teeth. Angelina's light brown eyes sparkled with mischief.

They chatted informally for a few minutes before Tom got down to business. She knew how to cross her shapely, long legs to disrupt Bradshaw's concentration and did so.

"Angelina, I'm a kidnap and ransom negotiator. If you or any of your relatives are kidnapped, I would immediately handle all communications between the family and the snatchers and try to get you released as quickly as possible."

"My grandfather has talked about you. He likes you, and he doesn't like many people," she said as she uncrossed and crossed her legs again.

"If you are kidnapped and finally released, you'll never get back to normal. You'll try, but you'll feel vulnerable forever. Life as you knew it before would be over," he emphasized.

"I think you're trying to frighten me," she said.

"Women, and particularly beautiful women such as yourself, are very vulnerable. The kidnappers could take turns raping you until your mind is shattered. It's happened before."

The smile faded from her lips.

Tom continued. "When you're kidnapped, it's like you've been taken and nailed in a box. In one case, that's exactly what happened. He was in a fetal position in a small box and was only let out to eat and piss in a pail, then he was put back in. He fought them at first, then pretty much gave up on life."

Angelina's eyes were riveted on Tom. "You're just trying to frighten me." She got up as if to end the conversation.

"Sit down," Tom commanded.

She reluctantly did so and crossed her arms across her chest.

"In most cases, you're alone in a dark room. You're left there in silence and darkness while the rest of the world goes on with their lives. In some ways, being kidnapped is worse than murder. At least with murder, you're dead and not being tortured by the hour in absolute darkness," Tom said in a hard voice.

Angelina stared at Tom but said nothing.

"When I get you back, you'll have some really dark moments. You'll have psychological scars from this horrible captivity for the rest of your life. You'll see a psychiatrist twice a week at the beginning of your transition back to the real world. It can go on for months."

The dynamic young woman and the dedicated negotiator gazed at each other. Angelina uncrossed her arms.

"Are you married?" she asked.

Tom growled softly and looked at the ceiling as if seeking divine guidance. He got up from his chair. "Wait here. I'll get your grandfather."

Bradshaw walked into Felix's private office and sat down opposite his desk. Ramirez shook his head from side to side.

"You didn't scare her, but you frightened the hell out of me. You didn't tell me these things in our earlier conversations," Felix said.

"If I had, you'd have been much more worried. As it turned out, I was left with no alternative but to try to frighten some sense into her. I don't think it worked."

Felix's large dark eyes registered alarm as he stared at Tom. "Will they really gang rape her over and over again?"

"It has happened. But I have an idea about how to keep that from happening in this case," Tom replied.

The two men talked for another five minutes before Ramirez asked if there was any way to lessen the effects of a kidnapping.

"Yes, and that's to leave the country. The most incredible feeling for Angelina would be the day she goes to the airport, passes through security, and boards a plane for the United States. Then she'll be completely free. When she reaches the United States, assuming that's where she wants to go, she'll just walk. She won't have to visit cathedrals, museums, fancy restaurants, or thunderous nightclubs. She'll just walk. It'll be wonderful to be free and without fear."

"Jesus Christ, Tom. We're talking about her as if she's already been kidnapped," the usually self-confident, dynamic businessman blurted out. The forceful leader with hundreds of thousands of employees looked defeated. His head dropped to his chest, and he exhaled sharply.

Bradshaw realized his outline of kidnapping events that could occur didn't faze Angelina but tore at her grandfather's heartstrings.

"You've done everything you can to protect your family. If a family member is kidnapped, you'll feel guilt, but it's not your fault. You can't be a universal savior for everyone. Life doesn't work that way," Tom emphasized.

"I love her so much. She's beautiful, spirited, and intelligent and loves to have a good time. I just watch her and smile," Felix said.

"Let's go back into the conference room. I'll have another short talk with her with you being present," Tom recommended.

"All right."

They walked into the room and sat down on either side of Angelina, who was busy doing her nails. She looked up and smiled. "This looks like an ambush to me."

"We're not here to force you to do anything. I'd like to ask you a few questions so I can better understand you and your feelings," Tom replied.

Their eyes locked, and she shrugged her shoulders. "Go ahead."

"You try to ditch the bodyguards every chance you get. Why?" he asked.

Angelina stopped painting her nails and thought for a moment. "It's like they're always around, like they're seeing everything I do and say. It's like I have no private life."

"It sounds as if you're rebelling because of a lack of privacy," he pointed out.

"That's part of it. Do you know how hard it is for me to

develop a relationship with a guy? It's like everything I say and do is being studied by the security men," Angelina said in an angry voice. "I'm tired of it."

"You've made some good points. Your grandfather could pull the bodyguards back so they would watch you from a distance. They wouldn't hear anything you say. But in return, you'd have to stop ditching them so the broader protective screen would work," Bradshaw emphasized.

"What about if I'd want to be alone with a guy?"

"Tell the bodyguards where you're going and if you'll be there all night. They don't care if you're with a boyfriend. They just want to know where you are so they can protect you, even at night. They will follow you to your destination, but discreetly."

"That's a possibility," she replied.

"Think of bodyguards as chauffeurs. Learn to use them. If you and your girlfriends want to go shopping, let the bodyguards chauffeur you. If you and your sorority sisters want to go to the beach over spring break, let the bodyguards drive you in a limo," Tom pointed out.

Angelina's eyes opened wide as she suddenly thought of the possibilities. "Let's try it."

Tom was invited to have lunch with Felix and his granddaughter. The exclusive restaurant was known for its ten-course tasting meal and burnt corn ice cream for dessert. Bradshaw had crisp-skinned trout with clams, peas, and wild spinach. Looking at the menu, he noted that there were no prices.

The men were kept laughing by Angelina's antics. Ramirez could see that his granddaughter took more than a passing interest in Tom and continually flirted with him.

"You didn't answer my question, are you married?" she asked again.

"I'm...I was seriously involved with a Spanish lady from Madrid. There were some problems, but I think we may end up together," Tom said.

"It sounds as if it's up in the air," Angelina said.

Tom had a pained look on his face. Felix looked away, trying to mask a grin.

"It's really complicated and difficult to explain," Tom said. He looked at Felix for help, but none was forthcoming. At the end of lunch, Angelina excused herself and went to the ladies room. Felix and Tom stood nearby and chatted while they waited.

"I'll be leaving California Fidelity in the near future. It's time for me to move on. I'll make sure you have a couple of top negotiators to choose from when selecting my replacement," he said.

"What do you want to do next?" Felix asked.

"I'm just completing a global economics degree online at The University of Southern California. Although lately, I've been too busy to finish the remaining courses," Tom said.

"Your strong points are analysis and negotiations. I'd love to have you join my corporation," Ramirez emphasized. "Whenever you're ready, come and see me."

They chatted for a few minutes. Both men began looking at the women's restroom door, wondering why Angelina had not come out. Felix signaled a waitress and asked her to check on his granddaughter. A minute later, she exited the ladies room and told Felix that no women were in the restroom.

"My God, she's gone," Ramirez said loudly, a look of disbelief on his face. He signaled with his hand, and three bodyguards came on the run. "Did you see where Angelina went?" he asked them in a worried voice. None of them had seen her leave, they said.

"Tom, could someone have grabbed her?" he asked in an anxious voice.

Before Bradshaw could answer, Angelina jumped out from behind a floor to ceiling set of drapes.

"Surprise!" she yelled and laughed at the expressions on the faces of the assembled group of worried men.

CHAPTER 30

Sergio Ramirez, the son of Felix Ramirez' brother, Sebastian, was one of the billionaire's favorite relatives. Sergio was short, clean shaven, and always dressed in a dark suit and tie. He had worked his way upward in the corporate structure through hard work, tenacity, and solid decision making. Currently, he was in charge of Ramirez Enterprises' chain of oil companies. Sergio was mild-mannered, somewhat introverted, and very much in love with his charming wife of one year.

He and his bodyguard took the elevator to the basement parking garage at 4 p.m., got into his new Honda Accord, and proceeded to drive the route they normally followed to his beautiful home in an upscale gated community. Sergio's driver/bodyguard always took a shortcut, crossing two major boulevards on a narrow two-lane street to save time and eliminate traffic congestion.

An old blue van pulled out in front of his car, causing the bodyguard to jam on his brakes. A black SUV came up behind, thereby boxing in the Honda. A masked man carrying a sledgehammer ran to the driver's side window and swung hard, smashing out the entire window, covering the bodyguard with broken glass.

A second kidnapper stuck a shotgun in the broken out

window. "Reach for your gun, and I'll blow your head off," the snatcher yelled.

The bodyguard raised his hands slowly, barely able to move under the blanket of glass shards. A third snatcher opened the passenger side door, reached in, and pulled Sergio from the vehicle. Sergio cried out in terror as he was yanked over to the van and deposited inside.

The second kidnapper grabbed the bodyguard's pistol from his shoulder holster.

"Don't move until we're gone," he was told. The bodyguard was speechless, dozens of pieces of glass biting into his upper torso and face. His eyes moved from side to side, but his head remained frozen in place.

One kidnapper drove the van while a second used duct tape to secure Sergio's hands and legs. The third kidnapper drove away in the SUV.

"If you yell or make any noise, I'll cut your tongue out," a snatcher warned. A black hood was pulled down over his head.

Forty-five minutes later, the vehicles pulled into a long driveway that circled a Spanish-style white adobe home with a red tile roof. Dense trees shielded the house from the road. The older home was in the center of a six-acre parcel with overgrown shrubs, bushes, and trees encircling the entire estate.

Sergio was pulled from the van, and the duct tape was removed from his legs. All three snatchers wore ski masks. His abductors walked him into the beautifully furnished home and into a rear bedroom. They took the duct tape off his wrists and sat him down in an overstuffed chair. Besides the chair, the room contained a queen-sized bed, a large flat screen TV on the wall, and a small table and chairs for eating. Books and magazines were piled on the table.

An interior door led to a small private bathroom complete with a shower, toilet, and free-standing sink. The lone window in the bedroom and the small window in the bathroom had both been professionally boarded up. The kidnappers were planning on running a string of Felix Ramirez's relatives through the safe house, and the leader wanted them kept healthy and reasonably comfortable.

"You can move around this room, watch television, take a shower, and do whatever you want. If you yell, scream, shout, or make noise in any way, you'll be taped up, including your mouth. Do you understand me?" the short, rotund kidnapper growled.

"Yes, I understand," Sergio replied in a frightened voice.

The kidnappers walked out of the bedroom and shut the door. Sergio was shaking, his face white and blood pressure nearing maximum level. He lay down on the bed in a fetal position and moaned.

***

Tom Bradshaw was preparing to board a plane for Los Angeles when he received a call from his boss, Mark Danforth, that Felix Ramirez's nephew, Sergio Ramirez, had been kidnapped. Minutes later, a call came in from the richest man in Mexico telling him the same thing.

An hour later, Tom entered the huge complex of Ramirez office buildings and was escorted to Ramirez's private office.

"I'm glad I caught you before you took off for Los Angeles. Sergio is the hardest working member of my family involved in my corporate dealings. Besides that, he's one of the nicest young men you'll ever meet," Felix emphasized.

Ramirez looked apprehensive, his expression fearful and his anxious movements denoting stress. He explained the particulars of the kidnapping to Tom, who had already heard most of the details from Danforth.

Tom gave orders to two secretaries on how the next door conference room should be set up with recording equipment and additional telephones. The work was completed within an hour. Calls at night regarding the kidnapping would immediately be transferred to Tom's cell phone.

"We'll probably get the first call tomorrow morning. You can let your secretaries go home now," Tom said. "I assume family members are with Sergio's wife."

"Yes. My brother and his wife are comforting her."

"Let's talk for a while," Tom suggested.

Felix dismissed his remaining staff members. He poured two glasses of brandy, and the men sat at the conference table. Tom rested his arms on the mahogany table and looked directly into the entrepreneur's eyes.

"There's been an attempted kidnapping and a successful snatch within a few days of each other. It could be coincidence, but I doubt it," Bradshaw said.

"What are you saying?"

"I'm saying that someone within your corporate structure is providing information to the kidnappers," Tom emphasized. "Tomorrow, I want you to have your private secretary determine if the human resources files on Angelina and Sergio have been viewed lately and by whom."

***

Laura Figueroa had been the private secretary to Felix Ramirez for nearly twenty years and was his most trusted employee. She was almost sixty-five years old, had neatly styled grey hair, and wore conservative dark dresses to work. Laura was soft-spoken, highly intelligent, and totally reliable. Tom agreed with Felix that she was above suspicion and therefore was informed about what had transpired and what they wanted done.

"It's quite possible that files could be secretly accessed. A hacker can steal information and erase his entry," Laura pointed out.

"Who do we have who can do an in depth investigation into the electronic data stored in our computers?" Felix asked.

"No one. It would take the expertise of a digital forensic

examiner. Remember when we had money missing from the cell phone corporation? We had to bring in an examiner named Pasquale Gonzales to find who was secretly stealing the funds," she replied. "He's a strange man but a genius."

"I remember him. He's short, thin, and bald, and has huge ears. The lenses in the glasses he wears look like the bottoms of Coke bottles," Felix said, and smiled. "He found the thief. Can you reach him by phone now?"

"Yes," she responded as she got up from a chair and walked into her office.

"She always has the answers and every bit of information I need, day in and day out. A man never had a better secretary," Felix maintained.

Laura returned in five minutes. "He says he can't provide service for another week. He's so busy. But I had him hold until I talked with you. He's on line four."

Felix punched the button. "Hello, Pasquale. I need your help now. Come over to my office immediately, and I'll pay you four times the going rate. And if you're successful, I'll pay you a five thousand American dollar bonus." After a few seconds, Ramirez hung up. "I think he was running to his car," Felix commented.

Forty-five minutes later, Pasquale Gonzales arrived carrying two large, black equipment cases. They were heavy, and Pasquale was breathing like he'd run a one hundred meter dash. "I'm ready," he gasped.

Felix explained about wanting to know who had gained entry recently into two personnel files and were they accessed by the same man. Second, was a private Ramirez file hacked?

Bradshaw had been quiet, listening to Ramirez explain the situation to Pasquale. The forensic examiner shifted his attention back and forth between Tom and Felix. His head moved forward as he stared through magnifying glasses so thick his brown eyes were four times normal size.

"Who are you?" he growled, looking at Tom.

"I'm Tom Bradshaw, a business associate of Felix Ramirez."

"Has he passed a security check? I don't want just any worker knowing what I'm doing for you," Pasquale said in a malicious voice.

"He's all right, Pasquale. Tom's investigative abilities have resulted in your being here," Felix said.

Pasquale continued to stare at Tom through his Coke bottle lenses. "I've seen you somewhere before."

"That's doubtful," Tom replied.

"Can we get on with the investigation?" Felix said in an authoritarian voice. "Explain a little bit about what you're going to do."

Pasquale muttered to himself, then said, "If a hacker has detailed technical knowledge, he can break into your computer system and steal, alter, or destroy any information. For instance, he can install a key logger and capture every username and password on the keyboard. Then, he can log into your secret file and basically steal everything."

"How do you go about investigating for security breaches?" Tom asked.

"You wouldn't understand if I told you," Pasquale replied in an unpleasant voice. "To simplify it so a child can understand, I'll be using electronic discovery techniques to analyze the information that only a digital forensic expert, like myself, can obtain. I'll be using state of the art technology to determine if a file has been accessed and the entry erased. Then, I'll reproduce the erased entry data."

Bradshaw wanted to wrap his hands around Pasquale's scrawny neck and squeeze, but showed masterful restraint. "Very interesting," he replied.

Pasquale used a second conference room, spread out his equipment on the table, and tied into a corner computer. "Try not to bother me," he said, looking at Tom.

Felix showed him which personnel files he wanted examined, as well as the private electronic file containing the names and information on all relatives and employees covered by California Fidelity's kidnap and ransom insurance policy.

"Is he going to do the work tonight?" Tom asked Felix.

"I guess so," Felix responded.

"I'd like to stay as well," Laura said.

Felix, Tom, and Laura ordered take out dinners, and they were delivered a half hour later. They talked about Felix's extended family, Laura's two sons and six grandchildren, and Tom's desire to marry Bianca in the near future.

The door to Felix's private office opened, and the little man with the elephant ears entered. "I'm done," he announced in a loud voice.

"You are?" Tom exclaimed, eyes wide.

"I have the username and password of the man you're looking for."

"You do?" Felix said in disbelief.

"His tactics and technical knowledge were old school, not up to date. It was easy to reproduce the erased entry data," Pasquale said proudly.

"Did the same man who accessed the personnel files gain entry into Felix's private file?" Tom asked.

"Yes. And, by the way, I remember where I'd seen you before."

"Give the username and password to Laura. She'll match it up with a name," Ramirez told Pasquale.

He handed a slip of paper with the information on it to Laura.

"It was in the lobby of the Hilton Hotel where I saw you. You were dressed in a painter's old clothes and looked like a homeless person. I still remember what you smelled like," Pasquale said loudly. "You stunk."

Felix and Laura had astonished looks on their faces as

their eyes turned to look at Tom. Bradshaw looked horrified as if he'd been struck a powerful blow. His surprise and distress kept him from responding.

"Let's get back to business here," Felix said loudly. "I owe you four times your usual fee of one thousand dollars, so the total is four thousand. Add another five thousand for a job well done. I'll round it off to ten thousand for fast, excellent service. Laura will give you a check."

The little man's face beamed with pride, and he grinned. Laura and Pasquale walked to her office, where she quickly made out a check and signed it.

"You're a woman. Do you have the authority to sign corporate checks?" he asked in a questioning voice.

Laura's grey eyes blazed, but she maintained total control. "Take it and go," she said in a sharp-tongued voice.

Pasquale headed back to the conference room, where he packed up his equipment and walked to the exit door. A guard met him and escorted him to his car.

Laura Figueroa studied the paper containing the username and password. Her mouth dropped open, and her face turned white. "I...I know who this person is," she stammered.

"Who is it?" Felix asked anxiously.

"It's your administrative assistant, Anselmo Garcia," she replied. "There were times I had to do work on his behalf, so he gave me his username and password."

Ramirez groaned. "How could he have done something like that? I pay him an excellent salary."

"He watches you turn millions into billions. Jealousy and a burning desire to become rich have corrupted more than one man," Tom maintained.

"When does he come back from vacation?" Felix asked.

"Day after tomorrow," Laura replied.

"Call him tomorrow and see if he can return a day early. Tell him I have some important work for him to do," Felix responded in a less than enthusiastic voice.

"I will," said Laura.

"Tom, how are we going to...approach the issues?" Felix asked, his face mirroring skepticism.

"Leave it to me to do the questioning. I know exactly how to get information out of him," Tom emphasized in a hard voice.

***

The following morning at nine, Tom and Felix were sitting in the conference room talking when a secretary opened the door. "The call you were expecting is on line three," she said, a worried expression on her face.

"Here we go," Tom said as he switched on the recorder and put the call on speakerphone. "Hello, this is Ajax. I'll be doing the negotiating for Felix Ramirez."

"I don't want to talk with you. Put Felix on the line," a deep baritone voice said loudly.

"I've been hired as a negotiator to handle this transaction. I'll be in the office from eight to five, Monday through Friday. If you call at night or on weekends, it might take longer to switch the call through to me," Tom said in a calm, business-like voice.

"Listen, asshole, put Felix on the line and don't play games," the deep voice commanded.

"We want to give you money for the safe return of Sergio. Remember, my name is Ajax," Tom responded.

"I told you I want to talk with Felix and only Felix. Now put him on the line, or I'll beat the crap out of Sergio and let you hear him scream over the phone," the abductor shouted.

"Once again, my name is Ajax, and I'll be handling the negotiations for Felix Ramirez."

"Go screw yourself," the kidnapper yelled, and hung up.

Felix had a worried look on his face. "Is he really going to beat him?"

"No. Actually, this first conversation went more smoothly than most. There weren't any death threats or any threat to cut off body parts and mail them to you," Tom said. "Often, the first conversation is laced with profanity and threats as the kidnapper tries to show he's in charge."

Felix looked distressed. "What will happen next?"

"He'll call again, probably tomorrow. I made four points during the conversation: who I am, that I'll be doing the negotiating, during what hours he can reach me at the office, and the fact that we want to give him money in exchange for the safe release of Sergio."

Felix was quiet as he reviewed the conversation in his mind. "It's so difficult to think of this as a business transaction, where a person is bought or sold."

***

Anselmo Garcia entered his boss's office at eleven. Dressed in an immaculate, dark blue suit, the handsome, black-haired administrative assistant suddenly stopped when he saw Tom Bradshaw sitting next to Felix Ramirez.

"What's he doing here?" Garcia asked, his unfriendly dark eyes suddenly suspicious as he stared at Bradshaw.

"Sit down. He's going to ask you some questions," Ramirez responded.

"Felix, this guy and I don't get along," Garcia said as he sat down opposite the two men.

"I know. You've told me that. Just answer his questions," Felix said in a firm voice.

The adversaries sized each other up for a few moments. Garcia's expression was one of anger, and his dark eyes looked mean. Bradshaw had his arms crossed across his chest as he studied his opponent.

Tom was perfectly calm, poised, and confident. His mouth was drawn into a hard, grim line as the moment for decisive action arrived. Tom's green eyes bore into Anselmo.

"Why did you access the personnel files on Angelina Ramirez and Sergio Ramirez?" Tom asked in a strong voice.

Garcia was taken aback. His eyes narrowed, and he suddenly looked away. "I don't know what you're talking about," he growled.

"We know that you looked at the files and then erased your username and password. Why did you do that?" Tom asked again.

Garcia grimaced, and he blinked his eyes several times. Anselmo turned his head to the right and looked upward. "I access files every day. I could have looked at their files."

"Why those two files?"

"Felix, do I have to answer these ridiculous questions? This man is a gringo prick," Anselmo said.

"Yes, you do. Answer the question," Felix replied.

"I don't remember," he said through tight, pursed lips.

"Why did you hack into Felix's private file on family members covered by kidnap and ransom insurance?" Tom asked in a steady voice as he continued to fix Anselmo with an unyielding stare.

Garcia jumped to his feet. "I don't have to take this kind of treatment. I've served you faithfully for years. I'm through being insulted by this gringo bastard. I'm through," he yelled and headed for the door.

Anselmo pulled open the door and froze. A bodyguard, the size of a small Fiat, blocked his path. He looked at Anselmo much the way a robin stares at a grub.

"Get over here and sit down," Felix ordered. "You're not going anywhere until we get the information we're after."

Sweat began pouring down Anselmo's forehead and dripped off his nose. His expression was one of terror as he looked from one man to the other.

"You have the opportunity now of giving us the information we want and staying alive. Otherwise, you'll end up feeding worms," Tom said in a harsh voice, his green eyes menacing as he stared at a man who was disintegrating in front of him.

"What do you want to know?" Garcia asked in a barely audible voice. His head dropped to his chest, and he appeared about to cry.

"We know you gave the information about Angelina and Sergio to a kidnapping gang. Who was the person you gave the info to?" Tom barked.

"He'll kill me if I tell you," Garcia said and groaned.

"I'm not going to let you out of here alive unless you cooperate. Now answer the question, goddamn it!" Tom yelled at him.

Felix stared at Tom, hardly recognizing him as being the smooth negotiator he'd come to like and respect.

Anselmo began trembling. His mouth hung open, and saliva began running out. Garcia wiped his mouth on his sleeve. "His name is Ivan Ortega."

Felix sat up in his chair. "The racehorse man?"

"Yes," Anselmo said quietly.

Ramirez looked at Tom. "He breeds racehorses. A few years ago, his horses were winning big-time. I haven't heard much about him winning lately."

"Why would he get involved in a kidnapping ring?" Tom asked Garcia.

"He needs money badly," Anselmo said.

"I used to play the horses and got to know people in the industry," Felix said to Tom. "It takes a lot of money to keep a large breeding ranch operating. His horses haven't won lately, so I guess it's hard to find buyers for his stock."

"So, he has financial problems," Tom reasoned. "How did you get to know him?"

Anselmo began rubbing one hand with the other. "He approached me at the race track. We became friends, and he asked if I would like to make a million dollars or more on a continuing basis."

"Weren't you suspicious at all?" Tom asked.

"Sure, but he's a very good salesman. Little by little, he won me over to the idea that I could supply information about Felix's family, and we could make tens of millions of dollars together. And he said none of the Ramirez family members would be harmed. They're to be kept in hotel-like accommodations," Anselmo pointed out. His eyes darted from one man to the other, looking for absolution.

"Was the kidnapping attempt on Angelina the first venture by Ivan Ortega and his gang?" Tom asked.

"Yeah. They were just getting started. She fought like a she-devil and got away," Anselmo related. "Ivan wasn't about to let that happen again."

"Where are the captors holding Sergio?" Felix asked.

Anselmo thought for a moment. "I don't know the location. I know he leased an estate for privacy to hold the Ramirez family members as they're abducted. He wanted to do it over and over again."

"What else do you know about the location?" Tom asked.

"It's not too far from his horse ranch. That's all I know," Anselmo said.

"All right, here's what you're going to do. You'll come to the office each day and spend it with me in the conference room. You'll answer all your phone calls and pretend everything is normal. Hopefully, you'll get a call from Ivan Ortega so we can possibly gain more information about Sergio and his whereabouts. If you do everything you're told, I'll see to it that you're able to leave Mexico alive," Tom declared.

Felix leaned forward in his chair. "If you try to run, I'll send a death squad after you," the entrepreneur promised.

"I won't run, I promise," Anselmo said in a worried voice.

CHAPTER 31

Security expert Maximiliano "Max" Santos sat in Felix's office later that day listening as Tom and Felix explained about the kidnapping and showed him photos of Ivan Ortega. The pictures of Ortega at the race track and at his horse ranch had just been emailed to Felix.

"I've seen him at the race track," Max said. "He's a big guy, flamboyant, and likes to talk about his horse racing expertise. He stands out in a crowd because of his size and the fact that he always wears white suits."

"Do you play the horses?" Tom asked.

"No. But over the years, I've been a bodyguard to a lot of men who do. It's really an elitist sport," Max maintained. "So I'm familiar with the Hippodromo of the Americas and its huge clubhouse and grandstand that seats twenty thousand people. The stable area can accommodate seventeen hundred horses."

"I had no idea it was that large," Tom said.

"Do you have any more questions about what we want you to do?" Felix asked in an impatient manner.

"No. My men and I will find him this afternoon and begin following him. He should take us to the estate they're using to hold Sergio," Max said.

Max was tall and had a manicured moustache and dark

eyes that focused intently on whoever he was talking to. He'd been a police officer, a Mexican army officer involved in fighting drug cartels, and a private bodyguard before Felix hired him to head his security division. His primary focus was to protect the Ramirez Enterprises' two square block concentration of three-story glass and steel buildings.

The flow of people in and out of the complex was done smoothly with everything captured on film. Security personnel dressed in dark blue uniforms were everywhere, especially at the entrances and exits. Thus far, his security plan was functioning flawlessly. Employees felt safe within the confines of the gigantic corporate headquarters complex, and visitors were quickly escorted to their destinations.

Tom and Felix continued to discuss the kidnapping. Everything had transpired quickly involving the kidnapping of Sergio and the discovery that one of Felix's most trusted employees was a traitor. Felix was still trying to grasp the reality of the situation. For the third time that day, he asked Tom if he thought Ivan Ortega would call again soon.

"I think he will tomorrow morning if he's the point man," Tom replied. "I believe he is."

"Maybe we should just pay him and bring Sergio home," Felix said. "My family is terribly upset, the women are crying, the men are damn near hysterical, and they're all over me."

"No, Felix, we can't. Ivan Ortega, or whoever the lead snatcher is, will ask for a huge amount of money to open negotiations. They'll want to see just how easily persuaded you might be."

"What's your guess about the first monetary demand?" Felix asked.

"One hundred million, or maybe even one hundred and fifty million."

Ramirez's mouth fell open. "Oh my God."

"The figure will drop down to reality in a very short time

after we counter back," Tom explained.

Felix looked as if he hadn't slept the previous night. He exhaled sharply and took another sip of his coffee, the fifth cup that day. "There's just no end to the pressure right now. They cry and plead, and it makes me feel like I'm partly to blame."

"You're in the unenviable position of being the patriarch of a large family. Your relatives all look to you to solve their most difficult problems. Normally, when a man is kidnapped, let's say a banker, his family relies on the support of relatives, and they keep in close contact with me. But they can't cry, scream, and shout at me. I'm a business professional, not a family member," Tom pointed out.

"Any suggestions?" Felix asked.

"No. But you're tough, resilient, and intelligent. Just handle each call from a relative in a business-like manner. That's all you can do. Except for one thing," Tom said.

"What's that?" Felix asked in an anxious voice.

"Turn your phone off when you go to bed."

***

The following morning the call from the kidnapper came in at nine.

"Hello, this is Ajax."

"Goddamn it. I told you I want to talk with Felix. Now put him on the line."

"I've been hired to handle the negotiations for Felix. We do want to pay you money for the safe return of Sergio," Tom said in a calm voice.

"Shit," the snatcher growled. "I guess I'll have to deal with you. I want eighty million dollars American for Sergio."

"I'll pass that on to Felix. You'll have an answer within twenty-four hours," Tom replied and prepared to hang up the phone.

"Why does it take so long to get an answer?" the kidnapper asked in his deep, baritone voice.

Tom was taken aback, and his expression mirrored surprise. "If you want to call back in two hours, I'll try to have an answer for you."

"Tell Felix not to screw around with me. I'm ready to beat the shit out of that kid to prove that I'm serious."

"I'll tell him," Tom responded.

The line went dead, and Tom leaned back in his chair. Felix's eyes were wide as he stared at Tom.

"Interesting," Tom said as he pondered the conversation.

"What do you mean?" Felix asked. "He's threatening to hurt Sergio again."

"Sergio will be okay. Generally speaking, kidnappers will throw out a dollar amount and hang up. This gang leader wants a quick negotiation. He doesn't even want to wait twenty-four hours for a response," Tom pointed out. "My guess is that he needs money and needs it now."

"How should we counter the eighty million dollar demand?" Ramirez asked.

"I'd recommend eight million."

Felix's eyes opened wide, and his head jerked backwards. "Are you joking? That's only ten percent of the asking price. I don't want Sergio to be harmed because they think I'm not negotiating in good faith."

"I'd recommend less if you were someone other than Felix Ramirez. The kidnappers have stars in their eyes. They have to be brought back to reality. Sergio won't be harmed. He's just a commodity to them," Tom maintained.

"I don't want him to be hurt," Felix said loudly.

"He's already emotionally injured. Sergio will never be the same again. We discussed the aftermath of a kidnapping and how victims are psychologically scarred for life," Tom said in a business-like voice.

"I'm putting my trust in you. I'm relying on you. I feel… helpless," Felix said in an anxious voice. He allowed Tom to see his vulnerable side when no one else was allowed the same privilege.

The next two hours were difficult for both men. Felix had to deal with both his corporate issues and calls from his wife and other relatives. As the workday progressed, he began to look increasingly stressed. Anxiety made his facial features sag.

Tom's main emphasis was on trying to calm Felix and give him the emotional support necessary to survive until the next phone call from the gang leader arrived. It came in precisely at 11 a.m.

"This is Ajax."

"Well, what's his response?"

"He's willing to pay you eight million dollars American. There's a lot you can do with eight million dollars," Tom replied.

"You tell that lousy, rotten son-of-a-bitch that I'm going to pulverize his piss-ant nephew. The next thing you're going to hear are screams over the phone," the captor yelled.

Undeterred by shouts from the gang leader, Tom continued in his usual business-like manner. "Remember, this is a negotiation. Mr. Ramirez is willing to go higher, but he has to hear what your counteroffer is first. Do you have a figure? If so, I hope it's realistic. You can have the ransom money in your hands in twenty-four hours."

The snatcher was breathing hard on the other end of the line. "I'll call you back in an hour," he growled, and hung up.

Tom hung up the phone and smiled. "We're getting closer."

***

Previously, Max Santos was parked some distance from Ivan Ortega's home near his cattle ranch. Santos's reconnaissance officer, Paco Perez, was in the car with him. He'd been watching the gang leader's house since Ortega arrived home at ten the previous night.

"He hasn't gone anywhere, boss," Perez said.

The men sat in Perez's silver Camry drinking coffee and eating donuts. An hour later, Ivan Ortega exited the home, dressed in one of his numerous white suits, and climbed into his red Lexus. He peeled out of the driveway and headed down the street at a high rate of speed. The security men followed at a distance.

Ivan turned down a side street and then turned onto a gravel road. The horse farm owner stopped in front of an iron gate, got out, and pulled the gate open. He drove through, stopped, and returned to close the gate, then got back in his car and drove forward. Ivan's Lexus disappeared through the trees surrounding the property.

The Camry stopped in front of the gate. "I'll go in here. You drive to the end of the property and work your way around to the rear. Let's figure out what we're dealing with here," Max told Perez. "I'll meet you back here in half an hour."

The surveillance concluded, and the men were back at the starting point thirty minutes later. Max Santos got back in Paco Perez's car, and they parked a quarter mile down the road.

"What do you think?" Max asked.

"There's one man patrolling the outside. Ain't much security there," Perez noted.

"It looks like a safe house to me. There's three cars there, including the red Lexus. It means there's two, probably three snatchers using this house as a base of operations. Smart. It's pretty isolated, yet close to Ivan Ortega's home and horse farm," Max pointed out.

"What do you want me to do?" Paco asked.

"Keep following him. I'm going to go talk with Felix Ramirez. I think we can bust in anytime and take the man who's being held captive. We'll see if he wants us to do it," Max replied.

***

A secretary opened the door and looked at Tom. "Mr. Ajax, a man is on line three for you."

Felix stiffened in his chair, his back rigid and eyes wide. Tom picked up the phone and pushed the button. "This is Ajax."

"I want forty million, and don't screw around with me," the deep voice demanded.

"I've been authorized to give you ten million dollars. That's a lot of cash that can be in your pocket in twenty-four hours. Think of what you can do with ten million," Tom said.

"Goddamn you, you son-of-a-bitch. I'm going to bust up Sergio. You need to hear him scream over the phone. I'm through playing games," the voice shouted.

"I'd like you to think about this for a minute. As a negotiator, the most money I've ever paid out was three million dollars for a banker. You'll be getting more than three times that amount for a relative who's not part of the immediate family. So think about having all that money in your hands tomorrow. We'll make the swap wherever you want, whenever you want," Tom insisted.

The gang leader was silent. Tom could hear labored breathing on the other end of the line. Felix also was breathing hard.

"All right, here's the deal. I want twelve million. There won't be any more negotiating. If I don't get twelve, I'll begin breaking his bones," the kidnapper growled.

Tom pointed his finger at Felix. The patriarch mouthed the word, "Yes."

"All right, you've got a deal. How do you want to make the exchange?" Tom asked.

The man on the other end of the line exhaled sharply. "There's a truck stop on highway fifty where it intersects with route seven, south of Mexico City about twenty-five miles. Be at the payphone at noon tomorrow. I'll give you directions from there. If I see anyone resembling a cop or security man, I'll cut Sergio's dick off and mail it to Felix. Got that, asshole?"

"I understand. I'll come alone with duffle bags filled with

cash. I'm tall and will be wearing a light tan suit," Tom said.

"All right," Ivan responded, and hung up.

"Oh my God, it's over," Felix said in a relieved voice. "I thought we'd never reach this point."

Tom took a deep breath and relaxed in his chair. "It's time to round up the money, Felix."

"Not a problem," he said, and began a series of phone calls to his banks.

They ate a catered lunch, and within an hour, the details for obtaining the cash had been worked out.

CHAPTER 32

A short while later, a secretary opened the door to the conference room and announced that Max Santos had arrived. Santos entered the room, along with his second-in-command, Paco Perez.

"We found what we think is the safe house. It matches the description that Anselmo Garcia gave you. We followed Ivan Ortega to the home earlier today," Max told Felix and Tom.

Perez explained that there was one kidnapper making the rounds outside the home. It would be comparatively easy to subdue the guard and simultaneously smash through the front and rear doors, he claimed. "We can get the kidnap victim back without a great deal of effort," Paco maintained.

Tom was suddenly alarmed. "We just concluded the kidnap negotiations and agreed upon a price for the safe return of Sergio tomorrow."

Felix got up from his chair. He walked slowly around the conference room table, deep in thought. When he reached Tom, he stopped. "What do you think, Tom?"

"We've discussed the fact that kidnap victims are sometimes injured or killed during rescue operations," Tom pointed out. "My advice to you would be to pay the ransom."

The richest man in Mexico continued walking slowly

around the table. "The agreed upon ransom, itself, is not a real issue. It's hardly a blip in my bottom line. I guess it's a question of moral values. Do I want to pay these bastards for returning my nephew? Or do we take him back using force because they're morally corrupt?"

Felix continued walking, still trying to make a decision. Tom stood up and blocked Felix's path around the table.

"If something unforeseen happens, you'll never forgive yourself for not going ahead and paying the ransom," Tom said quietly.

Felix looked at his head of security. Max Santos's eyes glittered. "I don't think there'll be a problem. We might have to pop a couple of the snatchers, but we should be able to retrieve him unharmed. The kidnappers will be so occupied during the assault that Sergio will be left alone," Santos said in a determined voice.

Felix looked from Tom to Max. "One man is a negotiator, and the other is an action taker. Which do I go with?" he said, and sat down again. "Give me a moment alone."

Tom, Max, and Paco Perez left the room and entered a smaller conference room and sat down. They talked about the negotiations, and Max was surprised that Tom had gotten the gang leader to agree to twelve million. Tom questioned the two men about the safe house and how they would implement the rescue. It seemed to be a sound, operable plan, he thought. Finally, the men became quiet, each caught up in his own thoughts.

Five minutes later, a secretary opened the door. "He's ready for you now," she said. The men returned to the larger conference room and sat down.

Felix's large, piercing brown eyes were framed by his salt and pepper colored hair that hung down around his ears. His silver and black moustache and goatee completed the picture of a dynamic businessman, determined and unafraid.

"I've made up my mind. Go ahead with the rescue,

Max. Tom, I'm sorry. You've worked tirelessly to arrange for Sergio's release. I just want to nail these rotten bastards," Felix emphasized. "They've made my life miserable over the past few days. My family members are distraught, and, according to you, Sergio's future life is permanently damaged."

Tom appeared outwardly calm and poised as he stared at Felix. The hours of intense investigation and negotiation were over, and the decision had been made to attempt a rescue. Ensuing events were now in the hands of others. The resilience of his character was visible in the way he accepted defeat without recrimination. He nodded his head in understanding.

Felix waited for Tom to make a comment. None came forth. "I know it's a blind choice, a leap in the dark, but I can't see paying those bastards twelve million dollars. It's thanking them for making my life miserable and possibly ruining Sergio's life."

Tom glanced at Max. "What time frame do you have in mind?"

"I think we should hit them tonight just about dusk. They'll want to eat and get comfortable for the evening. The day will have been uneventful for the kidnappers, and their guard should be down. Plus, tomorrow is the big payday," Max pointed out.

"I understand," Tom said.

"Tom, you'll stay with me?" Felix asked.

"Of course I will."

***

Max Santos and his six men moved into position among the trees at the rear of the Spanish-style home with its white stucco walls and red tile roof. They watched the fat guard make infrequent circles around the house before sitting down each time in a lounge chair near the front door. The bearded kidnapper appeared bored and tired from his movement throughout the morning and afternoon. He began frequently checking his watch as it came time for him to be relieved.

The assault team members were dressed in sand and

green patterned combat fatigues similar to those worn by the U. S. Army. His men also wore bulletproof vests and brown military boots so that there would be no mistaking rescuers for kidnappers when the fighting began.

Santos used his pocket-sized two-way radio and contacted his men. "I'll give the go ahead in sixty seconds, so be ready," he said quietly into the radio. A minute passed, and he gave the order. Three men moved stealthily towards the rear door. The other three security members circled the home and stuck their guns in the face of the surprised snatcher. The kidnapper's eyes opened wide as he raised his hands.

"Don't shoot," he pleaded as they disarmed him.

"Is the front door locked?" Max asked.

The short, fat gang member's lower jaw quivered. "Yes."

"How many kidnappers are in there?"

"Three. Please don't kill me," he said as sweat drained down his face and dripped from his beard.

"Where are they likely to be inside the house?"

"Probably in the living room watching TV or playing cards on a game table," the guard replied.

"Just keep answering questions, and you'll stay alive. Where is the kidnap victim being held?" Max asked.

"In a bedroom at the rear of the house," the kidnapper said, and began to whimper softly. "I don't want to die."

"Cheer up. I'm not going to kill you. How do you signal that you want to be let inside?"

"Knock on the door three times," the gang member said as he began to shake.

"Go to the door and knock three times when I tell you to," Max instructed.

The assault leader pushed the fat man forward and turned him around so he faced the peephole, then sank to his knees.

"Now," Max ordered.

The bearded guard hesitated. "What should I say?"

"Knock on the door, you son-of-a-bitch. Tell them you have to take a crap."

He knocked on the door, and moments later, a muffled voice asked, "What do you want, Jose?"

"I have to take a crap."

"Can't it wait? Your shift is almost over."

Max jammed his pistol in Jose's back.

"No. It's urgent," he cried out.

Max heard the door being unlocked. As it swung open, he pushed the fat snatcher forward, and he and his men rushed inside. Two of the kidnappers were lounging on a couch watching television. The third man, who had opened the door, fell backwards, a shocked expression on his face.

"Hands in the air, and you won't be harmed," Max shouted.

Both men on the couch jumped to their feet, grabbed pistols from their holsters, and prepared to fire. The assault team started shooting. Both of the kidnappers were wounded, but one returned fire, striking an attacker in the shoulder. The gang member who had fallen backwards at the front door grabbed his revolver and shot another of Max's men through the head, killing him.

Max and the remaining member of his assault team shot the kidnapper several times, and he went down on the floor. They then turned their attention to the two wounded kidnappers near the couch. One lay motionless on his back. The second gang member pulled himself up to a sitting position just in time to die from repeated bullets to the face and chest. The fat guard lay on his face with his arms crossed over his head.

A long hallway extended from front to back inside the home. A man dressed in a white suit came out from one of the rear bedrooms, took one look at the firefight in progress, and ducked back inside the bedroom.

Then the rear door to the house shattered as more attackers

used a handheld battering ram to demolish the door lock. A second battering ram struck the door frame, and pieces of wood flew inward. Max's men pulled the door open and rushed into the hallway.

Max and his remaining team member ran down the hallway and joined the other group.

"Check that bedroom," Max ordered.

An assault team member opened the door and found it empty. The men then turned their attention to the bedroom on the other side of the hallway. Max tried the doorknob, but the door was locked.

A deep voice yelled at the attackers. "I've got Felix Ramirez's nephew. If anyone comes through that door, I'll kill him."

Inside, Ivan Ortega grabbed Sergio by the arm and pulled him off the bed. The young man began yelling, "Don't hurt me."

"Shut up, you little asshole," Ivan growled. His block-like face mirrored anger as he prepared to use Sergio as a shield. Ivan's eyes were mere slits above his large nose and big cheeks. He snarled like an animal and cocked his pistol.

"Let's do it," Max said loudly when he heard Sergio yelling inside the room.

Max kicked the doorknob, and the flimsy door flew inward. Ivan pulled Sergio in front of him just as Max and his second in command, Paco Perez, fired at the racehorse owner. One of the bullets struck Sergio in the side. A second shot hit Ivan in the throat, causing his eyes to bulge out.

Ivan was dying as he lurched sideways, but his death grip on the trigger caused his pistol to continue firing. One of the bullets hit Paco Perez in the forehead. Ivan stumbled forward, a look of amazement on his face as death closed in.

The tall horse breeder slumped to the floor, blood covering the front of his white suit. The last bullet out of his gun accidentally hit Sergio in the left thigh, striking an artery. Blood began pumping out of the wound.

"Oh my God," Max said in an astonished voice. Seeing that Paco Perez was dead, he rushed over to Sergio and began applying a tourniquet, using his belt to stop the spurting blood coming from his leg.

An emergency medical services ambulance had been standing by and arrived within minutes. They treated Sergio's wounds and checked out Max's wounded team member, who had been shot in the shoulder. Then they headed for the hospital.

Max bent down on one knee and grabbed Paco by the shoulders. He put his arms around his dead companion and held him tightly, crying unashamedly.

Jose, the kidnapper guarding the front of the home, had run out the front door during the firefight and disappeared into the trees. An hour later, Max and two of his men were about four miles from the scene of the shooting, driving towards downtown Mexico City.

"Hey, isn't that the fat kidnapper who let us in the front door?" one of his men asked.

Max studied the snatcher for a moment. "Pull up next to him," Max ordered. "Hop in, buddy, and we'll give you a ride," Max said loudly.

"Oh, thanks. I'm exhausted." Jose slumped in the rear seat next to Max. "Haven't we met someplace before?" the gang member asked.

***

Felix Ramirez and Tom Bradshaw sat in large leather chairs in the patriarch's private office. Ramirez was downing large gulps of whiskey while Bradshaw was sipping a brandy. Max Santos had just left after recounting the bloodbath in play by play format. Two of his men were dead and a third badly injured. Max apologized for the debacle. Felix said the fault did not lie with Max but with his own decision to pursue a rescue.

"I should have listened to you," Felix said in a low, quiet

voice. "If he dies, I'll never forgive myself. I'm going to the hospital now and don't know how to explain my decision to my wife, my brother, and his wife—"

Tom cut off Felix's self-incrimination. "Do you want my opinion on how to move forward?"

"Yes," said Felix, a hint of hope in his voice.

"In life and death situations, there are no standards against which to measure your conduct and decision making. The full weight of your responsibilities are yours alone. I once badly misjudged a gang leader, and he did not like my answers to his questions. He had the victim's index finger delivered to me," Tom said.

"Jesus," Felix replied, and took another drink of whiskey.

"Sergio's young and strong, and Max got him to the hospital in time to save his life. Yes, he's in an intensive care unit, but as the doctor told you over the phone, his condition is stable, and he's resting comfortably. He'll recover," Tom pointed out.

"How do I tell them I could have paid a ransom?" Felix said, his eyes searching for an answer.

"You don't. You never mention it," Tom said emphatically. "Right now, your family members think you're a hero for rescuing him."

"But that's not true."

"What could you possibly gain from telling your family you chose a rescue scenario overpaying a ransom? Nothing," Tom emphasized loudly.

Felix glanced down at his drink. "I don't know."

"Do you suddenly want your family to look at you as being a moneygrubbing villain? Some might never forgive you. Being honest, for the sake of honesty, could permanently damage your family. Don't do that," Tom stressed.

Felix looked into Tom's eyes. "You're not telling me this just to make me feel better, are you?"

Tom lied. "Of course not. You have to think about the

mental well-being of your family members. They look to you for leadership. They must continue to love and believe in you. They need you," he pointed out.

Felix sighed and gazed out the window. "All right. I see the logic in what you're saying. You've lifted a huge weight off my chest."

"If we don't see each other again, I want you to know I'll always like and respect you. You're a fine man, Felix," Tom emphasized.

Ramirez suddenly looked alarmed. "Are you saying goodbye to me?"

"Tomorrow, I'm flying back to Los Angeles to hand in my resignation. Mark Danforth knows it's coming. I need a change in my lifestyle."

"Please promise me that you'll talk with me before you accept any other job," Felix implored.

"I will, I promise," Tom said, an earnest expression on his face.

The men stood up, and Felix suddenly threw his arms around Tom and hugged him.

***

Tom packed his suitcase and was ready to depart for the airport when his cell phone rang.

"Is this Tom Bradshaw?"

"Yes," Tom answered, hoping it wasn't a person selling something.

"This is Oscar Nance. I'm an investigator for California Title and Trust. I'm told that you were friends with the woman who moved into the condo next to you."

"Yes, Vivian Fairchild. Has something happened to her?"

"Well, not exactly. I'll level with you, so you understand why I'm calling. That woman is not Vivian Fairchild. Her real name is Doris Gooch."

"What?" Tom said in amazement.

"She was Mrs. Fairchild's live in caretaker at her New York home. It seems that Mrs. Fairchild passed away, and Doris assumed her identity. She put Mrs. Fairchild's body in a freezer in the garage and proceeded to empty her savings and checking accounts."

"What?" Tom said in an astonished voice. He attempted to sit down on the bed but slid down to the floor.

"Why I'm calling is that Doris had the original closing package on the Santa Monica condo. She obtained a fraudulent New York driver's license showing that she was Vivian Fairchild and had Vivian's social security card. She sold that condo for two million dollars and walked away with the money. Our title company is on the hook for the full amount," Nance explained.

"That's amazing," Tom said.

"You talked with her on several occasions, right?"

"Yes."

"Did she ever talk with you about her future plans? Or where she might go on vacation?" Nance asked.

"No. She was not very friendly and didn't talk much about herself. Wait a minute. She did say the people in Palm Beach were friendlier than in California," Tom remembered.

"Okay. Well, I guess I'll be traveling to Palm Beach. If you remember anything else, please call me," Nance said.

"I sure will."

Tom wrote down Nance's phone number, and the call ended. He sat there on the floor, shaking his head in disbelief.

CHAPTER 33

Less than five minutes later, his phone rang again.

"This is Tom."

"Hi Tom, this is Samantha Rosario. I work at the kiosk in the building housing the Mexico City Banking Association and numerous other offices. I found out who the man is that wears St. Johns Bay Rum Cologne. His name is Christian Salamanca."

Tom jumped in the air as if he'd been touched with a red hot poker. "Oh, my God. How did you find out?" Tom asked excitedly.

"When he walked by the kiosk, I smelled that cologne. I grabbed a couple of packages I was to deliver and got on the elevator with him. I exited with him and saw that he went into an office opposite the banking association. The name on the door is Salamanca Accounting Corporation. My girlfriend, Paulina, is the office receptionist in the banking association. She said Salamanca handles all of the accounting for the banking group," Samantha explained.

"You're sure he's Christian Salamanca?"

"Yes. The other employees are all women," she replied.

"Fantastic. I'll be at your building in an hour. You'll have a bonus coming,"

Tom promised.

He hung up and called Victor Chapa. The banker had been abducted by Salamanca's kidnap gang, and Tom negotiated his release.

"Hi, Tom. How's the negotiation business going?" Chapa asked.

"Great, and I'm about to give you the name of the gang leader responsible for your kidnapping."

"Jesus Christ. You've found him?" he asked excitedly.

"His name is Christian Salamanca, and he's a CPA who does the accounting for the banking association," Tom replied.

"No wonder the son-of-a-bitch knows everything about bankers. Well, he's a dead man, I'll see to that," Victor said loudly.

"Just relax. First, I need a photo of Salamanca so I can make a positive identification. Any idea where I can get one?"

Victor thought for a moment. "The Mexico Institute of Public Accountants should have one on file. I'll have our CPA check immediately. I'll be back to you in a few minutes."

They hung up. Tom stood on the balcony, looking out at the city, deep in thought. Then he walked back inside and called down to the lobby. Tom received the courtesy email address and determined that incoming photos could be printed there. Victor called back a half hour later with news that a photo would be emailed as soon as he had an email address. Tom gave it to him.

Minutes later, he held the photo of Salamanca in his hand. The CPA looked like the average man on the street. He had no distinguishing facial characteristics and was clean shaven. Tom thought he could pass Salamanca on the street and never remember what he looked like.

His next stop was the building that housed the banking association. He showed Samantha Rosario the picture of Christian Salamanca, and she positively identified him. Tom gave her one thousand dollars in cash, which caused her eyes and mouth to open wide. He cautioned her about being careful around Salamanca because he was extremely dangerous.

Tom returned to the Hilton Hotel, then turned and walked down the street to a restaurant with an outside patio. He ordered coffee and a pastry and stared at the bustling city activity, cars and buses moving by and men and women hurrying to business meetings. But Tom was lost in thought and didn't focus on the liveliness in front of him.

Sunlight fell upon a face containing bright green eyes, broad cheeks, strong nose, and a rugged chin. His mouth, shaped for laughter, was now a hard, grim line as he formulated a plan. He knew the final responsibility for decisive action was his alone, and the time had come.

Tom used his cell phone and called Max Santos. "How's Sergio doing?"

"He's out of intensive care and in a hospital suite. Private nurses and doctors are everywhere," Max reported.

"Can you get me a Glock pistol?" Tom asked.

"Sure. I've got one in the car. Do you need it now?"

"Yes. I'm at the Hilton Hotel downtown."

"I'll be there in half an hour to forty-five minutes."

Tom gave him the suite number and hung up. Thirty minutes later, Max arrived, and Tom checked the weapon.

"Do you need me for backup?" Max asked, realizing Tom was preparing for a sortie.

Tom briefly explained about the large number of bankers being kidnapped, and that he had identified the leader of the kidnapping gang.

"I know the leader's voice by heart. I've heard it so many times over the phone. Now I've got to hear it in person in order to positively identify him," Bradshaw explained.

Max nodded in understanding. "Do you want me to come along as backup?"

"All right. But I need to do it myself."

***

It was early afternoon when the two men walked into the

office building housing The Mexico City Banking Association. Tom waved to Samantha Rosario as they passed near the kiosk and got on the elevator. The two men exited and walked up to Salamanca's office door.

"See you shortly," Tom told Max as he opened the door and entered.

Salamanca looked up from reviewing paperwork on one of the desks. He straightened up. The two men stood facing each other, recognition on both their faces.

"Good to see you, Ajax—or should I call you Tom Bradshaw?" Salamanca said. A small grin and sparkling light brown eyes dominated his facial features.

"It's time for us to meet, Carlos—or should I call you Christian Salamanca?" Tom replied.

Salamanca threw a file of papers on the desk, freeing up his hands.

"You're a hell of an investigator, as well as being a darn good negotiator. I had to kill my men after you identified them. Damn shame. They performed well as a team. I did you a favor, though, when I shot Rodrigo Castio, the police captain. He was going to kill you," Salamanca pointed out.

"You'll understand if I don't thank you," Tom said.

"This is my last day in the office. I'm leaving Mexico. What do you say we just walk away from one another and part as friends?" Salamanca asked.

Tom shook his head. "No, that won't work."

"Supposing I sweeten the deal with a million dollars cash?"

"Nope. I'm not for sale, and you need to face the courts because of the kidnappings."

"That won't happen, so I guess this is goodbye," Salamanca said.

The gang leader's eyes narrowed, and his mouth became a firm line. The kidnapper quickly reached inside his coat and pulled a pistol from a shoulder holster. Tom grabbed the Glock from his waistband, and both men fired at each other from a distance of fifteen feet.

Bradshaw was hit in the left shoulder and fell over backwards. Salamanca took a bullet to the chest and fell forward, a shocked expression on his face. Both men were lying on the floor, looking at one another, realizing that years of cat and mouse games had ended. Salamanca's expression was one of disbelief as he tried to raise his weapon. Tom managed to point his pistol at Salamanca's head and pulled the trigger.

The sound of the shot coincided with Max Santos's entry into the office. He ran over to Salamanca and saw that he was dead.

"Are you hit bad?" he asked Tom as he moved to help him.

"No. But, it hurts like hell. This is the second time I've been shot in the same shoulder."

Santos called for an ambulance, stopped the bleeding, and Bradshaw was off to the hospital within minutes.

***

Douglas Bradshaw pushed his son's wheelchair toward the LAX parking lot.

"I can walk, you know."

"Not very far. Did you really tell your boss you're resigning?" Douglas asked.

"I did. He knew I was going to resign."

"Any idea about what you'd like to do now?"

Tom sighed. "I haven't even thought about it."

"What about Bianca?"

"I talked with her from the Mexico City hospital. She acted emotionally disturbed, and I wasn't too lucid. I'd been sedated, and I don't remember much about the conversation. I'll call her again from your house."

His father hit Tom with question after question during

the ride to his Brentwood home. Tom was relieved when they arrived, and he slowly got out of the car. The front door opened, and Tom was met by Rusty, the labradoodle, who tried to climb his leg.

Tom grinned, and then his face took on a shocked expression as Bianca Santana came running towards him. She stood in front of him, tears rolling down her cheeks.

"You can hold me. I won't break," Tom said.

She rushed into his arms and nearly knocked him over.

"Ouch!" he responded, but kept smiling.

The End

Following college at the University of Missouri and a stint in the U. S. Army, **Lee Bishop** began a newspaper career at *The Phoenix Gazette* in Phoenix, Arizona. He had more than two thousand news stories and feature articles published during that period.

His main work emphasis was government and politics, and most of his career was spent writing about Arizona State Government, the Arizona House of Representatives and the State Senate. Lee also covered the Phoenix City Council and Maricopa County governmental issues. He wrote numerous stories about prominent Arizona politicians and their successes and blunders that shaped Arizona.

Lee switched professions and has been a real estate broker for more than twenty-five years, selling land, businesses and homes. He still owns a real estate company, Southwestern Homes Realty, but has returned to writing novels and screenplays on a full-time basis.

He and his wife, Sue, have four children who live in the Phoenix metropolitan area with their families. Lee and Sue enjoy traveling and spend most of their vacations on the west coast.

Lee is an avid hiker whose favorite hike is to the bottom of the Grand Canyon every year. He also loves golf and plays frequently.